MERCURY
INK

SIMON
PULSE

MICHAEL VEY
HUNT FOR JADE DRAGON

BOOK FOUR OF SEVEN

MICHAEL VEY

HUNT FOR JADE DRAGON

BOOK FOUR OF SEVEN

RICHARD PAUL EVANS

MERCURY INK

SIMON PULSE

NEW YORK   LONDON   TORONTO   SYDNEY   NEW DELHI

SIMON PULSE / MERCURY INK
An imprint of Simon & Schuster Children's Publishing Division
1230 Avenue of the Americas, New York, NY 10020
First Simon Pulse/Mercury Ink paperback edition May 2015
Text copyright © 2014 by Richard Paul Evans
Cover illustration © 2014 by Owen Richardson
All rights reserved, including the right of reproduction in whole or in part in any form.
Simon Pulse and colophon are registered trademarks of Simon & Schuster, Inc.
Mercury Ink is a trademark of Mercury Radio Arts, Inc.
For information about special discounts for bulk purchases, please contact
Simon & Schuster Special Sales at 1-866-506-1949 or business@simonandschuster.com.
The Simon & Schuster Speakers Bureau can bring authors to your live event. For more
information or to book an event contact the Simon & Schuster Speakers Bureau at
1-866-248-3049 or visit our website at www.simonspeakers.com.
Cover designed by Jessica Handelman
Interior designed by Mike Rosamilia
The text of this book was set in Berling LT Std.
Manufactured in the United States of America
2 4 6 8 10 9 7 5 3
The Library of Congress has cataloged the hardcover edition as follows:
Evans, Richard Paul.
Michael Vey. 4, Hunt for Jade Dragon : book four of a seven book series /
by Richard Paul Evans. — First Simon Pulse hardcover edition.
pages cm
Sequel to: Michael Vey. 3, Battle of the Ampere.
Summary: Michael, Taylor, Ostin, and the rest of the Electroclan head to
Taiwan in search of nine-year-old child prodigy Lin Julung, or Jade Dragon,
who the Elgen kidnapped for Hatch's army of electric children.
[1. Friendship—Fiction. 2. Electricity—Fiction. 3. Tourette syndrome—Fiction.
4. Gifted children—Fiction. 5. Genius—Fiction. 6. Kidnapping—Fiction.
7. Taiwan—Fiction. 8. Science fiction.] I. Title. II. Title: Hunt for Jade Dragon.
PZ7.E89227Mg 2014
[Fic]—dc23 2014026196
ISBN 978-1-4814-2438-7 (hc)
ISBN 978-1-4814-2439-4 (pbk)
ISBN 978-1-4814-2440-0 (eBook)

To my Allyson,
You are a joy and a blessing in my life.

PROLOGUE

The ES *Faraday*
Port of Callao Harbor, Peru

"This is a cattle ship," Hatch shouted, throwing his half-full glass of Scotch against the wall. "Do you hear me? I'm living on a stinking cattle ship!"

"Yes, sir," his servant said, scrambling to clean up the mess. Even though she was accustomed to Hatch's volcanic temper, his outbursts still frightened her.

After the Electroclan sank the *Ampere*—the Elgen's luxury superyacht—Hatch and the remaining Elgen onboard had taken up residence on the *Faraday*, the Elgen troop ship and the largest boat of the Elgen fleet. "Vey and his terrorist friends will pay for this," Hatch grumbled. He reached for his glass before remembering he'd just thrown it. "Hurry and clean up that mess," he said to his servant, who was still on her knees collecting shards of glass in the palm of her hand. "Then get me another drink."

"Yes, sir," she replied.

Someone rapped lightly on the door.

"Who is it?" Hatch said.

"It's Captain Welch, sir. I have a report." Captain Welch was the head of the Elite Global Guard and one of the few Elgen allowed to speak directly to the admiral.

"What are you waiting for, EGG?" Hatch said.

Welch saluted as he entered the room, forcing himself not to look at the woman kneeling on the ground. "Excuse the interruption, Admiral. But we've captured the Chinese girl. Jade Dragon."

"Where is she?"

"She's in the custody of the Lung Li. They've smuggled her out of China. They're now in Taipei on their way to the Starxource plant."

"Have they gotten her to talk?"

"No, sir."

"Why not?"

"There's a problem."

Hatch's eyes flashed. "I don't want *problems*, EGG. I want *results*. Make her talk. Threaten her. Threaten her family. Threaten her dog if you have to."

"Sir, I'm afraid it will take more than threats."

"Then torture her!"

"We don't think she'll understand torture."

Hatch pounded his fist on his desk. "What is there to understand about torture? Quit talking in circles, Welch."

"The girl is deaf and mute. And she's autistic. It's unlikely that she'll make the correlation between the pain we inflict and the information we're trying to get from her. Torture may have a deterring effect."

The servant set another glass of scotch in front of Hatch, which calmed him. He took a drink, then said, "This *genius* we've captured is a deaf, mute, autistic child?"

"Yes, sir. She's an autistic savant."

He nodded slowly. "A *savant*. How did we not know this?"

"We knew little about her except the brilliance of her work, sir."

Hatch pondered the predicament, then said, "Get her to our scientists on the *Volta*. They'll know what to do with her."

"Shall we fly her there?"

"No, the *Volta* is already at sea. Have them change course to Taiwan. And find an expert on autism. I want someone who knows how to make the girl talk, so to speak."

"Shall we leave her in the custody of the Lung Li?"

He shook his head. "Not just the Lung Li. I want my Eagles to personally guard her."

"Your Eagles?"

"My Glows," he said. "Quentin will be in charge."

"Where are the youths, sir?"

"They're in Beverly Hills. I want them in Taiwan by the day after tomorrow, except for Torstyn and Tara. I'm going to need their services in Switzerland."

"Yes, sir. Anything else, sir?"

"While you're waiting for the *Volta* to arrive, I want you to spread the word around the plant that we have the girl."

"That seems unwise, sir. Word may leak to the resistance."

"I'm counting on it," Hatch said.

"I don't understand."

"If they know we have the girl, they'll send that snake, Michael Vey, to rescue her."

Welch's forehead furrowed. "You want Vey in Taiwan?"

"More than you can imagine." Hatch leaned forward over his glass. "You know how to kill a snake, don't you? Decapitation. You cut off its head and the body dies. We've underestimated Vey. He's been at the head of every Elgen conflict. Without Vey, there is no resistance." Hatch drained the glass, then his voice fell to a low, guttural tone, almost as if he were talking to himself. "I've had enough of this boy and his Electroclan. It's time we cut off some heads."

PART ONE

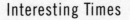

1

Interesting Times

My best friend, Ostin Liss, told me that there is an ancient Chinese curse that says:

MAY YOU LIVE IN INTERESTING TIMES

My name is Michael Vey, and I'm definitely living in interesting times. Just a year ago that wasn't true. In fact, my life was about as exciting as one of Ostin's clogging recitals. I was just an average, no-name freshman at Meridian High School in Meridian, Idaho—a small town where the only thing above average is the cow-to-human ratio. Don't feel bad if you've never heard of Meridian, Idaho. Neither has anyone else.

I lived with my mother, who worked as a checker at the grocery store, in a tiny apartment with eggshell-white walls and green shag carpet. I walked to school every day; avoided bullies, the principal, most types of math, and organized sports; and played video games with my best (and only) friend, Ostin, six out of seven days of the week. And I watched Shark Week twice a year. That pretty much summed up my life.

I suppose the only thing vaguely interesting about me was my Tourette's syndrome, which isn't really that interesting because I don't do any of the fascinating things that some people with Tourette's do, like shout out swear words in public or make animal noises. I mostly just blink or gulp a lot. I know, boring.

Actually, what I just said about Tourette's being the only interesting thing about me isn't really true. There's something about me that has always been very interesting—I'm just not allowed to tell anyone. I'm electric.

Which is what's led to my new and very interesting life. For those keeping score, in the last year I've done the following:

- Made friends with a group of kids with electric powers like mine.

- Been locked up in a cell and tortured.

- Shut down a private school.

- Scored a really hot girlfriend. (Still can't believe that one.)

- Flown to Peru and rescued my mother.

- Been tied up and almost fed to rats.

- Blown up a major power plant.

- Made Peru's list of most wanted criminals.

- Been chased through the jungle by helicopters with flamethrowers.

- Lived with the Amacarra tribe in the Amazon jungle.

- Attacked the Peruvian army and rescued my friends before they could be executed for terrorism.

- Blew up the *Ampere*, a billion-dollar superyacht, before the Elgen could take over and enslave the entire island nation of Tuvalu (which, like Meridian, Idaho, you've also never heard of).

Now we're preparing to fly to Taiwan to rescue a nine-year-old Chinese girl from the Taiwanese army and a group of Elgen superninjas called the Lung Li.

I have a feeling things are about to get a whole lot more interesting.

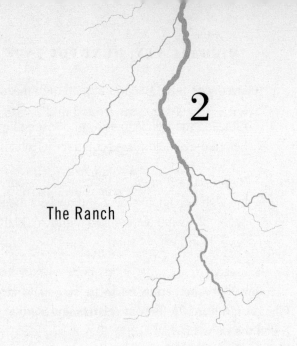

2

The Ranch

"**M**ichael, wake up. You're dreaming." I opened my eyes to see my girlfriend, Taylor, leaning over me. "It's okay, you're just dreaming."

I rubbed my eyes, then slowly sat up. "Where are we?"

"Still in the van."

I took a deep breath, then exhaled slowly. The right side of my mouth was ticking like crazy. "I had another nightmare."

"I know. I saw it."

"You saw my nightmare?"

Taylor nodded. "It was terrifying. This time I was in it."

Ever since we blew up the *Ampere* I'd been having recurring nightmares of the explosion and the boat sinking. I could see people trapped inside the boat, screaming as they tried to get out before they drowned. But lately they had been people I knew, like my mother or Ostin. This time it was Taylor.

"It was awful," I said.

Taylor wrapped her arms around me. "I wish I knew how to take them away. I tried."

"Maybe that's why you were in it," I said.

We had left Peru before sunrise and flown for about six hours, finally landing on a dirt runway in the middle of nowhere. As we got off the plane we were met by two men wearing suits and dark sunglasses who said little other than to tell us to board their van. Now we had been traveling on the same dirt road for more than an hour, an unending landscape of meadow grass, cacti, and cypress and Joshua trees occasionally broken up by barbwire fences. I squinted against the late-afternoon sun as I looked out the window. "Any idea where we are?"

"No. Just more of the same," Taylor said. "I feel like we're in one of those cartoons where the same background keeps going by."

"Look, cows," Abigail said, pointing ahead of us. "Hundreds of them."

Everyone looked out to see a large herd scattered across the landscape.

"Actually they're Brangus cattle," Ostin said. "They're a cross between the Indian Brahman and the Scottish Angus breeds originating from hybrid research conducted in Jeanerette, Louisiana, in 1932."

"What did he say they were?" Jack asked.

"Cows," Abigail said.

"When are we going to get there?" McKenna asked.

"Where is *there*?" Tessa said. "Why do they have to be so secretive about everything? It's not like we're Elgen."

"Please don't say that," the man in the front passenger seat of the van said. It was the first time he'd spoken since we'd started driving.

"Say what . . . *Elgen*?" Tessa said, deliberately using the word.

"You never know who is listening," the man said.

Tessa groaned. "If someone was listening to us they would have already died of boredom."

"It's better we don't know where we are," I said, "in case we're captured and they torture us for information."

"You've got a way with words, Vey," Tessa said. "I feel *so* much better now." She asked the driver, "Are we there yet?"

"Yes, ma'am," the driver said without turning back. "This is the Timepiece Ranch."

"We're going to a ranch?" Taylor asked.

"Yes, ma'am," the driver said.

"A ranch makes sense," I said. "They'd have privacy. Room to do things. You could detonate a bomb out here and no one would know."

"Right," Tessa said. "They can't hear a bomb, but they can hear me whisper 'Elgen'?"

"She's got a point," Ostin said.

"Maybe they'll have horses we can ride," Taylor said to me. "Do you like horses?"

"I've never ridden one," I said.

She smiled. "It's fun. I'll teach you."

"Why are we going to a ranch?" Tessa asked. "Why aren't we flying to China to rescue the girl?"

"We're not going to China," Ostin said. "We're going to Taiwan."

"Same thing," Tessa said.

"Yeah, right," Ostin said, shaking his head. "That's like saying Cuba and the United States are the same country. Taiwan is a multiparty democratic state. China is a communist state. The Chinese government claims Taiwan as its twenty-third province, while the Taiwanese constitutionally claim sovereignty over all of China."

"Thanks for the geography lesson," Tessa said.

"Did you know the entire country of Taiwan could fit in the land mass of Massachusetts, yet, at one time, had more than twenty-five different languages?"

"How do you know so much?" McKenna asked.

"I'm a fact sponge," Ostin said.

Tessa slid down in her seat. "Someone just kill me."

Fifteen minutes later Tessa said to the driver, "I thought you said we were already there."

"We are," the driver said. "It's a fifty-thousand-acre ranch."

"Holy cow," Ostin said.

"He means holy *Brangus*," Abigail said.

Jack laughed. It was good to hear him laugh. Ever since Wade's death he rarely laughed anymore.

Five minutes later the van slowed to a halt at a steel-and-barbwire gate next to a wooden shed. There was a tall, muscular man standing in front of the gate. He wore a cowboy hat, boots, and a leather vest.

"A cowboy," Abigail said. "I love cowboys. They're hot." She turned to Jack. "You should get one of those hats. You'd look cute in it."

"I'm not going for *cute*," Jack said.

"Michael," Ian said, leaning over the back of my seat. "See that guy? The guard."

"Yeah."

"He looks like a cowboy, but he's all teched-up with a radio and remotes and he's wearing a bulletproof vest. That wooden shed behind him is actually a steel-reinforced concrete bunker with a fifty-millimeter machine gun and an antitank gun. And there are land-mines all along the road and fence line. I'm guessing they're remote controlled. He's got everyone fooled."

"Except you," Taylor said.

Ian smiled. "Except me."

"I'm glad you're on our side," I said.

Our driver got out of the van. He spoke to the guard for a moment, and then he got back in and the gate opened. The dirt road we had been riding on changed to asphalt as we drove forward about another hundred yards past a large communications tower where the road split. We took the right fork and our path wound down into a long, narrow valley before ending at a large compound.

There were three large buildings built around a central structure, which was several stories high. The roofs of the structures were covered with solar panels and wind turbines. There were similar turbines on the ridge of the opposite hill.

Behind the main building were several aluminum-sided garages, a helipad with a helicopter, and three corrugated-steel grain silos, all of which were taller than the one I had practiced climbing on in Peru. There was also a long rectangular structure that looked like one of the commercial chicken coops near Meridian.

"What's in the chicken-coop-looking building?" I asked. "Weapons?"

"Chickens," Ian said.

"It's really a chicken coop?"

"They've got to eat, right? And there's really wheat in those silos."

"What's in the garages?" Taylor asked. "Potatoes?"

"No, *those* are weapons. There's a tank in one, and an attack helicopter in the other."

"Looks like they're preparing for war," I said.

"Looks like they're *prepared* for war," Ian said. "There's a huge underground bunker behind the main house, and the buildings don't look like anything I've seen before. The outer walls are all lined with some kind of metal mesh. It looks like chicken wire."

"Maybe they used to be chicken coops too," Taylor said.

"Faraday cages," Ostin said.

"What?" I said.

"Faraday cages," Ostin repeated. "They block external static and electric fields by evenly channeling electricity through the cage and diffusing—"

"Explain in English," Taylor said.

"Sorry," Ostin said. "The metal mesh protects the building's wiring from electromagnetic pulses."

"Why would there be an electromagnetic pulse out here?" Taylor asked.

"It's what the Elgen are working on," I said. "EMP weaponry. Once they perfect it they'll be able to shut down the power of entire cities."

"Not here," Ostin said. "If there's a major EMP blast, this place will still function. Of course, they must have their own fuel tanks and electric generators."

"The fuel tanks are underground next to the silos," Ian said. "The third garage has two large generators." He turned to Ostin. "How did you know that?"

"It wouldn't do any good to wrap the house in mesh to protect the home's wiring if the source of their electricity is destroyed. Common sense."

"We should all be so common," Ian mumbled.

The man in the passenger seat lifted a handset and said, "Egret four descending."

"Egret four clear," a voice returned.

After another quarter mile, the slope leveled off and the van pulled up to the front of the central structure, a tall ranch-style building with a long, wood-planked porch. The driveway was lined with rusted, antique farm equipment and pale yellow and purple wildflowers. There were a couple dozen chickens pecking around the yard.

"This is the real deal," McKenna said. "Wish I had some cowboy boots."

"Pink ones," Abigail said.

After we had come to a stop our driver said, "Please, stay in your seats for just a moment."

The building's front door opened and a tall, muscularly built, sandy-haired man walked out, flanked by two other men and a woman. Something about the tall man and the woman seemed familiar.

"Who's that dude?" Zeus asked.

"Maybe he's the voice," Taylor answered.

"Maybe," I said.

The man in the passenger seat got out and opened the van's sliding door. "Everyone out, please."

"Let's go," I said.

As soon as we were all out of the van the man slid the door shut again and the driver pulled away without him.

The sandy-haired man looked us over. "Welcome to Timepiece Ranch. We're happy to see you in one piece."

"You mean alive?" Zeus said.

The man's mouth rose in a half smile. "Yes. We're especially glad to see you alive."

"Not all of us," Jack said.

The man's smile fell. For a moment he just looked at Jack; then he started walking toward him. I noticed the muscles in Jack's neck tense. "You must be Jack," the man said.

Jack stared defiantly into his eyes. "You got it, Tex."

The man put his hand on Jack's shoulder. "I'm sorry for your loss. You've sacrificed more than anyone here. I promise you, I will do everything in my power to see that Wade's life was not lost in vain. Wade is a hero. And so are you. We are all in your debt."

Jack's muscles relaxed and he blinked with sudden emotion. "Thank you, sir."

"No, thank *you*. We're not just in your debt; the whole world is in your debt. Whether they know it or not." He turned to the rest of us. "If it wasn't for you, the people of Tuvalu would be living a nightmare right now. Hundreds, maybe thousands, of innocent people would have died. I'm sure you're all very tired and hungry, and there are some people here who are very excited to see you. So let's get you checked into your rooms."

"I have a question," I said.

"Michael," he said. "What can I do for you?"

"Are you the voice?"

"No."

"Will we meet the voice?"

He hesitated, then said, "Maybe. That's all I can tell you."

"Who are you?" Jack asked.

"My name is Joel," he said. "I forgot to tell you, before you enter the compound there is one inconvenience. My men need to check you for RFIDs. Then we'll show you to your quarters. You have a few hours before the reception."

"Reception?" Taylor said.

"We've put together a reception in your honor. You'll have time to rest a little, then shower and change before then."

"Change into what?" Tessa said. "We don't have any other clothes."

"Sydney Lynn will take care of that," he said. He turned and walked back toward the building.

The woman who had walked out with Joel stepped forward

carrying a clipboard at her side. "I'm Sydney Lynn. After you are checked and cleared, I'll take you to your rooms, where you can rest, then clean up and change. I'll come get you when it's time for the reception. In the meantime, if you need anything, please let me know. I'm here to take care of you."

"Like I just said," Tessa said, "change into what? We don't have any clothes."

"We have clothes for you," Sydney Lynn replied. "They should fit." She looked at Ostin and me. "Michael, you've grown taller."

"I think so," I said, wondering how she knew.

"That which doesn't kill you only makes you taller," Tessa said.

"And Ostin, yours might be a bit loose. It looks like you've lost weight."

Ostin smiled. "Yes, ma'am."

"It's the Peruvian prisoner diet," Taylor whispered to me.

I suddenly realized why Sydney Lynn looked familiar. She was the woman who had handed me the cell phone at Jack's sister's tanning salon. "You helped us in Meridian."

She smiled. "Bronze Idaho," she replied. "It's good to see you again, Michael."

Just then a shrill Southern voice pierced the air. "Ostin!"

We looked over to see Ostin's mother running toward us from the side doorway, her arms flailing like she was going to sack a quarterback. A much more subdued Mr. Liss was a few yards behind her.

"Mom!" Ostin shouted.

As we watched their reunion I heard someone say, "Michael." I turned back. My mother was walking toward me from the front door.

"Mom!"

Her eyes were full of tears. We didn't say much, just hugged. When she could speak she asked, "Are you okay?"

"Yeah," I said.

She looked at me as if she couldn't believe we were really together, then she brushed the hair back from my forehead. "I heard about Wade. I'm so sorry."

"It was awful," I said. "Still is awful."

She hugged me tightly again. As we parted Taylor said, "Hi, Mrs. Vey."

"Taylor," my mother said. She hugged her.

Everyone gathered around my mother like she was a magnet, which, in a way, was true. Everyone except for Jack, who stood a few yards off, quietly watching.

My mother walked over to him. Without speaking, she hugged him, then gazed into his face. "I'm so sorry about Wade. I know what it's like to lose someone you love. If I can do anything for you, or you just need to talk, I'm here."

"Thank you, Mrs. Vey," Jack said.

"Call me Sharon," she said.

It was a little strange seeing my mother so familiar with everyone. The last time I'd seen her was just before everyone fled through the pipe at the Peruvian Starxource plant and I'd been captured. Since that time my mother had been through a lot with the rest of the Electroclan.

"Zeus, who is your friend?" my mother said, looking at Tessa.

Tessa stepped forward. "I'm Tessa."

"Tessa," she repeated. "Is that short for Contessa?"

Tessa shrugged. "I was pretty young when the Elgen took me. I don't know where my name came from."

"It's nice to meet you, Tessa. I'm Sharon. I'm Michael's mother."

"I met Tessa in the jungle," I said. "She was living with the Amacarra tribe when they saved me."

"It sounds like we have a lot to catch up on," my mother said, smiling at me. "I know you must be exhausted. They want us to let you get checked in, then get some rest before tonight's reception, which I'm in charge of, so I'd better get back to work. I'll see you in a few hours." She looked back into my eyes. "I love you."

"I love you too, Mom."

Just then Ostin walked up, flanked by his parents. "Hi, Mrs. V."

"Hello, Ostin," my mother said. "It's good to see you back with your parents. They've been a little worried."

"A *little?*" Mrs. Liss said.

"I know," Ostin said. "But all's well that ends well."

"Yes, it is." My mother turned back to me. "We'll have fun at the reception tonight. Get some rest." We hugged again, then she hurried back to the ranch house.

Ostin watched her go. "She's *so* hot."

"Ostin!" his mother said.

I shook my head. "Dude, she's my mom."

3

Bunk Hall

After separating Ostin from his mother, the men checked us for RFIDs, then Sydney Lynn led us inside the main building, which she called the Ranch House. We entered through the front doors—which had handles made from horseshoes—into a large open room with hallways in three directions.

Like the deceptively simple wooden shack we had passed near the ranch's gate entrance, the outside of the Ranch House looked rustic, but the inside was filled with high-tech surveillance and communication equipment. In a way it reminded me of the Elgen Academy—but with cowboy art.

The main room interior was Western design. It had polished hardwood floors and a high, vaulted ceiling with exposed wooden beams. On one end of the room there was a massive stone fireplace that rose nearly two stories to the ceiling, tapering off near the top like a keystone.

Sydney Lynn led us to the right. "This way to the bunk hall, please." We followed her through a doorway and down a long, wood-paneled corridor. All of the doors were numbered.

"I'm sorry there aren't enough rooms for each of you to have your own, but I think you'll still find your accommodations comfortable. There are two beds in each room, so pick a roommate. Ladies, let's get you settled first. Who would like room one?"

"McKenna and I can take it," Abigail said.

"Very good," Sydney Lynn said, writing on her clipboard. "I'll have your clothes sent right over. Next?"

"Looks like it's me and Tessa," Taylor said.

Tessa put her hands on her hips. "Poor you," she said. "Having to share a room with me."

"I didn't mean that," Taylor said.

"It sounded like it."

"Sorry. That's not what I meant."

"Taylor and Tessa, room two," Sydney Lynn said, ignoring the drama. "And room three is occupied."

"Who's in room three?" I asked.

"Grace," she said.

Tessa's expression changed. "Grace is here? Grace and I used to be buddies."

"Maybe you could bunk with her," Ostin said.

Both Taylor and Tessa glared at him.

Ostin wilted. "Just sayin'."

"Michael," Sydney Lynn said, "who are you bunking with?"

"Ostin."

"Let's put you in room four." She turned to Zeus. "Zeus, room five is reserved especially for you and whomever you're bunking with."

"What's so special about room five?" Zeus asked.

"You can shower," she said. "The water is distilled."

Zeus stared at her in wonder. "Are you kidding?"

Sydney Lynn smiled. "Why would I be kidding?"

"I'll bunk with you," Jack said, then added wryly, "Now that you won't stink."

"Yeah, thanks, man," Zeus said.

Nothing against Zeus, but it made me a little sad that Jack was paired up with him. Up to that point it had always been a given that Jack would be bunking with Wade.

"Ian, that leaves you with your own room."

"Make that my own *suite*," Ian said with a smile. "Comfort over company. I'll take the privacy."

"And I'll take a nap," Abigail said. "See you, boys." She blew Jack a kiss.

I walked up to Taylor. "What are you going to do?"

"I think I'll take a bath," she said. "Want to go for a walk later?"

"Sure."

"Great, see you in an hour." She kissed me on the cheek, then followed Tessa into their room.

I headed toward my own room. I wondered how long we would be here.

4

Bugatti Veyron

The room Ostin and I were sharing was at least twice the size of my room at home. There was Western art on the walls, mostly paintings of coyotes and buffalo, and a framed woven Native American blanket.

Ostin had already claimed one of the beds and was lying on his back eating something, evidenced by an empty cellophane candy wrapper on the bed next to him. "Look, man. Licorice." He threw me a package of red licorice, which landed on the floor about ten feet from me.

I picked it up. "Thanks."

"There's a bunch of snacks in that cupboard."

I was amazed at how quickly he'd rooted it out, like a pig hunting for truffles. I took off my shoes, then sat down on the bed. "So what do you think of these guys?"

He stopped chewing. "Why? Don't you trust them?"

"I didn't say that. Do you trust them?"

"I think we need to be careful."

After what we'd been through in the last month, the word sounded ridiculous. "*Careful*," I said. "You mean like wearing a helmet at chess tournaments or knee pads to clogging practice?"

"Shut up," he said.

Within five minutes Ostin was snoring. I couldn't sleep, in part because of the noise, but also because I was afraid to. Almost every time I closed my eyes the nightmares returned. After enduring a half hour of Ostin's snoring, I put my shoes back on and left the room.

I was a little curious to see what the other rooms in the place looked like, so I opened the first door past Ian's. A tall, redheaded boy lying on his side looked up from a book. "Didn't anyone teach you to knock?" he said.

"Apparently not," I replied.

He grinned. "Hi, Mike."

"Hey, Tanner."

"You made it back in one piece."

"Barely."

"I heard you blew up the *Ampere*."

"Yeah."

I thought that maybe he saw the flash of pain in my eyes, because he looked at me for a moment as if he wanted to say something more about it. Or maybe I just hoped he would. If anyone would understand how I felt it would be Tanner. From what I'd heard, he also had nightmares about the planes he'd brought down. Instead he just said, "Too bad Hatch wasn't on it."

"He was. He just got off." I looked around his room. It looked more lived-in than ours. It was customized. There were stacks of books, framed photographs of Tanner's family, and posters on the walls, mostly of cars. Cool cars. Lamborghinis, Ferraris, and one I'd never seen before. I walked over to it.

"What's this?"

"It's a Bugatti Veyron," he said. "*Vey*, like your name. If your name was Ron, that would be my nickname for you."

"Is it fast?"

He laughed. "Are you electric? It can go two hundred and fifty-four miles per hour. At top speed it burns out its tires in fifteen minutes. And it only costs one point four million dollars."

I turned back. "Are you kidding?"

"Nope."

"I couldn't afford the tires," I said.

"I'm sure Hatch would buy you one . . ." I looked at him, surprised that he would say something like that. ". . . in exchange for your soul."

"*There's* a trade," I said. "Cool room."

"It's good here. The people are good. Intense, but good."

"What are you reading?" I asked.

He held up his book. "*Lord of the Flies.*"

The book had been required reading in my last English class. "That's pretty dark," I said.

"The world's dark. Or didn't you notice?"

"Yeah," I said. "I noticed." I took a step back toward him. "You look different."

"You mean since you last saw me and I was strapped down, psychotic, and drugged?"

I cocked my head. "Yeah."

"The medication helps." He gestured to a row of plastic pill bottles on his dresser. "So does the V."

"What's the V?"

"That's what they call themselves around here. Sometimes they call themselves 'the resistance,' but usually just the V. Like victory. Or Vey." He sat up a little. "By the way, your mom rocks. She got me through the jungle. I owe her."

"I owe *you*," I said. "Thanks for dropping those flamethrower helicopters. I thought I was toast."

"Burnt toast," he said. "I already owed you for breaking me out of that place. Hatch was ready to feed me to his rats."

"We'll call it even," I said.

"You guys going back out?" Tanner asked.

"We're planning on it. The Elgen kidnapped some little Chinese girl."

"That's what I heard. So you're off to China or Taiwan— someplace with chopsticks."

"Taiwan. Are you coming with us?"

"No. I'm still in recovery mode."

"We'll miss you." I turned back toward the door. "I'll let you get back to your book. See you around."

"I'll see you at the reception tonight," he said.

As I grabbed the doorknob he said, "Mike."

"Yeah?"

"It's good to see you again."

"You too," I said.

I walked back out into the hall, shutting the door behind me. Tanner looked completely different from the last time I'd seen him, but, like he'd said, considering the circumstances, I shouldn't have been surprised.

I walked down the hall to Taylor's room and knocked. She opened the door. Tessa was standing behind her looking over some clothes laid out on her bed.

"They brought your clothes?" I asked.

"Just a few minutes ago."

"How are they?"

"Pretty cute, actually."

"Do you still want to go for a walk?"

"Yes," she said, stepping out into the hallway.

We walked back to the Ranch House's main room, then out the same set of doors where we'd entered. Except for the chickens, the front yard was deserted. We walked west, which I only knew because the sun had started its late-afternoon decline.

"How's your room?" I asked.

"It's nice."

"Anything's nice compared to a Peruvian jail," I said.

"I was comparing it to my room at home." Her eyes immediately darkened. Her homesickness was taking a deeper and deeper toll. I reached out and took her hand.

"Where do you think we are?" she asked.

I looked around. "I don't know. It looks like Texas."

"Have you ever been to Texas?"

"No."

"Me neither," she said. "But I was thinking Texas too. Or Arizona."

We walked to the end of the Ranch House, then followed it around back. About fifty yards behind the building was a stable.

"Horses," Taylor said. As we walked toward them she said, "It's good to see your mother again."

"I wish your parents were here," I said. "I'm sure you'll see them soon."

Taylor didn't speak for a moment; then she said softly, "I don't think so. We're headed to Asia. Who knows if we'll ever come back?"

"I wouldn't go if I didn't think we'd come back."

She shook her head. "You'd still go. You're a hero that way." She looked back at me. "Do you think Taiwan will be as bad as Peru?"

"What do you mean by 'bad'?"

"Dangerous."

"I don't know," I said, then added, "But at least the food's got to be better."

She grinned. "I like Chinese food."

When we got to the stable, Taylor walked up to an Appaloosa colt standing next to a railing. "Hey, baby," she said. She rubbed the horse's nose and he nuzzled against her. "I love horses. When I was little I tried to talk my parents into getting me one, but it was too expensive."

"How much does a horse cost?"

"It depends on what kind. But it's not just the cost of buying one, it's also the upkeep—like feeding it and the stable rental. On my father's police salary, that wasn't going to happen." She sighed. "In my dream world I'd live on a ranch like this with a hundred acres of horse property, and every day I would go riding." She turned back and looked at me. "You love me."

"You read my mind," I said.

"I don't have to. You show me." In spite of what she'd just said, she looked sad. "I think it's strange that I don't have to guess anyone's feelings and everyone else in the world has to."

"You're lucky."

"Not always." She looked into my eyes. "Sometimes I wish you could read my mind. Sometimes it's hard explaining how I feel."

The way she said that made my heart ache. "How do you feel?"

She looked down for a moment, then back into my eyes. "When I was kidnapped, I kept telling myself that it was just a matter of time before I'd be rescued and things would go back to the way they were—cheerleading, after-game parties, hanging out with my friends at the Bagelmeister. . . ." Her eyes filled with tears. "I've finally realized that there is no going back."

"We'll go back someday," I said.

"No," she said, shaking her head. "Even if the Elgen and Hatch and all the bad guys in the world just disappeared, we still couldn't go back. We can go back to our homes and families, but it won't be the same. It never will be. The world didn't change, we did. We've seen too much evil. We grew up too fast." She covered her eyes with her hand and began to cry. I put my arms around her and pulled her into me. She laid her head on my shoulder.

"I'm sorry," I said.

Without looking up she said, "I never even went to a prom."

I held her until the sun began to dip below the western mountain range. We didn't talk, though a few times I purposely thought things knowing that she would hear them. Finally I said, "We'd better go back. We have that reception."

Taylor wiped her eyes. "All right."

We walked back to the Ranch House in silence. We stopped outside her bedroom door and I looked into her beautiful face. "Are you okay?"

She shook her head. "I probably look like I've been bawling."

"You're entitled," I said. I took her hand. "I'll talk to these guys about your parents. Maybe they can do something. They owe us, right?"

"Thank you." She leaned forward and kissed me. "I'll see you in an hour." As I turned to go she said, "I love you too, Michael."

I turned back. "I know. I still don't believe it, but I know."

5

The Reception

After showering I dressed in some of the new clothes they had brought, then lay back on my bed, waiting for them to come for us. Ostin was still snoring like a band-saw. As I lay there listening to him, all I could think about was what Taylor had said about never going back. She was right. I suppose I hadn't thought as much about it as she had because I wasn't really giving up anything. Everyone I cared about was here.

About ten minutes later someone knocked on our door. "Mr. Vey, Mr. Liss. It's time for the reception."

"C'mon, Ostin," I said, sitting up. "It's time."

"Time for what?" he said groggily.

"To go to the reception."

He yawned loudly, then rolled over. "There'd better be food at this thing."

* * *

By the time we walked out of our room, everyone else was already standing in the hallway. Zeus, McKenna, Abigail, and Ian were talking to Tanner.

Taylor walked up to me and took my hand. She looked like she was feeling a little better. Or at least she was doing a better job of hiding her pain. "Did you see Tanner?" she asked.

"I talked to him this afternoon."

"I hardly recognized him," she said. "He doesn't even look like the same person."

"That's exactly what I said."

Just then Tanner walked over to us. "Hey, Taylor. Mike."

"I was just saying how great you look," Taylor said.

"You look great too. Want to go out?"

Taylor grinned. "Flattered, but you'll have to ask my boyfriend."

"That's not going to happen," I said.

"Even after I dropped those helicopter gunships?"

"Even," I said.

He laughed. "Like my father used to say, if you don't ask, the answer is always no." He leaned in closer and his voice lowered. "Have you guys seen Zeus?"

"We see him every day," I said.

"I mean, *post*shower. He, like, doesn't stink. He smells good."

"We'll go right over and sniff him," Taylor said wryly.

Just then a voice from the end of the hall said, "You all clean up nicely." We all looked over to see Joel walking up the corridor. "Are we missing anyone?"

"Just me," Grace said, walking out of her room.

"Grace!" Tessa shouted. The girls hugged. "Where have you been?" Tessa asked.

"You know, after these guys took down the academy, I thought I'd come here for a while. How about you? I hear you've been hanging out in the jungle."

"It's true," Tessa said proudly. "I've been eating mashed tree larvae and fishing for piranha."

"That's crazy," Grace said.

"Seeing you is crazy," Tessa replied.

Like Tanner, Grace also looked different to me. Lighter. Healthier. I suppose being away from Hatch had that effect on people.

"The reunions are just beginning," Joel said. "Let's go to the party."

I was pleased to hear that the event had been upgraded from a reception to a party. We followed Joel back down the hallway, through a set of double doors, then outside to another building. The night air was cool and filled with the song of crickets.

"Is there food at this thing?" Ostin asked.

"What kind of a celebration would it be without food?" Joel replied. "I promise, there will be more than you can eat, including what may be the best steak you've ever had. It's dry-aged from range-fed beef raised right here on our ranch."

"I'm so happy," Ostin said.

"Good, because tonight is in your honor," Joel said. "Have a good time."

I took Taylor's hand. "That's an *order*," I whispered.

"Yes, it is," Joel said. I blushed, embarrassed that he'd heard me. He looked at Taylor. "I'm certain that Ms. Ridley will have an especially good time. In fact, I think I can guarantee it."

He doesn't know what he's guaranteed, I thought.

We stopped outside another set of double doors and Joel waited until everyone had caught up. "Are you ready?"

"Let's do this," Ian said, already knowing what was behind the doors.

Joel opened the doors, exposing a large dining hall filled with people. At the sight of us everyone burst into applause.

My mother was standing near the doorway, waiting to greet us, a broad smile on her face. "This is for you, my heroes."

We walked into the festivities. The room was decorated with crepe paper and balloons and a large sign that said WELCOME HEROES.

We were swarmed by people who wanted to shake our hands. After just a few minutes my mother pulled Taylor and me aside. "Taylor, are you okay?" she asked.

"Yes. This is really great."

My mother just looked at her. "You can tell me the truth."

Taylor half smiled. "I thought *I* was the mind reader."

"I'm a mother," she said. "I have intuition."

Taylor looked down. "I miss my family."

My mother nodded knowingly. "Of course you do. But not for much longer."

"What?"

"Didn't Joel tell you? They're working on bringing your parents here."

Taylor threw her arms around my mother. "Thank you, thank you, thank you."

My mother laughed. "It's the least they could do, right?"

Taylor's reaction filled me with both relief and joy.

A minute later Ostin walked over to us, dragging his parents with him. They all looked as happy as almonds in chocolate.

"Michael, honey," Mrs. Liss said. "It's so very good to see you."

"It's good to see you too," I said. It was. As eccentric as Ostin's mother was, I really liked her. She had always been good to me.

Ostin grinned mischievously. "I told them how we went back home and there were Elgen guards inside our apartment."

"You boys have had some excitement," Mrs. Liss said, not looking very happy about the fact.

"I'm watching out for him," I said.

"We know, Michael," Mr. Liss said. "Don't think we don't appreciate it."

Ostin squinted. "Who's watching over whom?"

"You're not watching over his diet," Mrs. Liss said. "He's not eating enough. I hardly recognized him. He's wasting away."

"Ruth," Mr. Liss said. "He's becoming a man."

McKenna sidled up to Ostin. "Are these your parents?"

"I'm sorry," Ostin said, realizing he'd abandoned her. "This is McKenna. She's my . . ." He hesitated.

"I'm his girlfriend," McKenna said.

Ostin's father looked both surprised and happy with the announcement. Mrs. Liss looked stunned. There was an awkward silence. "You're very pretty," Mrs. Liss finally said, making it sound like a bad thing. "Are you Japanese?"

Ostin groaned with embarrassment. "She's American, Mom."

"I'm Chinese-American," McKenna said.

"It's a pleasure to meet you," Mr. Liss said, shaking McKenna's hand.

Mrs. Liss said nothing, eyeing McKenna the way a boxer eyes an opponent before a match.

McKenna seemed unfazed. "It's a pleasure meeting you both as well."

Just then Taylor screamed so loudly the whole room stopped. "Mom!"

I turned around to see Mrs. Ridley standing in the open doorway. For a moment she just stared at Taylor in disbelief, then she shouted, "My baby!" The two of them ran to each other and embraced. Mrs. Ridley held Taylor tightly, crying over and over, "I can't believe it. I can't believe you're really here."

I turned to my mom, who was watching them joyfully. "Did you know Mrs. Ridley was already here?"

"I knew they had gone to get her," she said, her eyes still fixed on them. "She must have just arrived."

"Why didn't you tell her?"

She turned to me with a wise expression on her face. "Would you have wanted to spoil that surprise?"

After Taylor and her mother parted, Taylor brought her mother to me. "Mom, this is Michael, my boyfriend."

"We met once before," she said. "Your father and I went to his apartment after you disappeared."

I remembered that night well. Mr. and Mrs. Ridley had come to my apartment to see if I knew where Taylor was. I suddenly felt embarrassed. "I wasn't lying, I . . ."

"You don't need to explain," Mrs. Ridley said. "I've been briefed about everything. I don't know how to thank you for rescuing my daughter." She looked at Taylor and broke down crying again. "I'm never going to let you out of my sight again. Never, never, never again."

No one has told her about Taiwan, I thought.

About ten minutes later there was a loud squeal from a

microphone, then Joel said, "Good evening and welcome, everyone. There are some happy reunions going on tonight and I won't keep you from them. I just wanted to inform you that dinner is ready, so if everyone will find a seat, we'll begin serving."

My mother and I sat down at a table for eight with McKenna, the Lisses, Taylor, and her mother. After we were seated I asked Taylor's mom, "Where's Mr. Ridley?"

"He's at home," she said.

"He couldn't come?"

"If he knew Taylor was here he would have definitely come. He thinks I'm on a business trip for my travel company. In fact, until two hours ago, so did I."

"What do you mean?" Taylor asked.

"A few days ago, a woman came into my office. She said she represented a very wealthy Arizona businessman who was looking for someone to handle his company's travel, but wanted to meet me first. She said he would send his private jet. So just a little after noon we flew out from Boise. I thought we were headed to Scottsdale, Arizona, not wherever this place is."

"You don't know where we are either?" Taylor asked.

She shook her head. "Just an idea. It looks like Texas, but it could be Southern Arizona, New Mexico, or even Mexico. So after four hours in the air I asked the woman where we were. All she said was, 'On course.'

"It was only after the plane had landed on a private landing strip and these guys with guns met us that I began to panic. That's when the woman told me that they were taking me to see my daughter." She teared up. "At first I thought they had kidnapped me, too. But then on the drive here they explained things. It was all so strange, but when they told me that Taylor had these *powers* . . ." She turned to Taylor. "This is still so hard to believe—not just what is going on in the world, but that you can do what they say you can. Is it true?"

Taylor nodded. "Yes."

"Honey, why didn't you just tell us?"

"I was scared. It took me years to understand my powers, and once I finally did I didn't know how to tell you." She looked at me. "When I saw Michael use his powers it was the first time I thought someone might understand."

"It's lucky she met you," Mrs. Ridley said to me.

"Lucky for me," I said.

The dinner was as good as Joel promised. We had tomato and onion salad, sautéed mushrooms, mashed potatoes and gravy, sweet potato and pecan casserole, and huge T-bone steaks. While we were eating, Joel walked up to our table. "Is everyone having a good time?"

My mother looked up at him with a large smile. "Everything is wonderful. Thank you."

A similar smile crossed his face. The way they looked at each other made me wonder if there was more to their relationship.

"Thank you," Mrs. Ridley said. "For bringing us together."

"It's our pleasure," Joel replied. He looked at Taylor. "I guaranteed you an especially good evening. Was I right?"

"Yes, sir," Taylor said. "Thank you."

"It's the least we could do." He looked back over the table, his gaze again settling on my mother. "I'll let you enjoy your meals. But, sincerely, thank you for all you've done." He turned and walked off to another table.

About a half hour later the servers brought out coffee and a dessert of fresh berries with sweet cream, and Joel lifted the microphone again. "I hope you've all had a good time this evening. It's getting late and we start early tomorrow, so it's about time we wrapped things up. Tomorrow morning we will be meeting in this same room at eight o'clock for breakfast. For those assigned to Operation Jade Dragon, which includes all of our young guests, please come dressed and ready for your first briefing. Thank you again, and good night."

A few minutes later we all got up from the table. After telling everyone good night, I walked my mother to her room in the eastern wing of the Ranch House.

"You know, what Joel said earlier about you being a hero is true," my mother said. "Your father would have been just as proud of you as

I am." She looked me in the eyes. "But remember, you're still my son. You don't have to save the world."

"What if I'm the only one who can?"

Her expression was a mix of pride and sadness. "That's something you're going to have to answer yourself."

By the time I got back to my room the lights were out and Ostin was already asleep. At least I thought he was. As I quietly undressed and slipped into bed, Ostin said, "Good night."

"Good night," I answered. After a moment I added, "It was cool seeing your parents tonight."

"Yeah. It was. Sleep well."

"You too."

I had just closed my eyes when Ostin blurted out, "Did you know that the first woman to win a Nobel Peace Prize was from Taiwan?"

I think that could have waited until morning, I thought. "No."

"Did you know that Taiwan's national sport is American baseball? In 1995 they won the Little League World Series in the U.S."

"No," I said again. "Didn't know that either." For a moment I lay there wondering why he was sharing these random factoids—not that this was unprecedented for Ostin. I sometimes wondered if there was so much information in his head that it occasionally just burst out. At my thirteenth birthday party I was about to blow out the candles on my cake when he said, "Did you know that Stalin tried to create a humanzee—a hybrid of men and chimpanzees— hoping to create ape-men superwarriors?"

Suddenly it occurred to me why he was pelting me with facts about Taiwan. "Are you worried about Taiwan?"

"A little," he said quietly. "Are you?"

"I'm always worried."

"You don't act like it."

"I'm just good at faking." I was quiet a moment, then said, "You know, you don't have to go."

"If you go, I go."

"Thanks, buddy."

More silence.

"Michael."

"Yeah?"

"Something's really been bothering me."

"What's that?"

He hesitated for such a long time that for a moment I thought he'd fallen back asleep. "I know Hatch is a demon and all that, but what if he's right?"

"Right about what?"

"About making an electric species."

I wasn't sure what to say. "Why would he be right?"

"Everything evolves. That's how nature survives. What if an electric species is the natural evolution of humans?"

"There's nothing natural about what Hatch is doing."

"But wouldn't the world be a better place if we didn't have to worry about electricity anymore?"

"Better for whom? The humans the Elgen kill or the ones they enslave?"

"You're right."

"It's not electric power I'm worried about. Hatch doesn't care about the world or clean energy or a better species. He uses those things to manipulate people into doing what he wants them to do. Just think how much oil those boats of his need. He probably uses more oil in a second than most people use in three or four lifetimes."

"You're right," Ostin said. "It's subterfuge."

"Exactly," I said. *Whatever that means.* "Good night."

"Night," he echoed. I had almost fallen asleep when he said, "Michael."

"Yeah?"

"You won't tell anyone I said that, will you?"

"No."

"Okay. Good night."

"Good night," I said, rolling over. Now my eyes were open. I was ticking. *What if the devil was right?*

6

The Council

When I woke the next morning Ostin was dressed and sitting cross-legged on his bed, reading. "Did you hear that rooster?" he asked. "It was crowing at like four in the morning."

"No, I was too tired."

"If I were you I would have thrown a lightning ball at it."

"Should have," I said.

Actually, I felt more rested than I had in days. It was the first time I'd gone through an entire night without having a nightmare since we'd sunk the *Ampere*. "What time is it?"

"It's after seven. I was about to wake you up. Breakfast is in a half hour."

"I'm going to shower," I said. I grabbed some clothes, then walked into the bathroom. A hot shower is one of those luxuries you don't think about until you've been deprived of it. I stood under the water until Ostin banged on the door.

"It's time to go," he shouted.

"I'll meet you there," I said. "Save me some food."

By the time I arrived for breakfast the dining room was crowded. Taylor waved to me as I entered. She was sitting at a table next to both of our mothers. Ostin was sitting with his parents at the table behind them. The rest of our group, including Tanner and Grace, was sitting together.

Taylor got up to meet me. "Good morning, sunshine."

"Looks like I'm the last one here," I said.

"As usual," she said, smiling. "The food's over there. You just help yourself."

The food was served buffet-style from long tables at one end of the room. There was thick bacon and sausage, scrambled eggs, hash browns with cheese and red and green peppers, and blueberry pancakes. I loaded up with everything, then, after saying hi to the rest of our group, sat down next to my mother.

"How did you sleep?" my mom asked.

"Good. I didn't hear the four a.m. rooster alarm."

"I did," Taylor said. "It went on for like ten minutes before I rebooted it."

"You rebooted a rooster?"

"I think so. It stopped mid-crow."

"You should eat," my mother said. "The food here is really good. They grow everything. Even the wild blueberries in the pancakes. They're completely off the grid."

"This is where I want to be for the zombie apocalypse," Taylor said.

"Or the Elgen one," I said. I looked at Taylor's mother. "How are you, Mrs. Ridley?"

"Thank you for asking," she said. "I woke this morning thinking I had dreamed it all."

"Sometimes I still do too," I said. I took a bite of blueberry pancake. It was delicious.

"Tell us about Peru," Mrs. Ridley said. "And this tribe you were with."

"You should let him eat," Taylor said.

"It's okay," I said. "I wasn't with the Amacarra that long. But they were good to me. They saved me from the Elgen."

"I'd like to meet them someday," my mother said.

"You can't," I said, frowning. "They don't exist anymore. The Elgen and the Peruvian army wiped them out for helping us."

Her expression fell. "I'm so sorry. That's horrible."

"It's hard to believe that their entire civilization is gone," I said.

"If Hatch has his way that will be true of all of us," Taylor said.

Just the mention of Hatch's name brought a cloud over the table.

As we finished eating, Joel walked in. He greeted a few people, then went to the front of the room. "Excuse me, I have an announcement. For members of the Electroclan, we'll be meeting in this same room at nine thirty, so you'll have a little time to go back to your rooms or walk around the grounds before then, but please don't be late. Thank you."

As soon as he finished he headed to our table. I again noticed the unspoken interaction between him and my mother.

"Good morning," he said to all of us. Then he turned to me. "Michael, before things get started, the council would like to meet with you."

"What's the council?" I asked.

"They're the leadership of the resistance," my mother said.

"They're waiting in the conference room right now," Joel said.

"They're waiting for me?"

"Yes. As soon as you're ready."

I glanced at Taylor. "What about everyone else?"

"This time they'd just like to see you," Joel said.

I stood. "All right. Let's go."

My mother and I followed Joel back to the Ranch House, then across the main room, through a doorway, and down the central wing. At the end of the hallway Joel opened a door for me. "Go on in," he said.

I stepped into a large, sparse room with a long, oval table with nearly a dozen people sitting around it. They all stood as I entered. I recognized most of them from the night before, but with the exception of Joel and Sydney Lynn, I hadn't known who they were.

The man at the head of the table walked toward me. He was a little older than the others, handsome with graying temples. He extended his hand. "Michael, welcome. I'm Simon."

"You're not the voice," I said.

He shook his head. "No. I'm not. I'm the council chairman."

"You're the main guy?"

He smiled. "I am here. The council runs most of the day-to-day operations of the resistance, but the overall leadership is elsewhere. The threat and power of the Elgen is such that it's vital that we not keep all our eggs in the same basket. The council communicates with the voice, who directs operations from a confidential location."

"I'd just like to meet this person who keeps asking us to risk our lives," I said. "I think it's only fair."

"And so you shall," Simon said. "When the time is right. Please, have a seat at the table."

I sat down alongside Joel and my mom. Everyone else sat down as well.

"Welcome to the Timepiece Ranch," Simon said. "We have many questions for you, and I'm certain you have many for us as well. So please, if there's anything you would like to ask first, go right ahead."

I looked around the room, then said, "Where did you all come from?"

Simon smiled at my forthrightness. "That's a good question," he said. "The great physicist Newton said, 'To each action there is an equal and opposite reaction.' Simply put, we are the reaction to the rise of the Elgen."

"But who started *this*?"

Simon hesitated, then leaned toward me. "Your father was the founder."

I glanced at my mother, who nodded. "My father?"

"He was the first to realize what the Elgen had done. Back in those days, the Elgen's goals were different than what they are today.

They were all financial. Our group started when your father realized that everyone who was involved with the Elgen's initial MEI
tests was in danger and he began gathering us to protect one another.
I was one of the original members of that group as well. Almost
everyone at this table was somehow involved with those tests. The
Elgen brought us together by giving us something in common—they
threatened our lives."

My head spun a little. "I can't believe this is all because of my
father."

"I understand," Simon said. "What other questions do you have?"

"Why is everything such a secret?"

"Anonymity has always been our greatest weapon. Up until a few
weeks ago, the Elgen didn't even know that we existed. Now they do.
If they knew where we are right now, they would hunt us down and,
if possible, destroy us.

"We keep things secret for your safety as well as ours. As you well
know, the Elgen are not above torturing for information. That's why
we don't know the whereabouts of the voice. But we communicate
what we know to the voice and he guides us. This way, if something
were to happen to us, the resistance would continue. It must continue. Failure is not an option. Does that answer your question?"

"Yes, sir."

"If we fail, the world will fall into a state of captivity it has never
before experienced—not in its thousands of years of recorded history.
It would be Orwellian."

"So what is it that you do?"

"Whatever we need to do to hinder the Elgen," he replied. "We
began purely as a means of self-defense. We tracked the Elgen's
movements. As they grew, we began to infiltrate their organization.
Of course I can't tell you where or who our informants are, but when
the *Ampere* exploded, one of our people was killed."

I began ticking. "We . . . we killed one of the good guys?"

Simon shook his head. "It couldn't be helped."

"But if we knew they were there . . ."

"You didn't," Simon said. "As it was, you barely escaped with your lives. There was no way we could have alerted you. He died in the explosion, but whether the *Ampere* was destroyed or not, he would have died. Hatch had discovered who he was. He would have tortured and killed him. In that way, you did him a favor. He died instantly."

I was still ticking. Simon leaned forward. "Son, this is not your concern. Our agent knew the risk he was taking and he was willing to accept it. Just as you and your friends have risked your lives. Just as Wade *gave* his life. This is war. Lives have been lost. And unfortunately, more will be lost before it is all over."

Simon looked around the table at the other council members, then said, "Michael, we asked you here this morning so we could explain where we are in our struggle. Throughout history there have been men who have launched movements that have changed the world. Men like Genghis Khan or Adolf Hitler. At one point in their climb to power all of these men could have been stopped. But once their plans gained momentum, no one could stop them until their revolution had run its course. It is a cycle too familiar in history. By the time the world starts taking these revolutions seriously, it's already too late. They are like pythons in the jungle. The smallest child can crush a python egg. But let the snake hatch and grow and the python will squeeze and devour the child.

"Dr. C. James Hatch and his Elgen are on such a trajectory. In the last six months Dr. Hatch has taken complete control of the Elgen organization. He has built an elite guard of highly trained soldiers more than two thousand strong. We believe this number will double in the next six months, then double again the next year. He has an army. And they're better equipped than most police forces and militaries.

"Make no mistake, when the Elgen are ready, they will attempt to take over the world. The fact that they were prepared and willing to take over the country of Tuvalu demonstrates this.

"Last week in Lima, you and your Electroclan almost put an end to Hatch's climb. Almost. If it weren't for you he would have attacked and conquered the island nation of Tuvalu this week. I regret to inform you that he has not abandoned his original plans. You have slowed the Elgen but not stopped them. They will not be stopped so easily.

"In spite of your successes, we are losing this battle. The world views the Elgen as a blessing, because they promise them free, clean energy. They don't know—they don't *want* to know—the cost they will be forced to pay.

"I tell you this to prepare you. As you saw in Peru, you were not celebrated for liberating their country—you were demonized. That is often the way of heroes. And why, more times than not, we build monuments to those our fathers stoned. Someday you may be celebrated, but it might not be in your lifetime. Heroes are heroes precisely because they are willing to do what everyone else won't— oppose the popular voice. But we will know what you have done. And in your heart, so will you. And that is more than heroic. It is noble."

I let his words sink in. "We'll do our best," I said.

Simon smiled. "And that is noble too."

7

Gervaso

When I returned to the dining room the rest of the Electroclan was seated around two tables at one end of the room. A man I had never seen before was standing in front of them. He was dark-skinned, tall, and powerfully built. His hair was trimmed close to his scalp, revealing a thick scar that ran from the nape of his neck nearly to the top of his head. He had a narrow waist and biceps as large as my thighs. He reminded me of an action figure.

As I sat down he said with a slight Hispanic accent, "Welcome, Michael. We were waiting for you."

"I'm sorry," I said. "The council wanted to see me."

"I was told." He turned back toward the group. "Let's begin. My name is Gervaso. You don't need to know my last name, because we don't use them here. First, let me say that it's an honor to meet the brave young men and women of the Electroclan. I've been closely following your activities and what you have done is courageous and heroic. That's precisely what it's going to take to stop the Elgen."

He put his hands behind his back. "Today, I am here to brief you on our enemy. To understand why the Elgen do what they do, it helps to understand their history. The Elgen Corporation was founded in 1984 as a medical products company specializing in electroanalgesia—the technology of relieving pain through nerve stimulation. Much like what our Abigail here does."

We all looked at Abigail. She smiled and bowed.

"Their technology sounds modern, but in reality it is ancient science. More than two thousand years ago the Greek philosopher Socrates noticed that standing in a pool with some types of fish could produce numbing sensations. The Elgen's first patent was for an electric nerve implant to stop back pain.

"As they experimented with electricity, a brilliant scientist named Dr. Steven R. Coonradt discovered the original science that the MEI technology is based on. Recognizing its potential, the Elgen Corporation brought on some significant investors to pursue the technology, which took nearly three years longer to develop than they had planned. The investors—former chairman Schema was one of them—became impatient, and the CEO of Elgen, Dr. Hatch, was pressured for results. Against Dr. Coonradt's advice, the MEI was tested before it was ready. You know the results of that test as *you* are the results of that test. Seventeen surviving babies were born electric. The rest of the children born during that period died at birth or within days.

"It took only a few days for the Elgen to realize the connection between their experiments and the infant deaths and shut down the MEI. But there were others outside the Elgen Corporation who also made the connection. Not so coincidentally, these people mysteriously disappeared. Most of them died of electricity-related deaths." He looked at me. "Carl Vey, Michael's father, was one of those people.

"At this time, there was another important death. Dr. Coonradt, the only man who understood the science on which the MEI machine was built, also 'disappeared.' It was a grave mistake on the

Elgen's part but a blessing for the world. Had Dr. Coonradt lived he likely would have solved the problem with the MEI, and the Elgen would already be producing their new species.

"Faced with the possibility of lawsuits, the Elgen Corporation shut down the MEI project. The company was taken over by the investors and Schema became the new CEO. Dr. Hatch, who should have been thrown out, was demoted to executive director. We don't know why he wasn't fired, but knowing how Dr. Hatch works, I would wager that he threatened to go public with the Elgen deaths, which would have no doubt resulted in massive lawsuits and destroyed the company.

"At any rate, Hatch remained involved with the Elgen. He was ordered to find and follow the remaining seventeen children just in case they began dying later as well.

"It was about five years after the MEI experiment that the first electric child was discovered. That was Nichelle. She was in foster care and had been sent from home to home. Her record showed that wherever she went the home suffered damage to its electrical system. A few of them burned down.

"Because she had no permanent home and a history of running away, she was easily taken in by the Elgen. They began running tests on her and discovered her power. That's when they began, without the board's consent, kidnapping the other electric children. As you know, the last to be found were Michael and Taylor.

"It was likely during this time that Dr. Hatch came up with the idea that the MEI could be used to create a super-race of humans. This is nothing new. Throughout history, others have tried to create a super-race. Unfortunately for Hatch, with Dr. Coonradt gone, their ongoing experiments with the MEI were largely unsuccessful, with one big exception—they accidentally discovered how to electrify rats.

"The timing of this 'accident' was fortunate for Hatch. The board had just become aware of Dr. Hatch's crimes and had resolved to terminate him. Instead, Hatch won them over with a small machine he had created called the Elecage—a prototype to the Starxource plants.

Hatch demonstrated to the board how this dishwasher-size box was able to produce enough energy to power the entire Elgen building without pollution or fossil fuels and at a fraction of the cost of conventional energy sources.

"Chairman Schema and the board immediately recognized the potential of what Hatch had developed and the very real possibility of controlling the world's electricity. They would make trillions of dollars.

"Of course Hatch also realized the potential of his discovery, but he never lost sight of his original plan—to create a master race. Hatch still believes that he will someday be the father of a race that will dominate the world and rule the Nonels."

"What's a Nonel?" Jack asked.

"You're a Nonel," Gervaso said. "So am I. Nonel is the term Hatch uses to refer to nonelectric humans. It is ironic that Hatch himself *is* a Nonel.

"In the meantime, the Elgen have continued to build Starxource plants, which, for the most part, have been very successful. The Elgen are already earning more than seven billion dollars a year selling electricity. Hatch has used the plants' success to appease the board over his continual experiments with producing more electric children—something most of the board was opposed to.

"Hatch knew that his conflict with the board would someday come to a head, so he prepared for it. He trained an army of Elgen guards with the stated purpose of protecting their Starxource plants, but his real reason was to someday take over the company, which is what he did less than a month ago.

"This brings us to where we are today. A few weeks ago a scientific paper surfaced online from the Chinese province of Shanxi. It was written by a Chinese scientist named Lin YuLong, which, translated to English, means 'jade dragon.'

"The paper theorized that human DNA could be electrically altered through the use of magnetically altered electrons. As with many major discoveries, only a few understood the importance of the theory, and the paper was largely ignored by the scientific world. The first paper YuLong wrote hypothesized that the result would likely kill 71.43 percent of the species, which, remarkably, is within a half percent of the actual mortality rate of the MEI.

"Then YuLong claimed to have solved the problem, predicting a 0.003 percent mortality rate. Fortunately, the scientist did not divulge the mathematical formula used on the alteration.

"We immediately sent our Taiwanese associate to China to track down this scientist. We were surprised to discover that Jade Dragon wasn't a scientist, but rather a nine-year-old girl, and that only days before she had been kidnapped."

"How do you know that the Elgen kidnapped her?" Ostin asked.

"We don't. But this is what we do know. First, we know that the Elgen desperately want the information she has. Second, we know that the Elgen Lung Li force was called to the Shanxi province of China just days before Jade Dragon disappeared."

Ostin looked at me. "What's a Lung Li?" he whispered. I shrugged.

"And third, we know that the *Volta*, the Elgen's floating laboratory, has changed course and is now sailing to Taiwan. The pieces all fit."

"Why would they need the *Volta*?" I asked.

"It's where the original MEI is. And more important, it's where their scientists are."

"How long ago was she kidnapped?" Ostin asked.

"It's been seven days."

"Then it may already be too late," Ostin said. "Once they have the information, it's over."

"We have hope that she will not turn the information over to them."

"They'll get it from her," Jack said. "They'll torture her."

"You know better than anyone that the Elgen are not above torture—even with a child. But in the case of Jade Dragon it probably won't do them any good. Jade Dragon is not only deaf and mute, she's an autistic savant. She is, in all likelihood, extremely confused and frightened."

"What's a savant?" Abigail asked.

"Savants are highly gifted individuals capable of remarkable mental feats," Gervaso said. "For instance, an American autistic savant named Kim Peek could read two pages of a book at the same time in about three seconds and memorize everything on them. Before he died, he had read more than twelve thousand books and could recite any of them word for word.

"Another savant is Leslie Lemke; he was born blind and with such severe birth defects that he didn't learn how to walk until he was fifteen years old. When he was sixteen, his mother woke in the middle of the night to the sound of piano music and thought she'd left the television on. She discovered that it was her son. Even though Leslie had never had a single lesson, he was flawlessly playing a Tchaikovsky piano concerto after hearing it just once on the television.

"There are also reports of a savant who could learn a foreign language in less than a week, and another who could solve math equations as quickly as a calculator and recite pi up to twenty-eight thousand places."

"Ostin, to how many places can you recite pi?" Abigail asked.

Ostin gulped. "Maybe a couple hundred."

"You mean they're even smarter than Ostin?" Zeus asked.

Ostin frowned.

"Perhaps in a specific field," Gervaso said kindly. Ostin relaxed.

"How long until the *Volta* reaches Taiwan?" I asked.

"If she continues at her current speed, about two weeks. You'll need to be in Taiwan well in advance to prepare."

"So what do we do while we're here?" Taylor asked.

"We'd like to work with you in developing your powers," Gervaso said.

"Like the Elgen did," Zeus said.

"I do not like the comparison, but yes. The Elgen are evil, not stupid." Gervaso looked around the room. "Are there any more questions?"

"Is there a gym?" Jack asked.

"Yes. It's in building C, near the silos. There's also a pool and hot tub."

"That's where we're headed," Tessa said.

"By 'we' you mean 'you,'" Zeus said.

"I didn't say you have to get in," she replied.

"If there are no more questions," Gervaso said, "I think that's enough for now. You have the rest of the day free. I'll see you here tomorrow morning at nine thirty. Have a good day."

Gervaso stopped me on the way out. "Michael, I'd like to try something with your powers. Would that be all right?"

"Sure."

"I'll meet you here after lunch."

As we walked from the room Ostin said to me, "I know what I'm going to do to prepare."

"What?" I asked.

"I'm going to learn Chinese."

"In one week?"

"Probably not all of it," he said. Then added, "I'm not a savant."

I patted him on the back. "Trust me, you're close enough."

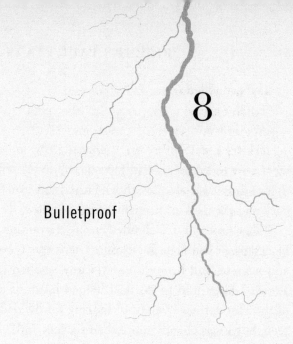

8

Bulletproof

Lunch was fried chicken, mashed potatoes with white gravy, and a homemade soda the lunch lady called sarsaparilla, which tasted like root beer. Taylor and I sat next to Jack and Abigail.

"So what's the story on this Gervaso guy?" I asked. "He looks like a Marine."

"He's tougher than that," Jack said. "He was Delta Force, the army's elite tactical-combat and antiterrorist unit. They only take the best of the best. They're trained in marksmanship, demolition and entry, hostage rescue, espionage, surveillance, and diplomatic protection. He's like a one-man army."

"Like you," Abigail said to Jack. He smiled.

Taylor looked at Jack for a moment, then asked, "How are you doing?"

"Fine," he said. Then he flinched a little. "You mean, with Wade?"

Taylor nodded. "Yes."

"I miss him."

"We do too," I said.

Jack took a deep breath, then said, "Around four summers ago I went over to Wade's house. He was still living with his old man back then. I didn't get along with his father, so I usually just went around back and climbed in through Wade's window.

"This time, after I climbed inside, I couldn't find Wade. Then I heard him. He was in his closet. There was blood all over the floor and his face and his eyes were nearly swollen shut. His father had almost beaten him to death. I helped him out and wiped off some of the blood, then I went out looking for his dad. I was only like fifteen, but I was already more than six feet and a hundred and ninety pounds. His father was a little man. He was drunk, sitting on the floor in the hall.

"The dude came at me with a bottle. I was crazy mad. I knocked him down, then started waling on him. Then Wade shouted, 'Stop! Please stop.' He had crawled out of his room to save his father. If it wasn't for Wade I might have killed that drunk." Jack slowly shook his head. "I was so pumped with adrenaline that I lifted the guy with one hand and shoved him against the wall. I told him if he ever touched Wade again that the next time I wouldn't stop." Jack looked down. "Child services took Wade out of the house the next week."

Abigail reached over and took Jack's hand.

"From then on, I felt like it was my job to protect him. That's what I can't get over. Failing him." Jack looked into my eyes. "I relive his death over and over. If I could just have those five minutes back. Just five minutes . . ."

Taylor's eyes welled up. "I'm so sorry."

Jack looked up at her. "Can you take the pain away from me? Like you did with Zeus?"

Taylor frowned. "Maybe. But I'd have to take away all your memories of Wade. Do you really want to forget him?"

Jack thought for a moment, then slowly shook his head. "No. It's all I have left of him." He put his hand over his eyes.

Abigail put her arm around Jack. I think she was using her power because I noticed that he relaxed a bit. We finished eating in silence.

About fifteen minutes later Gervaso walked into the dining room looking for me. "Are you ready?"

"Sure. How long will we be?"

"About half an hour."

"I'll be in my room," Taylor said. "Come find me when you're done."

I followed Gervaso outside the dining hall to a warehouse near the stables. He grabbed a green metal ammo box from a shelf, and then we got in one of the jeeps and drove about a half mile from the house to a shooting range. There were targets scattered all over the terrain and the ground was littered with brass bullet casings. Gervaso parked the jeep next to a gun mounted on a turret.

"Come," he said. We walked about a hundred feet to a round bull's-eye mounted to a bale of hay. "I've been speaking with Jaime," he said. "He told me that he saw you push an army truck with your magnetism. Is that true?"

"Yeah. It wasn't moving too fast; it was in a convoy."

"I want to try something. When I say 'now,' I want you to push like you did that jeep. That direction," he said, pointing away from me.

"What do you want me to push?"

"Just the air," he said. "Don't move, just push when I tell you to. Understand?"

I nodded. "Okay."

"Stand right here," he said, moving me toward the target. He turned and walked back to the mounted gun, then looked through the gun's scope and put his finger on the trigger. The gun was pointing right at me.

"Wait!" I shouted. "You're not going to shoot that thing at me are you?"

"Not at you. The target."

"Yeah, and I'm like six inches away from the target. No offense, but I don't know how good of a shot you are."

"It won't hit you. The gun's been calibrated to hit the target dead center each time."

"This is crazy," I mumbled. "How many bullets?"

"This is an M16 automatic, so I'm going to fire a thirty-round clip."

I stepped back. "Wait, you didn't tell me you're firing a freaking *machine gun* at me. What if you're off a few inches?"

"Don't worry, they'd definitely fire me if I killed you."

I just stared at him.

He grinned. "I'm joking." He looked back through the scope. "I've already tested more than three hundred rounds."

Shaking my head, I stepped back toward the target. "Whatever."

"Are you ready?"

"As I'll ever be," I said. I started ticking, blinking my right eye.

"Are you ready?" he repeated.

"All right. Ready!" I shouted.

"Now!"

I pulsed. Fire leaped from the gun barrel as it spit bullets toward the target. I suppose I was pretty hyped up from adrenaline because I pulsed hard enough to knock over a metal ammo box almost twenty yards away.

"Clear!" Gervaso shouted. He raised his head from the gun as smoke drifted up from its barrel.

I stepped back and examined the target. None of the bullets had hit the bull's-eye. Not one. "I thought you said this thing was calibrated!" I shouted.

Gervaso walked up to the target, counting the holes as he approached. "You're right. Only eight of thirty rounds even hit on the target."

"You could have killed me," I said, still ticking.

"No," he said calmly. "Not if I wanted to." He ran his finger down the target, then looked back at me. "The gun wasn't off. You moved those bullets."

"You're saying it's my fault you missed?"

He smiled. "I'm saying that with a little more practice, you're going to be bulletproof."

9

The Woman Out Back

That night after dinner I went out for a walk. I wanted to be alone. No, I *needed* to be alone. Since the moment we'd left Peru I hadn't had much privacy, and I had a lot to think about. I suppose that I needed some solitude to let everything settle before I took on the next phase of my bizarre new life. I think Taylor must have understood because she didn't say anything as I slipped out the back.

Even though the sun had set an hour earlier, it was still warm outside and the compound grounds were lit by a nearly full moon. I walked over to the helipad to look at the helicopter, then wandered farther back to where Taylor and I had talked the night before.

As I approached the stable I thought I heard someone crying. I walked quietly around the side of the Ranch House to see a woman leaning against the fence. The moon's illumination was bright enough that I could at least partially see her. She was older than me, probably in her late twenties, tall and thin with long dark hair that fell over half her face. I didn't remember seeing her at the reception.

She was crying. I felt awkward for intruding on her privacy, and I was about to turn back when she looked up at me with a startled expression. I think my glow must have frightened her. (If you've never seen one of us glow, it takes a little getting used to—just one of many reasons I was never allowed sleepovers as a child.) For a moment we just looked at each other.

"Are you okay?" I asked.

She wiped her eyes. "You're one of *them*."

Them? I wasn't sure how to respond. Finally I said, "Sorry, I'll leave you alone."

As I turned to leave she said, "I'm crying for my husband."

I turned back. "Your husband?"

"He was killed in action."

"I'm sorry," I said.

For a moment she just looked at me with dark, angry eyes. Then she said, "You should be. You killed him."

Her words rolled over me like a train. "I didn't kill your husband."

"He was on the *Ampere* when you blew it up."

For several moments I was speechless. Finally I said again, "I'm sorry."

"Me too," she said. She wiped her eyes, then turned and walked back to the house.

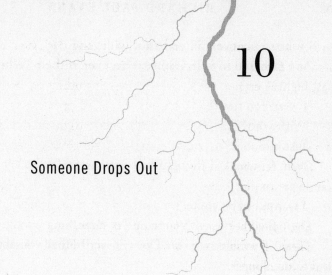

10

Someone Drops Out

I woke in the night drenched in sweat. I had dreamed about the *Ampere* again. This time I was trying to save someone trapped inside, but the smoke and flames and the force of the water kept me back. I wasn't sure who it was, I just knew it was someone important to me. When I finally got to them they were underwater, drowned, their limbs and hair floating, lifeless. Then I saw the person's face. It was white and swollen, and his eyes were wide open. It was me.

It took me several hours to fall asleep again. I felt like I'd only slept a few minutes when Ostin woke me.

"Michael, it's time to get up."

"You've got to be kidding," I groaned. "I didn't sleep."

"More nightmares?"

"Yeah."

"Just stay in bed. I'll tell them you're sick."

I rubbed my eyes. "No, I've got to get up."

As I gathered myself, Ostin sat back on his bed. "Where were you last night?"

"I went for a walk."

"With who?"

"Just me."

Ostin frowned. "I thought you were with Taylor. Why didn't you come get me?"

"I wanted to be alone."

He looked at me with concern. "Is something wrong?"

"Yeah." I exhaled slowly. "Does it ever bother you about what we did to the *Ampere*?"

"We did what we had to do."

"I know. But all those lives . . . there were innocent people on that boat."

"Not so innocent," he said. "If you take the beast's money, you are part of the beast. That's the way war is. There is no middle ground." He leaned forward. "We either stopped the Elgen from enslaving and killing more people or we didn't. That's the only issue." He looked at me quizzically. "Did something happen last night?"

"On my walk I met a woman. Her husband was on the *Ampere* when we blew it up. She said we killed him."

Ostin nodded slowly. "No wonder." He looked me in the eyes. "Listen, if he was on the *Ampere*, he knew what was going on. In fact, he might have been the one who told them that we had to sink the boat. He accepted the risk, just like we did. We almost died on that boat."

"But we didn't."

"No, we got lucky." He seemed to study me for a moment, then he said, "What you're feeling is called survivor's guilt. It happens in war. But you can't blame yourself for the chaos of war. You stood up to the bully to protect someone else. You didn't do it because you wanted to or for personal gain. You didn't act carelessly. You did it to protect others. That makes you a hero and no matter how awful war is, that doesn't change that fact. Don't let anyone tell you otherwise. Especially yourself."

I pondered his words for a moment, then said, "Thanks, buddy."

"That's what I'm here for," he said. "Now can we get some breakfast?"

After another big breakfast we met with Gervaso again. This time he had a map of the island of Taiwan taped to the wall behind him.

"Today we're going to talk about your mission. We now have positive verification from our informants that Jade Dragon is being held at the Taiwan Starxource plant, waiting for the *Volta*, the Elgen's science boat, to arrive." He walked over to his map. "The Starxource plant is located about here," he said, touching a point on the map with his finger, "in southwest Taiwan, just a few kilometers northwest of the city of Kaohsiung, the second largest city in Taiwan.

"The Taiwan Starxource plant is the largest in the world. It does not have the landmass around it that the Peruvian plant had, but the facility itself is larger. Like the Peruvian plant, it is also an Elgen training center, which means there will be more guards than usual."

We all groaned.

"Lovely," Ostin said.

"It gets worse," Gervaso said. "In addition to the Elgen, you will also be facing the Taiwanese army."

"Just like the Peruvian army," Zeus said.

"Not exactly. The Peruvian army is ranked fifty-ninth in the world. The Taiwanese army is ranked seventeenth, just below Canada. It is a much more powerful force."

"Why are they involved?" I asked.

"For good reason. The Starxource plant is vital to Taiwan's national security. Taiwan imports one hundred percent of their energy, so they are extremely vulnerable. After the destruction of the Peruvian plant, the Taiwanese army took up the defense of the plant.

"We do not recommend shutting down the Taiwanese plant if you can help it. It will cost many, many innocent lives if you do, and you will be regarded as terrorists. It is best if you just get into the plant, get the girl, and get out."

"Did he really say 'just'?" Tessa said.

"Piece of cake," Jack said sarcastically.

"You're saying that the nine of us are taking on the seventeenth-largest army in the world?" Taylor asked.

"*Eight* of you," Gervaso said. "Abigail will not be going to Taiwan."

We all looked over at her. Jack must have already known, because he was the only one who didn't look surprised.

"This is at our insistence," Gervaso said. "Her powers will not be useful in Taiwan. We do not want to risk any of your lives unnecessarily."

"I'm sorry," Abigail said, looking embarrassed.

"They're right," I said. "And if we're taking on such a big force, we're not going to succeed with numbers anyway."

"You can say that again," Ostin said.

"Exactly," Gervaso said. "This must be a covert operation."

Ostin raised his hand. "Yesterday you said something about the Lung Li. Who and what are they?"

Gervaso frowned. "The Lung Li is an elite branch of the Elgen guard made up of Asian mercenaries. They are mostly Chinese, but there are Japanese, Vietnamese, Korean, and Thai members as well. *Lung Li*, in Chinese, means 'dragon strength' or 'power.' It's fitting. They are a formidable group of warriors. They are highly disciplined, fierce fighters. They make the rest of the Elgen guard look like mall cops."

"This just keeps getting better," Taylor said.

"They are also highly superstitious," Gervaso continued. "They follow astrology and ancient mysticism. They believe that the electric children are the literal reincarnation of the lightning gods of ancient Chinese legend."

"So if I shock them crazy they'll all be worshipping me," Zeus said, grinning.

"I'm afraid not," Gervaso said. "They regard the Electroclan as fallen angels. Demons."

"That's creepy," Taylor said.

"Not surprisingly, they religiously follow the teachings of Sun Tzu's *The Art of War*."

"These guys sound like ninjas," Ostin said.

Gervaso nodded. "Precisely. They are very much a modern-day

version of the ninjas. They have all taken oaths to die for the Lung Li and the Elgen cause. When they take the oath they are branded with the Lung Li symbol, the fiery dragon head."

"Branded?" Taylor said. "Like cattle?"

Gervaso nodded. "With a red-hot poker. It's a sign of bravery."

"Or insanity," Tessa said.

I groaned. "Great. We're fighting high-tech ninjas who like pain."

"Hopefully you'll never see them," Gervaso said.

"Isn't that the point of ninjas?" Ostin said. "You're not *supposed* to see them."

"Let me get this straight," Tessa said. "The *eight* of us are taking on a Starxource plant with extra Elgen guards, the entire Taiwanese army, and a powerful group of ninjas?"

Gervaso nodded. "Yes, but it could get worse."

"How could it possibly get worse?" Zeus asked.

"There's a chance that Hatch may be sending his Glows to protect the girl. We will know within a few days."

"We're *so* dead," Tessa said.

No one else said anything.

That afternoon Gervaso and I practiced my magnetic-bullet thing again. This time it was my idea. After our morning meeting I felt even more motivated to prepare. Fear is a great motivator.

I experimented with focusing my pulse in different ways to see if I could increase the effect. It worked. Once I knocked a bullet out of range by more than eight feet.

"I can deflect bullets," I said.

"Not just bullets," Gervaso said. "If you can deflect something as small and fast as a bullet, you could deflect knives, axes, even Chinese stars."

"Like in the movies," I said.

"Yes. Just like in the movies," he replied.

I just hoped our movie had a happy ending.

PART TWO

11

The Four Horsemen

The ES *Faraday* Boardroom
Port of Callao Harbor, Peru

The Elgen board stood at attention as Hatch walked into the room. He sank into his throne-like leather chair, pausing a moment before saying, "You may be seated." He silently looked around the table, his gaze resting momentarily on each member of the board. Then he took a deep breath and leaned back in his chair. "I will be leaving for Switzerland in the morning. Our bankers are not cooperating with my demands, so I, along with Tara and Torstyn, will be paying them a visit. It's possible that Schema might be involved."

Hatch had sent out a memo to all Elgen that the former chairman was a traitor and criminal and should he still be alive, the reward for his capture was a million dollars.

"But, sir, wasn't Schema killed on the *Ampere?*" asked Six.

"So we hoped. But some recovered video footage has led us to believe that he and the other traitors escaped the *Ampere* before it was destroyed. If so, I'm certain he would seek out our bankers, which is all the more reason to pay them a visit." Hatch paused again, then added, "But that isn't why I convened this meeting."

Hatch stood, his expression growing impassioned. "We are entering a new age, Elgen. A golden age. A *renaissance.* We are on the cusp of fulfilling our vision. We are close to solving the problem with the MEI technology.

"This breakthrough came from a place we did not expect. A young Chinese girl named Jade Dragon is the first to fully understand the science behind the MEI since the brilliant scientist Dr. Coonradt. She will teach our scientists how to use the MEI to populate the world with a new species."

"But, sir," Seven said, "our scientists have been successfully using the MEI for years, electrifying rats."

"*Rats,*" Hatch said, shaking his head. "*Using* the MEI is simple. It's like a child playing a video game. He may know how to turn the machine on and even win the game, but he has no idea how the machine actually works. Until this girl came along, no one, including our scientists, has understood the actual dynamics of how the MEI alters human DNA. This child has figured it out without even knowing the MEI existed. It's only a matter of time before we have the information we need from her to make the necessary alterations to the MEI that will allow us to create electric children"—he paused— "instead of just dead ones."

Hatch looked around the room. "Are there any questions?"

Seven raised his hand. "After we solve the problems with the MEI, will we continue building Starxource plants?"

"Of course," Hatch replied. "Populating the world with a new species will take more than a century. In the meantime, there are already seven billion Nonels on this planet. It is time we brought those numbers down to a manageable number."

"What's a manageable number?" Six asked.

"A billion or so."

"Will the Nonels ever become completely extinct?" Seven asked.

"I've not yet decided, but probably not. Just as the horse has survived the automobile, there will always be a use for beasts of burden."

"Do you mean slave labor?" Seven asked.

"You make that sound like a bad thing," Hatch said with a dark smile. The rest of the board members laughed.

"In spite of our setback in Peru, things are moving forward at a tremendous pace. The world's hunger for energy has driven the Nonels to our door in increasing numbers. Dr. Benson will now give us our production report."

A woman sitting to the side of the table wearing a white lab coat stood. "Good afternoon. I'm pleased to report that the Chad, Greece, and Portugal plants will be fully operational by the end of next month. That will bring us to twenty-nine operating plants—though, after the recent terrorist attack, the Peruvian plant will not be fully operational for another eight months.

"We are currently generating 776 million kilowatt hours each year and providing power to 194 million people, or 3.6 percent of the world's energy. After we complete our Southern India, Pakistan, and Philippines plants we will be generating 2.8 billion kilowatt hours per year, providing power for about 11 percent of the world's population, and 13 percent of the electricity currently being generated in the world. We are slightly ahead of schedule to reach our twenty-four-month goal of providing power to 19.89 percent of the world's countries, comprising 46 percent of the global population."

Hatch smiled with satisfaction. "I should add that currently, more than a billion and a half people in the world have no access to electricity. We will remedy this in three years. We will be their saviors."

"Admiral, what if the oil producers pressure governments to stop us?" Six asked.

"Do you think I'm not prepared?" Hatch asked, his tone revealing his annoyance with the question.

Six wilted. "No, sir."

"I was prepared long before they considered us a threat. This is global fencing. *Pave* and *repave*. Should Japan declare war on us, the Taiwanese and Filipinos will declare war on them. How could they not? We are providing eighty-six percent of Taiwan's electricity and seventy-two percent of the Philippines' energy. To lose our electricity would create anarchy at home. They can have wars in their own streets or war abroad; it's an easy choice."

"Sir, you said that we will reduce the Earth's population. How?" Eleven asked.

"Efficiently, of course," Hatch said. "Our efforts will be of biblical proportions."

"Biblical?" Seven asked.

"Yes," Hatch said. "Biblical. We are the Four Horsemen of the Apocalypse prophesized to bring about the end of man's history. It was written thousands of years ago that 'They,' meaning us, 'were given power over the Earth to kill by sword, famine, plague, and the wild beasts.'

"Of course we will not dirty our hands by bearing swords. We will provide money and arms to those countries who follow us; then we shall lead them into conflict. We'll start with the small countries and, like the wars in Korea and Vietnam, these conflicts will draw bigger countries in behind them until we have World War Three. Hundreds of millions will die.

"But war is only the first horseman; next comes famine. War has always produced scarcity, but we shall add to it. We will shut down power to those producing food and to those who distribute it. There will be food riots and starvation and the human population will decrease still more.

"Then comes the third horseman—plagues. Our laboratories will release the plagues we have created—viruses that do not affect our electric species. Our GPs will be our carriers. We will infect them, then let them out into the world, and they will spread their diseases in public places. The death toll will dwarf the black plague of the fourteenth century.

"Then, when all is in commotion, and we have created a race of our superior electrical beings in sufficient number, we will unleash the wild beasts, our electric rats, to destroy and feast on what is left of the humans.

MICHAEL VEY: HUNT FOR JADE DRAGON 71

"Our scientists have just perfected the ER46, a strain of electric rat that will breed quickly and spread throughout cities, but that has been genetically disposed to survive for just three generations and then reproduce no more. The plague of beasts will last six years. The only thing that will be left in their wake will be the cities the Nonels have built, still intact." Hatch looked around the table. "Any other questions?"

Seven began clapping, soon followed by the others.

"Very well," Hatch said. "I'm off to Switzerland, then Taiwan. This meeting is adjourned."

PART THREE

12

Hungry Eagles

Beverly Hills Mall
Beverly Grove, Los Angeles, California

"Dude, we've got to go," Quentin shouted at Bryan, loud enough to be heard over the sounds of the video arcade.

"Just a minute," Bryan said. His eyes were glued to his game, as Quentin and Torstyn watched from behind. "I'm not done yet."

"Yes, you are," Quentin said. He raised his hand and the video game popped loudly and its screen went black.

"Dude, I was up to level eighteen! Turn it back on."

"Yeah, right." Quentin said. "I fried the circuitry. No one's ever turning that game back on."

"Thanks a lot," Bryan said, standing.

"It's time to go," Torstyn said. "We're meeting the girls for dinner at the food court before Tara and I have to leave."

Torstyn and Tara were scheduled to fly out from Beverly Hills to Switzerland at midnight, while Quentin, Kylee, and Bryan would fly directly to Taiwan the next morning, which was why they had decided to make one last trip to the mall.

"You didn't have to destroy the game," Bryan grumbled.

"You like that?" Quentin said as they walked out of the arcade. "Watch this." He raised his hand and pulsed. The entire arcade went dark. There was a moment of stunned silence; then everyone started shouting. Quentin grinned. "Do you have any idea how much it will cost them to fix that mess?"

Tara and Kylee were already in the food court when the boys arrived. They were leaning against a wall near the entrance, comparing their clothing purchases.

"Hey, beautifuls," Quentin said to the girls.

"It's about time you guys got here," Tara said. "We're starving."

"We had to drag Bryan away from Grand Theft Auto. Where do you want to eat? They've got sushi, Chinese, Mexican, Italian . . ."

"I'm getting Chinese," Bryan said. "I gotta have tofu."

"You've got tofu for brains," Torstyn said. "You're going to be eating nothing but Chinese food for the next month."

"I'm getting a calzone," Quentin said.

"Sounds good to me," Torstyn said.

"And me," Kylee said.

"Make that four," Tara said.

"I'm still getting Chinese," Bryan said, walking off alone.

"Suey yourself," Torstyn said.

Quentin led the rest of them over to DiSera's, an Italian café squeezed in between a corn dog restaurant and a sandwich shop.

"Do you know what 'calzone' means in Italian?" Quentin asked.

"Let me guess," Tara said. "Folded pizza?"

Quentin shook his head. "It means *socks*."

Tara grimaced. "You mean like the kind you wear on your feet?"

"*Esatto*," he replied.

"Makes you want the capellini instead," Kylee said.

"Capellini means hair," Quentin said.

"Now I'm totally grossed out," Tara said. "The Italians don't know how to name food."

"But they know how to make it," Quentin said.

Quentin ordered four calzones, two capellini with sage and pine nuts, and six garlic breads topped with mozzarella cheese. After they'd gotten their food they walked out to the courtyard.

"There's no place to sit," Tara said. "This place is a zoo."

"No," Quentin said. "It's a chicken pen. And these chickens are too stupid to know they should scatter when hungry Eagles arrive."

"I can take care of the chickens," Torstyn said. "Where do you want to sit?"

"Ladies?" Quentin said.

"How about that table right there?" Tara said, pointing to a rectangular table crowded with diners.

"You got it," Torstyn said. He reached out toward the table. Suddenly everyone jumped up screaming and clutching their backsides. Nearly half the people in the food court turned to look at them.

Two of the people tried sitting back down, but after Torstyn burned them again they grabbed their trays and left.

"Leaving so soon?" Torstyn said as he sat down at the now-abandoned table.

Quentin sat at the head of the table, with Torstyn on one side and Tara on the other. It had taken a while for Torstyn to accept Quentin's leadership of the group but now that he had, he had done so completely, assigning himself the role of enforcer.

"It's good to get back to Beverly Hills," Kylee said, sipping her Coke. "It feels like it's been years since I've been shopping."

"It's been a week," Quentin said. "If that."

"I mean *real* shopping," she said.

"As opposed to *fake* shopping?" Torstyn said.

"Don't mind them," Tara said. "I know what you mean."

"Enjoy it," Quentin said. "You're not going to get any shopping done in Taiwan."

"They have malls," Tara said. "I checked."

"You won't have time to shop," Quentin said. "We've got a job to do."

Kylee frowned. "I don't even know where Taiwan is."

"It's an island a hundred miles off the southeast coast of China," Quentin said.

"Why are we going there?"

"To guard a girl the Lung Li brought to the Starxource compound," Quentin said. "Didn't you hear anything Dr. Hatch said on the call last night?"

"I was thinking about something else."

"You were doing your nails," Torstyn said.

Kylee glared at him. "You have a problem with that?"

Torstyn speared his pasta. "Apparently you do. You can't paint your nails and think at the same time?"

"Chill," Quentin said.

"I don't understand what's so special about this girl," Tara said.

"She's a savant," Quentin said.

"What's that?"

"It means she's smart. Like genius smart."

Tara's brow fell. "And why does this concern us?"

Quentin glanced around, then said in a softer tone, "I'm not supposed to tell you this, but if you can keep it to yourself, I will."

"I can," Tara said. "Kylee?"

She looked up from her cell phone. "What?"

"She won't understand what you say anyway," Torstyn said.

"You're such a jerk," Kylee said.

Torstyn smiled. "Only to you."

"All right," Quentin said. "The Elgen scientists think this girl can show them how to make the MEI mass-produce Glows."

Tara frowned. "So what you're saying is that with her help, they're going to make a lot more of us."

Quentin nodded. "Exactly."

"And why is this a good thing? If there's a million of us, suddenly we're not special anymore."

"Yeah," Kylee said. "What if some of them have powers better than ours?"

"We're the pioneers," Quentin said. "We'll be their leaders. It's like when the Wright brothers invented the airplane. Within five years there were dozens of plane manufacturers, but the Wrights dominated aviation because they got there first. We're the firstborn. We'll be the leaders of the next generation."

"How do you know so much?" Tara asked.

"I'm smart," Quentin said.

Tara nodded in agreement.

"We won't be their leaders," Kylee said. "Dr. Hatch will."

"With *us*," Quentin said.

"So what if something happens to Dr. Hatch?" Kylee said.

"If something happens to him, we take over the Elgen," Quentin said.

"You mean *you* take over the Elgen," Kylee said.

"Do you really think one person can handle all of it?" Quentin said. "We'll split up the world. Torstyn will take Asia, Tara gets North and South America, Bryan takes Europe, and Kylee, you get Africa, Australia, and Antarctica."

"What do you take?" Tara asked.

"I'll oversee all of it."

Just then Bryan walked up to the table with a tray of orange chicken and fried rice with chunks of tofu. "How did you guys find a table in here?"

"They gave it to us," Torstyn said.

"Why does Bryan get Europe?" Kylee asked. "That's where the best shopping is. And why would I want Antarctica? It's just ice."

"Then give it to Bryan."

"Give what to me?" Bryan asked, sitting down.

"Antarctica," Quentin said. "When we take over the world you get Europe and Antarctica."

"I'll take Antarctica," he said. "They've got penguins. And ice fishing. I can cut through the ice without a saw."

"Good for you," Kylee said. "I still want Europe."

Tara asked Quentin, "Have you ever been to Taiwan?"

"Dr. Hatch took me there once when I was nine. I don't remember much about it, except there was something going on in the street outside the hotel. Dr. Hatch told me it was a Chinese opera, but it sounded more like an execution."

"Who are we guarding the girl from?" Tara asked.

"Vey and your sister," he said. "And the rest of the traitors."

"The next time I see Vey," Torstyn said, "I'm going to melt his brain into a little puddle that drains out his ears."

"That would make a very little puddle," Bryan said. "That guy's an idiot."

"If he's such an idiot, how does he keep outsmarting us?" Tara said.

"You suddenly a fan of his?" Torstyn asked.

"She's right," Quentin said. "The first rule of success is to never underestimate your enemy. Vey's no idiot." He shook his head, adding, "I hate that twitching little dork."

"Speaking of dorks," Kylee said, "want to see something funny? Watch that fat guy over there."

Everyone turned to see a smiling, overweight man on the other side of the courtyard walking toward a table in the middle of the most crowded section of the food court. He was dressed in a light beige suit and tie.

"The one with the tray?" Tara asked.

"The one who looks like he ate a tray," Torstyn said.

"He looks like he ate a stack of trays," Tara said. "What about him?"

Kylee grinned. "Just watch."

The man set his tray on the table, then pulled out a chair to sit. As he began sitting, Kylee reached out. "Wait for it, wait for it, now!" She magnetized, pulling the chair out from under the man. He fell back onto the ground, hitting his head on the chair and pulling the tray on top of himself.

The teens laughed. The man slowly sat up with Coke and spaghetti dripping from his face and chest. He was rubbing his head and looking around to see who had pulled out his chair.

"You did him a favor," Torstyn said. "You helped him start his diet."

"I can do one better than that," Tara said. "I've learned a new trick." She held up her hand, her palm facing the man, who was now standing back up, his face bright red with embarrassment.

Suddenly several women standing next to the man screamed. One fainted. Almost everyone around him ran except a few who held chairs up, as if warding him off. Then people began pelting him with trays and food. The confused man ran from the courtyard. The teens laughed again.

"That was awesome," Bryan said. "What did you do?"

"I made everyone around him think he's the thing they fear most."

"That's epic cool," Bryan said. "You're going to give him an inferiority complex."

"He's a human," Quentin said stoically. "He *is* inferior."

"I know, right?" Tara said.

Quentin looked at her. "So how did you do that?"

"It's a trick I've been working on with Dr. Hatch and the trainers. They say that fear is located in the amygdala region of the brain, but triggered by the hippocampus, so they taught me how to focus on it and trigger it. I can also make people think they're looking at anything or anyone."

"What do you mean?"

"Watch." Suddenly Tara turned into Dr. Hatch.

"Whoa," Torstyn said, sliding back.

"That's incredible," Quentin said. "How did you change?"

Tara turned back to herself. "I didn't. I just rerouted the part of your brains that recognizes images and made you see something else. I can prove it. You all saw Dr. Hatch, right?"

"Yes," Quentin said.

"What was he wearing?" She looked around at each of them. "What did you see?"

"A gray suit," Quentin said. "Red tie."

"No, it was a dark blue Armani," Kylee said. "I would know, I love Armani."

"He wasn't wearing a suit," Torstyn said. "And I don't think the tie was red. I think it was gold."

"I don't remember," Bryan said. "It could have been blue. Or black."

"So who was right?" Quentin asked.

"You were *all* right," Tara said. "Because the image came from your own minds. You saw what you expected to see."

"Fascinating," Quentin said. "So what did those people around the fat guy see?"

"That's the weird part. I don't know. It could have been a bear, a werewolf, a snake, a giant spider; it could have been their boss. Whatever they fear most. But I could have made him someone they like too. Like a famous movie star or singer."

"So you could make them think I'm the president of the United States?" Quentin asked.

Tara nodded. "I could make people think you look like anyone."

"That's very cool," Quentin said. "We'll have to play around with that."

Just then a large, muscular kid with bright red hair walked past their table. He smiled at Tara. "Hey, baby."

Tara rolled her eyes. "Did you really just call me baby, loser?"

He stopped next to her. "You have a problem with that?"

"Uh, yes, moron," she said.

"You think you're something special?"

"Please go away," she said.

He glared at her, then said, "Woof."

Tara's eyes flashed with anger. "What did you say?"

"I said 'woof,' dog face." He turned and began to walk away.

Tara turned red.

"I got this," Torstyn said. He shouted after the kid, "Hey, ginger, did anyone else survive the accident?"

The guy turned back. "Huh?"

"Dude, is that really your head or did your neck just throw up?"

The guy flushed. "What did you say?"

"You're ugly *and* deaf? I'll use small words so you can read my lips. Beg my friend's forgiveness; then I might let you run away."

The kid's fist clenched. "I'm going to rip your head off."

Torstyn smiled and calmly leaned back in his chair, his arms behind his head. "Show me."

The redhead took one step toward Torstyn, then froze. His mouth fell open and he grabbed his head, which was turning bright red. Then the blood vessels in his eyes began bursting. "Ah, ah, ah."

"Aren't you going to 'rip my head off,' tough guy?" Torstyn mocked.

"Ahhhh."

"What are you saying? Do you want me to stop?"

"Ahhhhhhh."

"I can't understand you, carrottop," Torstyn said. "I don't speak moron."

"That's enough," Tara said.

"Not for me."

The guy fell to his knees.

"You want to worship me now, huh? You better start praying."

"Stop it," Quentin said. "You're drawing too much attention."

Torstyn looked at him. "C'mon."

"I said *now*," Quentin said.

Torstyn pushed one more time, then lowered his hand. "Whatever."

The kid fell to his side, convulsing.

"What did you do to him?" Bryan asked.

"Dude was a hothead, so I added a little more heat."

"You heated his brain?"

"It was a little hard to find, but yes." Torstyn smiled darkly. "Not all of it. Just parts."

Kylee grimaced as the kid vomited. "Gross."

"Is it permanent?" Bryan asked.

"Maybe. He might have had an aneurysm. Dr. Hatch used to have me practice on GPs, but I melted too many of them, so then I started practicing on monkeys." He grinned. "One day I fried about a hundred of them in the Lima zoo. Scientists are still scratching their heads over that one."

"That was you?" Quentin said. "I read about it online. They're calling it the Capuchin Virus."

"That was me, bro. The virus."

Bryan laughed. "That's epic, man. That reminds me of that time at the X Games when Zeus shocked that . . ." He froze, realizing his slip. Everyone looked at him.

"Did you just say the Z word?" Quentin said.

Bryan swallowed. "Sorry, man. It was an accident."

"You think?" Kylee said.

"You're lucky Dr. Hatch wasn't around," Tara said. "You'd be on lockdown for a week."

"Like I was in Peru," Kylee said. "He needs to be punished."

Bryan looked afraid. "Please don't tell him. Please."

Quentin looked at the others. "I'll let you off this time. But don't do it again."

"Oh, come on," Kylee said. "No one let me off."

"That's because you were dumb enough to say it in front of Dr. Hatch," Torstyn said.

"Thanks, man," Bryan said. "Stupid mistake."

Quentin squinted. "You owe me a big favor. Don't forget."

"You got it. Thanks."

Just then an Asian woman knelt down next to the kid on the ground. "I'm a doctor," she said. She looked at Torstyn. "Did you see what happened?"

"Dude dropped to the ground like a fish," Quentin said.

"Will one of you call 911?"

"We're eating," Torstyn said, turning away.

The woman stared at him in disbelief. "He may be dying."

"Everyone goes sometime," Torstyn said.

The woman just gaped. Someone at a nearby table said, "I'll call."

As a large crowd started to gather, Quentin said, "We better get out of here. We've only got two more hours before we need to get back."

As they stood Kylee asked, "Will you bring us back some chocolate from Switzerland?"

"Of course," Tara said.

"Better get a lot," Quentin said. "There won't be any decent chocolate in Taiwan."

"I'll buy twenty pounds of it," Tara said.

The five of them walked away. As they left the food court Quentin raised his hand and shut the place down.

PART FOUR

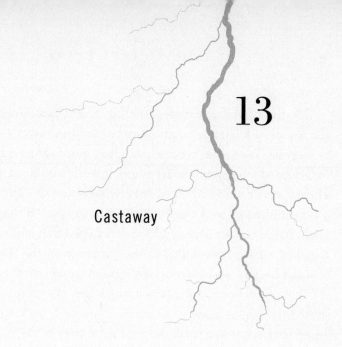

13

Castaway

Port of Lima, Peru

Schema and the surviving Elgen board members were about a mile up the Peruvian coast from the *Ampere* when the *Watt* exploded. They briefly slowed their raft and watched as a column of thick, black smoke billowed up into the twilight sky.

"It's the *Ampere*," Three said.

Schema turned back. "*Andiamo*, we must keep going. Once they recover from the attack, the whole Elgen guard and the Peruvian military will be looking to find who did that."

Ten minutes later there was a second explosion. "What was that?" Eight asked. "They got a second boat?"

"Hopefully they'll take out the entire fleet," Nine said.

"Maybe the first explosion wasn't the *Ampere*," Eight said.

"If it wasn't, Hatch may have gotten out," Schema said. He pointed toward the beach. "There. Cut back on power and head to shore."

"Yes, sir," Four said.

Schema carefully surveyed the beach but saw nothing but sand and a wall of foliage separating the beach from the city. They had to be careful. There were hundreds of Elgen guards around Lima, and six well-dressed foreigners coming ashore in a raft would not go unnoticed. The raft struck sand and the board members quickly climbed out.

"Send the raft back out," Schema said to Four. "If they find it they might figure out we survived." Schema hoped that anyone who knew they had escaped was killed in the explosion of the *Ampere*, but he couldn't be sure, and a wrong assumption could cost them their lives.

The other board members turned the raft around; then Four started the engine again and sent it, unmanned, back out to sea. The group took cover in a small grove of palm trees while Schema walked to the road alone. After sunrise he flagged down a passing cattle truck.

Schema spoke even better Spanish than he did English, and he bargained with the driver for a ride into downtown Lima, offering the man the only valuable he still carried—his twenty-thousand-dollar Rolex watch.

Schema, who was accustomed to elegant yachts and luxury cars, now sat on the alfalfa- and manure-covered floor of the cattle truck for the twenty-minute ride. But the discomfort and humiliation were not the source of his greatest pain. His love, Two, had died after Hatch had hung her upside down in the *Ampere*'s brig, taking Schema's place in death.

The truck reached downtown Lima a half hour later and Schema ordered the driver to stop a half block from the Hilton Hotel. "Wait here," Schema said to the driver and the other board members. "I'll be back."

He brushed himself off, then walked into the hotel and up to the concierge desk. A Peruvian man wearing thick-rimmed glasses and a black suit looked up. "May I help you?"

"Yes," Schema said. "What is your name, please?"

"I am Victor Perez."

"Mr. Perez, my name is Giacomo Schema. I am the CEO of the Elgen Corporation. I have no identification, but if you need confirmation you can verify my identity on the Internet. My associates and I have been the victims of a crime. We were kidnapped on our way into town. The thieves stole everything and I need your assistance. If I could have access to a telephone, I can wire money to your hotel and book a room. I would like your presidential suite or an equivalent."

Even though Schema's suit was disheveled, Perez recognized it as a twenty-thousand-dollar Ermenegildo Zegna.

"You are of what citizenship?" Perez asked.

"Italian."

"Shall I alert the Italian consulate?"

"Yes, of course," Schema said, not meaning it. "But if you please, I will do so later. I am tired and hungry and still a bit traumatized. If you can assist me, I guarantee that you will be properly rewarded." Schema took a pen from the desk and wrote his name and "Elgen Inc." Then, at the bottom of the page, he scrawled,

$1,000 for your kind assistance

Schema looked into the man's eyes. "Do you understand?"

"Yes, sir."

"Being who I am, there are obvious reasons this is best handled discreetly. If you need verification, check the website."

The man googled "Elgen Inc.," and then clicked on the website's Chairman/Board tab. He looked at Schema, then back at the screen. "Yes, this appears to be you. Just one moment, sir. I must speak with the hotel manager, Señor Castillo."

He spoke into his phone and a moment later a tall Peruvian man walked up to the desk.

"Good morning, sir," he said to Schema. "I am Señor Castillo, the manager of this hotel."

Perez spoke to Castillo in Spanish, not knowing that Schema could understand him perfectly.

"This gentleman claims that he was robbed and is now without money or identification. He says his name is Giacomo Schema and

he is the CEO of an international company called Elgen. I looked at
the website and there is a picture of him."

"What is it he wants?"

"He wishes some assistance to transfer money. And the president's
suite."

"That is correct," Schema said. "I would be most grateful for your
assistance in this matter."

Castillo glanced down at the computer screen, then back up at
Schema. He said in English, "I am sorry for this great tragedy. Our
country is usually more hospitable, but in all big cities there are
problems."

"Of course," Schema said.

"Please, follow me to my office."

Schema followed the hotel manager past the concierge desk to a
small back office.

"I need to call my banker in Switzerland," Schema said. "I will, of
course, take care of all expenses."

"Please," Castillo said. "You may sit at my desk."

Schema looked down at his wrist before remembering he'd given
his watch away. "I forgot that my watch was stolen. What time is it?"

"It is just past nine."

"Good. It is not closing time in Switzerland yet."

"I will give you some privacy," Castillo said, stepping toward the
door. "I will be right outside my office if you need me."

"Thank you," Schema said. He sat down at the desk and dialed
an eleven-digit number. "Please put me through to Florian Wyss. Tell
him this is Giacomo Schema."

A moment later a man answered in stilted English. "Giacomo, I
have been trying to reach you. You missed our dinner party. My wife
was so disappointed to not meet you."

Schema ignored the pleasantries. "Florian, I am calling with
urgency. There has been a mutiny. Our director, James Hatch, has
commandeered the company and the *Ampere*. He has murdered two
board members and imprisoned the rest of us. It was by sheer fortune
that we have managed to escape."

"*Mon dieu!*" Wyss exclaimed. "Now I understand. There was an order from President Hatch to immediately transfer eight hundred million dollars into an account in the Cayman Islands. Of course I would never make such a transfer without personally speaking with you."

"When did that order come?"

"Just a few hours ago. I have been trying to reach you."

"Then Hatch is still alive," Schema said. "This is most unfortunate. You did the right thing, Florian. I am in Lima, Peru. I need you to make arrangements to wire money to this hotel and move money to this account."

"Have you contacted the authorities?"

"The authorities of which country, Florian?"

"My apologies, Giacomo. What else do you require?"

"Send a jet for us. We will meet with you in Geneva to discuss our next move."

"How many will be flying with you?"

"There will be six, including me."

"Shall I freeze the Elgen accounts?"

Schema thought for a moment. "No. Hatch doesn't know we're still alive. Let's let him keep his false sense of security until I have determined a course of action."

"Where shall I wire the money?"

"I am at the Lima Hilton. Let me have you speak with the hotel manager." Schema walked to the door. "Señor Castillo, my banker would like a word with you."

While Castillo and Wyss worked out financial arrangements, Schema found some paper and made a list of everything he needed, including two changes of clothing. A few minutes later Castillo said, "Mr. Wyss would like to speak with you again."

"*Gracias,*" Schema said, taking the phone.

"Everything is taken care of, Giacomo," Wyss said. "Our bank has opened a line of credit with the hotel, so all your expenses will be covered. In the morning you will be delivered five thousand American dollars from the Banco de la Nación with a new credit card. The jet will take me a few more minutes to reserve, but it will be sent for you at the first moment possible and will reach you, at the latest, by the day after tomorrow. Señor Castillo will arrange transportation to the airport."

"Thank you, Florian. I look forward to seeing you, and meeting your lovely wife."

"I will be most pleased. I will see you soon. I look forward to helping you put an end to this mutiny."

"Indeed," Schema replied. He hung up the phone and turned to the hotel manager. "Thank you for your assistance. I will need my suite and four other rooms for my board members." He handed Castillo the list he had made. "Also, I will need these things delivered to my room as soon as possible."

"As you wish, sir. Is there anything else you will require?"

"Please have your finest wine, cheese, and fruit sent to my room. Also, your best steak with a cheese-and-mushroom omelet."

"Yes, sir."

"And one more thing. Give yourself a thousand-dollar tip. You've been most helpful."

By the time Schema retrieved the other board members and got to his own suite, there was a bottle of Peruvian wine waiting for him, along with a selection of crackers and cheeses, dates, apricots, and honey, as well as a T-bone steak and an omelet.

Schema examined the bottle of wine, poured himself a glass, then took a sip. "It isn't Château Margaux, but it will do." He drank the glass, then wolfed down his meal. He hadn't eaten for nearly twenty-four hours and he felt it.

When he'd finished eating, he took off his clothes and lay back on his bed. Now that the danger and hunger that had filled his mind were gone, his thoughts turned to the man who had caused him such pain. Hatch had taken everything from him—his company, his love, his future. Now that he knew Hatch was still alive, he wanted revenge. *He* will *pay*, Schema thought. *I will use every last dime, every means available to me, to make him pay for what he has done. I will destroy Hatch if it's the last thing I do.*

The question Schema struggled to answer was: *Just how desperate is Hatch?* Schema could employ a mercenary army to overthrow Hatch and his Elgen guard, but that could take weeks or months to organize. In the meantime, Hatch had full access to all the Starxource plants. He could destroy every Starxource plant in a matter of hours. Or, worse yet, he could release the rats into the countries they inhabited, causing mass destruction. Schema had no doubt that the attacked countries would destroy everything Elgen, leaving nothing for Schema to recover.

However he proceeded he had to be careful. Underestimating Hatch was a mistake he couldn't afford to make again.

14

Fugitive

**Bank of Geneva
Geneva, Switzerland**

The flight from Lima to Geneva took a little more than fourteen hours. Wyss had cars waiting for them at the airport and the board was taken to the Metropole Hotel, on the bank of Lake Geneva, while Schema, in a separate car, went directly to the offices of the Bank of Geneva.

"It's good to be back in Switzerland," Schema said to the driver as they left the hotel.

"It is always good to be in Switzerland," the driver replied. "Would you like me to wait for you?"

"Yes," Schema said. "I should only be an hour or so."

The car pulled up to the curb in front of the bank, and inside, Schema took the elevator to the seventh floor, to Wyss's office. Wyss's secretary, a mature Frenchwoman, greeted him as he entered.

"*Bienvenue*, Monsieur Schema. Mr. Wyss and his associates are expecting you. Please go on back."

"*Merci,*" Schema said as he walked past her desk. He suddenly turned back. "His associates?"

"Yes, *Monsieur.*"

Schema walked past the reception area to Wyss's office and opened the door. Florian Wyss was sitting at his desk. He looked up when Schema entered. His face was pale and his hand was wrapped in white gauze.

"Florian, what happened to your hand?"

Wyss shook his head. "I am very sorry, Giacomo. I had no choice."

Schema walked farther into the room. "What are you talking about?"

"He gave me no choice."

"Who?" Schema said.

"That would be me," Hatch said. He walked into the office flanked by Torstyn and Tara and four Elgen guards. The guards immediately surrounded Schema. "And I believe Mr. Wyss is referring to the sizable transfers we just made."

Schema turned white. "Call security," he said to Wyss.

"Giacomo, what kind of welcome is that?" Hatch said calmly. "After traveling halfway across the world I thought you would at least offer me a drink."

Schema glared at him, red with rage. He would have lunged at him were it not for the guards surrounding him.

"No?" Hatch said. "Then I'll help myself." He walked over to the credenza on the far side of the office and poured himself a drink from a crystal decanter. "Ah, the good stuff. No wonder you bank here." He stepped back toward Schema. "Of course, I would have preferred that you had gone down with the *Ampere,* but, as it turns out, it is fortuitous that you didn't. Otherwise I might have had some trouble locating a few of your accounts."

Schema looked back at Florian. "What have you done?"

"I had no choice, Giacomo. All the money has been transferred."

Schema leaned in. "Surely not . . . *everything.*"

Florian grimaced. "Everything."

"How could they have even known about those accounts?"

Florian glanced over at Tara, who smiled darkly. "They have ways of getting into your head."

"It's done, Giacomo," Hatch said. "Everything is gone. Except you, of course. You're still here. Now, I could easily remedy that and shoot you right now, but where would the fun be in that? So I propose a challenge. You are a fugitive from nearly every civilized country and now you have no money to run. Oh, and I put a million-dollar bounty on your head. Let's see just how long you can survive. Florian, call Interpol. Inform them that a known fugitive has entered your bank."

Wyss blotted his forehead with a handkerchief. "Please, Admiral Hatch . . ."

"Wrong answer," Hatch said. "Torstyn . . ."

"Yes, sir."

"Help Mr. Wyss understand how much I dislike being disobeyed. He still has one hand with flesh."

"Please, no," Florian said, lifting the phone. "I'll call right now. I'll alert Interpol immediately." He pushed a button on his phone. "Connect me with security."

Hatch turned to Schema. "It's pathetic, isn't it, how quickly loyalties turn? You really can't trust anyone these days. Now, if I were you, and thankfully I'm not, I would run. And joining the others isn't in your best interest. I've already sent guards to the Metropole to collect them." Hatch grinned. "Some of the EGGs and I have a bet on how long you can resist capture." He flourished a hand. "It's a game of sorts." He turned to Wyss. "If you please."

Wyss spoke into the phone. "This is Florian Wyss of Bank of Geneva. I would like to report a known fugitive who has been seen in our bank. Yes. Immediately." He hung up and looked at Schema. "I am very sorry."

"You will pay, Hatch," Schema said.

"Yes, so you've said," Hatch said. "But I'm still waiting for the bill." His dark gaze turned to amusement. "Now please hurry. If you're captured today I'll lose the bet. And you of all people should know"—he leaned forward and his voice dropped—"that I hate to lose."

An alarm sounded. Schema glanced once more at Florian, then turned and ran out of the building.

Hatch laughed. "That went well."

Wyss used his bandaged hand to blot the sweat from his forehead. "I've done everything you asked. You'll release my wife and daughter now?"

Hatch looked at him quizzically. "Of course not."

Florian blanched. "But you said that if I cooperated . . ."

"Yes, I did," Hatch said. "Allow me to explain. There is a fable about a man who comes to a riverbank and is about to cross when he sees a viper. The viper says to the man, 'I would also like to cross the river. Would you please carry me across?' The man replies, 'No, you're a viper. You'll bite me and I'll die.' 'Don't be foolish,' the viper says. 'If I bite you, we'll both drown.'

"The man, convinced by the snake's reasoning, puts the viper on his back and swims across the river. As he reaches the opposite bank the viper bites the man and slithers off. As the man lies dying he says, 'I carried you across. You said you wouldn't bite me.' 'Sorry,' the viper replied. 'I'm a viper. It's in my nature.'"

A broad smile crossed Hatch's face and he leaned forward. "Thanks for the lift, Florian, but I can't really help myself. It's in my nature."

"What will you do with my family?"

"Your wife and daughter will be held as GPs."

"What are GPs?"

"They'll find out soon enough. Unfortunately, you won't. Now, if you'll excuse me, we're needed in Taiwan." Hatch said to Torstyn, "We'll be in the car. Finish him." Hatch walked out of the office followed by Tara and his guards.

Wyss just stared at Torstyn in horror. "Please . . ."

Torstyn reached out his hand. "It won't hurt . . . for long."

PART FIVE

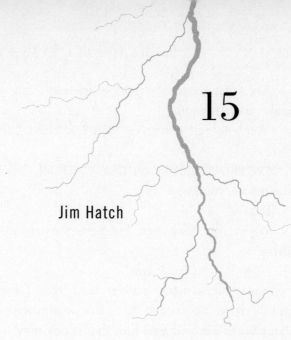

15

Jim Hatch

Timepiece Ranch

After my practice session with Gervaso I knocked on my mother's door. She answered, smiling as soon as she saw me. "I was just thinking about you."

"I need to ask you something," I said.

"Of course," she said. "Come in." As I stepped into the room she said, "This sounds serious."

"It is."

She closed the door, then looked at me, her arms folded at her chest. "What is it?"

"Is there something going on between you and that Joel guy?"

"Something?"

"You know." I hesitated and she tilted her head. *"Romantic."*

She thought for a moment, then said softly, "I don't know."

"What does that mean?"

"Just what I said. We're close friends. I care about him. I don't know where it's going."

I suddenly felt defensive. "You care about him? How long have you even known him?"

"I've known him longer than you think," she said. "You've met him before, you know."

"I have?"

"When you were four. He helped us move from Pasadena to Idaho."

"How did you know him?"

"Anna, Joel's sister, worked with your father at the hospital. Shortly after your father died, she disappeared. She had told Joel about the Elgen and told him that if anything happened to her he should help us hide."

For the first time in my life I realized that all our moving around wasn't just about me. "So you've known about the Elgen since I was born?"

"Of course. It was a company your father was working with. The MEI was something we thought might change the world, not the way Hatch does, but for the better. James Hatch worked with your father. In fact, we had him over for dinner."

I couldn't believe what I was hearing. "Dr. Hatch was in our *home*?"

My mother nodded. "We called him Jim back then. He came over to the house once for a barbecue."

I was speechless. It was like hearing my mother was in a book club with Hitler. "You barbecued with Dr. Hatch? The man who kidnapped you and tried to kill me?"

"He wasn't trying to kill anyone back then. In fact, you weren't even born. I was thirty-six weeks pregnant when they placed the MEI in the hospital. I gave birth to you the next week."

"Then why didn't you recognize him in the parking lot at PizzaMax?"

My mother smiled. "It had been almost fifteen years. He's changed a lot since then. *And* he was wearing sunglasses."

"This is unbelievable," I said.

"Believe it or not, Jim Hatch was a pretty normal guy. He brought me flowers in the hospital when you were born."

I struggled to process this. "What was he like?"

"He was a little insecure, but hardworking and very ambitious, which isn't always a bad thing. I don't know why he turned out the way he did. I think he got caught up in something that took him over. The lust for power can do that."

"He's insane now," I said. "And evil."

"Maybe. But he wasn't back then. It's easy to place people in black-and-white categories of good or bad, but the truth is there's a lot of both in all of us."

"You're nothing like Hatch," I said. "Neither am I."

"You're right. There's one big difference."

"What's that?"

"Love."

"He loves himself," I said.

My mother shook her head. "No. He feeds his hunger, but that's not self-love, just selfishness. Deep down he must hate himself or he could never be so cruel. When people do things contrary to their own moral foundation, they either feel guilty and change or try to break down the foundation of their belief.

"Jim Hatch has tortured and killed people. Unless you're a sociopath, the only way to do things like that and still live with yourself is to convince yourself that the end justifies the means."

I just sat quietly thinking.

"And, Michael, you don't have to worry about me. I'm not going to do anything foolish." She stepped closer. "I'm glad you came over. I wanted to talk to you about something too."

I looked up at her.

"I'm afraid." She breathed out slowly. "Afraid and conflicted. And I don't know what to tell you to do." She put her hands on my shoulders. "I'm terrified of you going to Taiwan. I feel like any mother must feel sending a son off to harm's way. If the reasons weren't so important, I'd never let you go." Her eyes filled with tears. "Part of me is so proud of you that I'm without words. The other part . . ." She wiped her eyes. "I'm still your mother. I'm supposed to protect you."

I bowed my head. I didn't know what to say.

"It's not fair that you've been placed in this position. You're so young."

"Alexander the Great was only sixteen when he ruled the world," I said. "And Joan of Arc was only seventeen when she led the French army."

"And she was nineteen when the English burned her at the stake."

"Maybe not the best example."

"One of the last things your father said to me before he died was to keep you safe. I haven't done a very good job at that." She looked me in the eyes. "I wonder if he would be disappointed in me."

"Is it better to be safe and worthless, or valuable and in danger?"

"Now you sound like your father."

"Is that a bad thing?"

She slowly shook her head. "No. It's not. But what do *you* want?"

"It doesn't matter what I want."

"It always matters," she said. "Do you want to go to Taiwan?"

"And face the Elgen? No. But I have to."

"No, you don't. You've already risked enough. Let someone else do it."

"Who?"

She looked at me for a moment, then put her arms around me. "When did you become so strong?"

"When they took you," I said.

"Just promise me that you'll always come back."

"I promise," I said. We both knew it was a promise I couldn't make.

After a moment she kissed my forehead and stepped back. "Is there anything I can do for you?"

"There's one thing," I said. I hesitated. "It's a little complicated."

"Whatever you want," she said.

"It's not for me. It's for Taylor."

She smiled. "Just tell me what to do."

16

Operation Jade Dragon

The next morning we gathered again for class. For the first time Gervaso was late. When he arrived there was something different about him. Not the way he dressed or anything, but the way he looked at us. There was a gravity to his demeanor.

"Good morning," he said. "Excuse me for being late. I've been in a meeting with the council. Operation Jade Dragon is a go."

While this wasn't a surprise to any of us, hearing Gervaso's pronouncement made it real in a way it hadn't been before.

Ostin was the first to speak. "When do we leave?"

"The day after tomorrow. That will give you time in Taiwan to prepare for the *Volta*'s arrival." He looked around at all of us. "There's no class today. I want you to have down time before you go. In the meantime, if I can do anything for you, just let me know."

"Will we meet again before we leave?" Ian asked.

"Tomorrow," he said.

As everyone walked out I approached Gervaso.

"I'd like to try the bullet thing again."

"Of course. When would you like to go?"

"Right now," I said. "If you have the time."

"I have the time."

We drove back out to the shooting range. As Gervaso loaded the gun, I stepped in front of the target so the bull's-eye was directly behind my stomach.

Gervaso looked up from behind the gun's scope. "What are you doing?"

"I don't want to find out I can't do this while they're shooting at me."

For the first time since I'd met him he looked truly worried. "Are you sure about this?"

"Just don't shoot before I'm ready."

"I'll guarantee that. We'll count down. Three, two, one, fire, okay?"

"Okay," I said.

He got behind the gun again. I took a deep breath and pulsed slightly, enough that electricity started sparking between my fingers.

"Ready?" he asked.

I was ticking like crazy. "Let's do this."

He put his finger on the trigger. "Here we go. Three, two"—I pulsed—"one, fire."

A single round exploded from the gun. It smashed into the cinderblock wall beside me. Gervaso stood and I could see relief on his face. He walked quickly toward me. "You did it."

We walked over and examined where the bullet had hit. It was nearly twelve feet off the mark.

"I think you overcompensated," he said.

"I was nervous."

He laughed. "Nervous." He put his hand on my shoulder. "You may be the bravest person I've ever met."

17

The Last Day

We met again the next morning, but only for a few minutes. Gervaso briefed us on what he knew of the Taiwan Starxource plant, concluding with, "Your Taiwanese operative will fill you in on the rest." Then, as he looked us over, he did something that surprised us all. He stood at attention and saluted us. Then he said, "It's been an honor knowing all of you."

Taylor whispered to me, "He's acting like he's never going to see us again."

As we got up to leave, Gervaso stopped me. "Michael."

"Yes, sir."

"May I talk to you a moment?"

"Of course." I looked at Taylor. "Where are you going?"

"I told my mother I'd go horseback riding with her," she said.

"Let me know when you're back," I said.

As she walked off I turned to Gervaso. "Yes, sir."

"I want to personally thank you for your leadership and bravery."

"Thank you," I said.

"I joined the military when I was just eighteen. I have served under many leaders. You are not only brave, you are also a very good leader, which is why your friends follow you into danger." He reached into his pocket and brought out something wrapped in a white handkerchief. He peeled back the cloth to reveal a bronze medal in the shape of a cross with an eagle with outspread wings in its center. A banner beneath the eagle read,

FOR VALOR

"Have you ever seen one of these before?"

I looked back up at him. "No."

"This is the Distinguished Service Cross. It is the United States Army's second-highest military award. It is given for extreme gallantry in battle."

"Is it yours?"

"It was," he said. "I received it during Operation Desert Storm in Iraq." Then he handed it to me. "I'm giving it to you."

I made no move to take it. "I can't take that."

"It would be an insult for you to refuse."

"It's too much. I don't deserve it."

"I know what you have done, Michael. I have studied the reports. You deserve this award more than I do. Please, don't refuse my offering."

For a moment we looked into each other's eyes. I reached out and took the medal. "I don't know what to say."

"Your actions have said enough." He saluted me again. This time I saluted back.

"I want a full report when you return with Jade Dragon."

"Yes, sir."

He stepped forward and hugged me. "Good luck." Then he turned and walked away. I looked back down at the medal. It was the greatest honor of my life.

18

An Unexpected Request

"Dude," Ostin said. "I can't believe he gave that to you. That's like the coolest thing ever. The only medal higher is the Medal of Honor."

"I can't believe it either."

Ostin reached out his hand. "Let me see it again."

I handed him the medal. "That's epic." He looked at it for a moment, then handed it back to me. "Gervaso gave me something too." He lifted a small burgundy book from his bed. *The Art of War.* "He thought it might come in handy if we face the Lung Li."

"Have you started reading it yet?"

"I'm not *reading* it; I'm *memorizing* it."

"Sorry." I put the medal in my pocket. "Have you seen my mom?"

"She was just here," he said. "She left that for you." He pointed to a large rectangular box on my bed. "Is that your . . ."

"Yeah, I think so."

"Then you're still doing it tonight?"

"Of course."

He looked concerned.

"Why? Don't you approve?"

"I mean, it's great and all, but why tonight? We leave in the morning."

"I'm doing it *because* we leave in the morning."

He thought for a moment, then said, "That makes sense."

Someone knocked on our door.

"Come in," I said, turning around.

Joel stepped inside. "Sorry to interrupt," he said. "Michael, could you come with me for a moment? The council would like to speak with you again."

"Right now?"

He nodded. "Yes, please."

I turned to Ostin. "If Taylor comes by, don't let her see the box."

"You got it," he said.

I followed Joel down to the council room. He opened the door for me and followed me in. There were only eight members around the table. Simon stepped forward to greet me. "Michael, thank you for coming."

"No problem," I said, wondering what this was about.

"Have a seat. Please."

I sat in the chair closest to the door.

Simon waited until I was settled, then said, "I imagine you must feel some apprehension as you prepare to go."

"Yes, sir."

"As do we," he said. "The reason we wanted to talk to you is because we've just received a report that Hatch has assigned his electric youth to oversee the transporting of Jade Dragon to the *Volta*. That means you may be facing Quentin, Bryan, Kylee, Torstyn, and Tara."

"I've faced them before," I said.

"But this time there will also be the Elgen guards and the Lung Li. Any one of those alone is dangerous. Together, we fear it is too much. We thought you might need some help."

"What kind of help?" I asked.

Simon looked over the table, then said, "We think you should take Nichelle with you to Taiwan."

I thought I must not have heard him correctly. "You mean Hatch's Nichelle? The one who tortured us?"

"Yes."

"Are you kidding?"

The council member sitting next to Simon, who had been introduced as Thomas, spoke up. "I know this must come as a surprise. We expect that it will to the Elgen as well. You're the only one of the electric youth who has been able to stop her, so she's still a viable threat to the others. She could be a powerful asset to the Electroclan."

"Have you ever met her?" I asked.

"No," Simon said. "And certainly not the way you have."

"We can't trust her."

"We believe we can," Thomas said. "We've been following her for some time now. She's very angry at Hatch for abandoning her."

"You know what they say," the woman sitting next to Thomas said. "Hell hath no fury like a woman scorned."

Thomas nodded in agreement. "She's very bitter."

"Nichelle is *always* bitter," I said. "She's psychotic." I looked around the table. Everyone was looking at me with concern.

Thomas lifted a folder and slid it across the table to me. "This is her dossier. After the Elgen abandoned her she lived on the streets around Pasadena for about a week until she met some men we believe are former gang members. She's living with them in a West Pasadena apartment. We don't know if she's been involved in any illegal activity but she has a job at a taco stand, so we think she's at least trying to make good."

Simon said, "We assume that these men she's with are dangerous. But not nearly as dangerous as you."

I looked around the table, then said, "I need to think this over."

"It's your decision, Michael," Simon said. "You're the leader of this mission. But we are unanimously for it. For *your* sake."

I scratched the back of my head as I thought. As crazy as it sounded, they were right about one thing: battling the Elgen, the Lung Li, *and* the Glows might be too much. "I could have Taylor read her mind," I said. "See where she's at." I took a deep breath, slowly exhaling. "If I decide to do this, how would we get her?"

"You would have to pick her up on your way to Taiwan," Thomas said. "Pasadena is only three hours from here. We've had an operative keep track of her, so we have an idea of her schedule. The safest place to approach her would be at work."

"Just give me the night to think about it."

"Of course," Simon said, standing. "Again, it is *your* decision."

"Just remember that war and politics make strange bedfellows," Thomas said.

Whatever that means, I thought. "I'll get back to you."

"We'll need to inform the pilots of your decision before you leave the ranch," Joel said, "so they can file a flight plan."

As I walked out I thought about what Ostin liked to say: "My enemy's enemy is my friend." Still, it seemed impossible to imagine Nichelle working with us. Almost as impossible as talking the rest of the Electroclan into it.

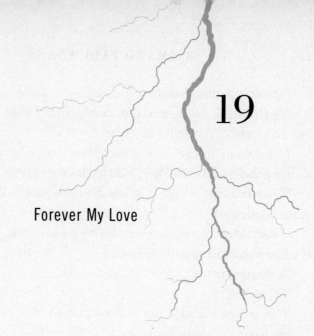

19

Forever My Love

When I got back to the room Ostin was packing what few things he possessed. "What did they want?"

"Nothing," I said.

"You mean nothing you want to tell me."

"Right," I said.

"Great," he said. "Now I'm going to spend the rest of the night trying to figure out what it is."

I grinned. "Did Taylor come by?"

"Oh yeah. I gave her the box."

"What?"

"I'm just kidding," he said. "I told her you'd be back in a few minutes."

"Thanks," I said. I picked up the box, then walked over to Taylor's room and knocked on the door.

Tessa opened. "Let me guess, you're looking for Taylor."

"You're a genius," I said.

"You can call me Ostin. No, don't. That's kind of creepy." She turned around. "Taylor, it's lover boy."

Taylor came to the door shaking her head. She stepped outside, shutting the door behind her. "She makes me crazy."

"Tessa *is* crazy," I said. "I think it's from eating all those mashed Amazon jungle slugs."

"I just threw up in my mouth," Taylor said. She looked down at the box I was carrying. "What's that?"

"It's a present."

"For me?"

"Of course." I handed her the box. "Open it."

She tore the paper from the box, then lifted its lid. "Oh, wow." She pulled a dark grape-colored chiffon dress from the box, then handed me the box and held the dress out in front of her. "Michael."

"Sydney Lynn and my mom took care it."

"It's beautiful." She looked into my eyes. "What's it for?"

"Tonight."

Her forehead furrowed. "What's tonight?"

"That's a surprise. I'll be back at seven to get you."

Taylor tilted her head. "What are you up to, Vey?"

"I'm not telling you."

She reached out to take my hand. "You can tell me."

I stepped back. "Don't read my mind, you'll ruin the surprise."

"You're finally on to me."

"I'll be back at seven." I smiled as I walked to my room.

Later that evening Ostin and my mother watched as I put on a suit coat and tie. The coat was a little large, but under the circumstances it was the best we could come up with.

"You look so handsome," my mother said. "Here's your corsage." She handed me a white glossy box containing a cluster of white roses. Considering where we were, I didn't know how she had managed the box, let alone the flowers.

"What time is it?"

"It's almost seven."

"Is everything ready?" I asked.

My mother smiled. "Yes."

"All right," I said. "So am I."

My mother and I walked to Taylor's room. I knocked, and her mother immediately answered.

"Hi, Michael. Come on in." As she stepped back, she opened the door all the way, revealing Taylor in her new dress. It fit perfectly. It was an elegant floor-length, sleeveless dress that wrapped tightly around her middle, accenting her slim waist. For the first time in months she was wearing makeup and her hair was pulled back in an updo. She looked Photoshopped beautiful—beautiful enough to make me tic.

I stepped inside her room. "You look . . . amazing."

Taylor looked at me dreamily. "And you look very handsome."

"I brought you this." I handed her the corsage.

She opened the box and took out the corsage. "Where did you get this?"

I looked at my mother and she just winked.

"I have connections," I said.

"Will you put it on?" she asked.

"I'll try." I fumbled awhile with the needle, but eventually pinned the flower to her dress without drawing blood. I took her hand. "Shall we go?"

"If you'll tell me where we're going."

"I'm taking you to the prom."

Her face was a mixed expression of surprise and gratitude. "The prom?"

"You said you wanted to go to one."

"Before you go," Mrs. Ridley said, "we need pictures."

"*Mom*," Taylor said.

"We are definitely taking pictures," she said. "And don't even think about rebooting me."

Between my mother and Mrs. Ridley, they took what seemed like a hundred pictures before Taylor finally said in exasperation, "Okay, we're good."

"It's just so exciting," Mrs. Ridley said.

Our mothers followed us out to the front of the Ranch House, where a horse-drawn carriage was waiting. Abigail and Jack were sitting on the front porch and Abi screamed when she saw Taylor. She ran over to us. "Omigosh! You look so beautiful!"

Taylor beamed. "Thank you."

"No really, you look like a princess." She looked at me. "You're a lucky guy."

"I know," I said.

Jack gave me a thumbs-up.

"Your carriage awaits," I said to Taylor.

The driver was standing to the side of the carriage wearing a cowboy hat, a Western-cut suit, and a bolo tie. He opened the door for us and I helped Taylor up.

"Have fun," my mother said. Jack and Abigail waved to us, and Taylor's mother began crying.

Our driver flicked the reins and the carriage started off.

When we were a little way off, Taylor asked, "Where are we going for prom?"

"Well, there isn't a school or a restaurant within a hundred miles of here, so we had to improvise a little."

The carriage drove us down a dirt road to a redbrick building about a mile from the compound. The driver pulled up to the front of the building, then got down and helped us out. "Have a good time," he said.

I opened the front door of the building and Taylor stepped inside. She took just a few steps in, then stopped. "Oh, Michael."

In the middle of the room was a small, square table set with crystal and china and lit by two long tapered candles. Strings of small lights hung from the ceiling. The floor was scattered with rose petals. There was some equipment that was too large to move, so it had been covered with sheets.

Taylor turned to me. "How did you do all this?"

"I had help," I said. "Our moms were busy."

I pulled a chair out from the table and Taylor sat down. Then I sat down across from her. A dark-haired man dressed in a white linen suit and vest with a baby-blue ascot walked out of a side door carrying a bottle in a bucket of ice. Following him with a bread basket was a beautiful, petite woman with short, curly dark hair and large brown eyes.

"*Monsieur, madame*, good evening," the man said. "My name is Benoit, I am your *serveur*. And this is my assistant, Monique."

Monique smiled and tipped her head a little. "Good evening."

"Hi," we said in unison.

Benoit continued, "Tonight's meal comes all the way from Paris. We begin with a bottle of fine sparkling grape juice and warm egg-basted croissants."

Monique set the basket of rolls on the table while Benoit uncorked the bottle and poured our glasses half full of the juice.

"We will return shortly with your hors d'oeuvre. *Bon appétite*," he said. They left the room.

"This is so much fun," Taylor said. "Do you know them?"

"My mom introduced me to Benoit this morning. He's the ranch's head chef."

"Is he really French?"

"I think so."

Benoit returned a few minutes later carrying a small oval plate with crackers and some salmon-colored pasty stuff I had never seen before.

"This is pâté de foie gras. It is a fine goose-liver pâté. Enjoy." He turned and left.

Taylor just looked at me with a funny expression.

"I'm sorry, I didn't order goose liver."

"It's not that," she said, smiling. "I just can't believe you would go to all this trouble for me."

"You mean like, compared to breaking into the academy?"

She laughed. "I shouldn't be surprised."

She spread the pâté on a cracker and took a bite. "Mmm, this is delicious."

"Really? You're a lot braver than I am."

"No," she said. "I'm definitely not." She held the rest of the cracker up to my mouth. "Try it."

I opened my mouth and she fed me. "What do you think?"

"It's good."

"Of course it's good. You didn't think Benoit would lead us astray, did you?"

"I don't really know Benoit," I said.

She reached over and took my hand. "So I've been thinking. I was complaining the other day about the things I've missed out on, but the truth is, I have something every girl dreams of: a real-life fairy tale. The brave knight stormed into the castle and rescued the princess from a fire-breathing dragon. How many girls can say that?"

"In this scenario, Hatch is the fire-breathing dragon?"

Taylor laughed. "Yes, he's the dragon." She looked at me a moment more, then added, "And I'm the princess."

"Yeah, I figured it out," I said.

Ten minutes later Benoit returned with two bowls of French onion soup. He waited for Taylor to try it. "*C'est à votre goût?*" he asked. "Do you like it?"

"It's delicious," Taylor said.

"*Très bien,*" he said, again leaving us.

For our main course we had lobster and filet mignon topped with blue cheese crumbles and burgundy wine sauce. On the side we had a baked potato and wild asparagus. Monique came out a few times to check on us and fill our water glasses. As the night waned Taylor spoke less.

After Monique brought out our dessert, a crème brûlée, I said to Taylor, "You're kind of quiet tonight."

"Sorry," she said. "I just have a lot on my mind. It's too bad you can't read my thoughts."

"You'll just have to tell me what you're thinking."

"I was just thinking about when we first met."

I nodded. "It's hard to believe how much things have changed."

"I know, right? Jack was bullying you. Now he practically worships you."

"And I practically worshipped you back then."

She playfully cocked her head. "You're saying that you don't practically worship me anymore?"

"Now I *actually* worship you."

She smiled.

"I've never told you this, but my first Valentine's Day at Meridian I made a Valentine's card for you. I was going to give it to you, but then I got scared. So when no one was looking, I shoved it in your locker."

Her eyes lit up. "I remember that card. That was you?"

"There's no way you remember that," I said.

She looked into my eyes. "It said, 'You are the most beautiful girl in the world.'"

I looked at her in surprise. "You do remember."

"How would a girl forget that?" She shook her head slowly. "The sad thing is, I had a boyfriend at the time. But I knew it wasn't from him because he wouldn't do anything that nice." She frowned. "What was wrong with me? Why would I go out with someone who didn't treat me very well? Why wasn't I with you?"

"Because I wasn't cool," I said.

Her frown grew. "That makes me feel bad."

"I'm sorry," I said. "Maybe it was because you didn't know I existed."

"I knew you existed. You were that cute boy who sat next to me."

"Who blinked a lot."

"Who blinked a lot," she said. She grinned. "I remember the first time I saw you, you winked at me. I didn't know you had Tourette's, so I just thought you were flirting."

"How do you know I wasn't?"

She leaned forward. "Because you were *way* too shy."

"I wasn't shy."

Her eyebrows rose in disbelief. "No?"

"No. I was just terrified."

She laughed.

* * *

After dinner Monique cleared away the table; then soft music started playing, Colby Cross's "Forever My Love."

"You know Colby's my favorite singer," Taylor said. "I got to sit in the front row at her concert when . . ." She stopped. I knew why. The pain of remembering was too much. Her smile fell. "I betrayed her."

"I know," I said. "You told me about it. But it was Hatch's fault. And it certainly hasn't hurt Colby's career."

She looked at me gratefully, then took my hand. "Let's dance."

I really didn't know how to dance, but I put my arms around her and we just kind of swayed to the music. Sometime during the second song she said, "Me too."

I looked at her. "Me too what?"

"I'm sorry. Your thoughts are so strong right now, I thought you said that out loud."

"Said what?"

"I wish this would never end."

I held her tighter.

We danced for a few more songs; then Taylor started crying, gently at first, then hard. Some of her tears ran down my cheek. I looked at her. "What's wrong?"

"Nothing," she said, laying her head on my shoulder.

"What is it?"

"It's just that, I've never felt this way before."

"What way?"

"So afraid." She looked up at me as another tear rolled down her cheek. "Tonight's been so wonderful, but it is going to end. And tomorrow we go to Taiwan. . . ." For a moment she couldn't speak. Then she said, "I'm scared. If something happens to you . . ."

"Nothing will happen to us," I said. But the second I said it, thoughts of Wade came to mind. I quickly forced the thoughts out, hoping she hadn't heard them.

She just clung to me tighter. "No, you're right. Nothing will happen."

I'm not sure what time it was when we returned to the Ranch House, but it was way past midnight and I had to wake our carriage rider, who had fallen asleep on his seat. After we got back I walked Taylor to her room and we stopped outside her door. She gazed at me sweetly. "Thank you, Michael."

"I just didn't want you to go through life without a prom."

"That was the best prom I could ever have." She leaned forward and we kissed. We must have kissed for a long time because Mrs. Ridley came to the door and neither of us even noticed her until she cleared her throat.

"It's late," she said.

"Sorry," I said to Taylor.

Taylor grinned. "I'm not." She leaned forward and kissed me again. "Good night, Michael."

"Good night."

Her mother looked at me and mouthed, "Thank you."

I turned and walked down the hall to my own room, where Ostin lay fast asleep. Even as late as it was, I couldn't sleep. For nearly an hour I just lay there thinking. I was new to this romance stuff, so maybe that's why it was so confusing, but I couldn't understand how tonight could simultaneously be the happiest and saddest night of my entire life.

20

Leaving the Ranch

I woke with the sun streaming in through the window. I looked over at the clock next to my bed. It was nearly six, almost time for us to leave for our flight. "Ostin?" I sat up and looked around the room, but he was gone. His bag was gone. "I can't believe he didn't wake me up," I said to myself. I pulled on my pants and shirt and ran out into the hall, but there was no one around. I walked down to Taylor's room and knocked on the door, but she didn't answer. Then I tried to open the door. It was locked. *They must all be having breakfast*, I thought. When I got to the dining hall my heart froze. It was also empty. No Electroclan. No staff. No one. *What's going on?*

I ran back to the Ranch House to my mother's room and knocked on her door. "Mom!" I shouted. Nothing. I opened her door. "Mom, it's me." I looked inside her room. She wasn't there. In fact the room was vacant, cleared out as if it had never been occupied. *Where is everyone?* I thought. I stepped back out into the hallway.

"Where is everyone?" I shouted. No one answered. I ran back to the main room of the Ranch House and out the front door onto the dirt drive. The buildings and vehicles surrounding the ranch were gone. Then I turned back and the Ranch House was also gone. I looked around me. There was nothing but miles and miles of tumbleweeds and dusty, barren landscape.

And then I woke from the nightmare.

The next morning came too early. *Way* too early. I reached over to hit the snooze button and I must have pulsed because the radio–alarm clock practically exploded. Ostin laughed.

"Dude, you fried it."

I groaned. "Someone had to."

"Time to get up, lover boy," he said.

I sat up and wiped the sleep from my eyes, then walked to the bathroom and showered. Ostin was already gone when I got out. I dressed, then went to the dining room for breakfast. My mother was waiting for me. Her eyes were red and I could tell that she had been crying, even though she tried to hide it. She smiled when she saw me. "How was last night?"

"It was perfect. Thank you."

"It was my pleasure."

A few minutes later Taylor walked in with her mother. They both looked tired and their eyes were red and puffy from crying, but she smiled when she saw me. She walked up to me and we hugged.

My mother said to her, "Michael said you two had a good time last night."

"Thank you so much," Taylor said. "It was one of the best nights of my life."

"I'm so glad," she said with a sigh. "Now we'd better get some food in you two. We only have an hour before you leave."

We all walked over to the buffet tables. "I asked the cooks to prepare something special," my mom said. "Waffles."

I piled a plate high with waffles, along with strawberry jam and whipped cream. Ostin was sitting with his parents. His stack of waffles was like six inches high.

As we ate, my mother got more emotional. She kept dabbing at her eyes with her napkin.

"Are you okay?" I asked.

"I hate good-byes."

"It's going to be okay," I said.

"You be safe," she said sternly. "You promised."

We had just finished eating when Joel walked into the room. "Electroclan, you have twenty minutes before your bus leaves."

"I'd better get my stuff," I said to my mother.

"I'll meet you out front," she replied.

I went back to my room and grabbed the bag with the clothes they had given me and carried it out to the front of the Ranch House. The van was idling in the center of the driveway where it had let us off five days earlier. Taylor, Mrs. Ridley, and my mother were standing next to it. Understandably, Mrs. Ridley was a mess. Ian, Tanner, and Zeus were standing next to them, and they all looked over as I walked out.

"Hey, dude," Tanner said.

"You changed your mind and you're coming with us," I said.

"In your dreams," he replied. We hugged. "You be careful."

"*Careful* is my middle name," I said.

"I thought *Danger* was your middle name."

"Not this time," I said.

Jack and Abigail walked out of the house holding hands. Abigail was crying, and Jack kept pulling her into him. They walked up to me.

"You guys come back safe," Abigail said. She hugged me. "Bring everyone back. Promise me."

"We'll be back," I said. "I promise."

Abigail whispered into my ear. "Don't let Jack do anything stupid, okay?"

"I'll do my best," I said.

She kissed my cheek. "I love you, Michael." She smiled at me again; then, holding Jack's hand, she went to say good-bye to Ian and McKenna.

I walked over to Taylor and our mothers. Mrs. Ridley seemed inconsolable and Taylor looked agonized by her mother's pain. My mother put her arm around me. "This is hard," she said softly.

Ostin was the last out. His eyes were puffy and Mrs. Liss was dabbing at her eyes with a Kleenex. Mr. Liss had his arms around both of them.

"You be careful," Mrs. Liss said when she was close to me. "No shenanigans."

I had no idea what she meant by that, but I hugged her and she turned back to Ostin, who was as emotional as I'd ever seen him.

A moment later Joel walked up to us. He glanced at my mother, then put his hand on my shoulder and pulled me away from everyone else. "I need to know what you've decided about Nichelle," he whispered.

"We'll bring her," I said.

He nodded in approval. "I think you're making the right choice."

"Take care of my mom," I said.

"I will." He looked at me seriously, then said, "Michael, no foolish risks. Rescue Jade Dragon if you can, but if you can't, we'll deal with it. I promised your mother you would come back safe."

"We'll do our best," I said.

He looked at me, then said, "I know you will." He looked around. "It's time to go." We walked back to my mother.

As we were about to board the van Gervaso walked out the front door. For a brief moment we looked at each other; then he saluted me. "*De oppresso liber*," he said.

"Liberate the oppressed," Ostin translated.

I saluted Gervaso back. I hugged my mother again; then we walked over to Taylor and her mother. Mrs. Ridley turned to me. "Keep her safe. I beg you."

"I'll protect her," I said. "I'll bring her back."

"I love you, Mom," Taylor said. "I'll see you soon."

She wiped her eyes with a tissue. "I just got you back. I can't believe I'm letting you go."

A minute later Joel said, "I'm sorry, but it's time."

Taylor and her mother hugged and kissed again; then Taylor stepped toward me. "Good-bye, Mrs. Vey."

"I'll see you both soon," my mother said, doing her best to be strong. "And, Taylor?"

"Yes?"

"You keep my son safe too," she said.

Taylor nodded seriously. "I'll do my best."

I hugged my mother once more, then picked up my bag, and Taylor and I climbed into the van. The vehicle shook as the driver started the engine. With the exception of Taylor's and Ostin's sniffles, everyone on board was quiet as the van pulled forward around the circular drive, then up the steep incline away from the compound.

I wondered if we would ever see this place again.

21

A Brief Stop

I wasn't sure when I was going to tell everyone about Nichelle. Initially, I was planning on breaking the news on the two-hour ride to the airstrip, but everyone was already so tired and emotionally drained that I decided against it. Taylor found out accidentally. About a half hour after we'd left the ranch I was lying against her in the back of the bus when she suddenly said, "You've got to be kidding."

"About what?"

She looked around to make sure that no one else could hear us; then she whispered, "We're really going to pick up Nichelle?"

I couldn't keep anything from her. "Yes."

"When were you going to tell us?"

"Why do you ask questions when you already know the answer?"

"I wouldn't do it now," she said. "Everyone's grumpy."

"I'm waiting until we're on the plane."

"They're going to freak, you know."

I took a deep breath, then exhaled slowly. "I know."

It was around nine o'clock when we boarded the same plane we'd flown in on—a Gulfstream G650. The copilot stored our bags in the back of the fuselage as we climbed aboard. Taylor and I sat in the back.

After we'd taken off, Ostin, who had finally regained his composure, said to me, "Based on where I believe we are, I'm guessing our flight to Taiwan will be about fifteen hours. Am I right?"

"Probably," I said. "Except our first flight isn't to Taiwan."

"I figured that," he said. "Our first stop is probably in Hawaii or Japan to refuel. Which is it?"

"Neither," I said.

"What?"

I looked at him for a moment, then stood. "All right, everyone, I have an announcement to make."

Everyone turned back to look at me.

"Before we go to Taiwan we're going to make a brief stop in California. We're going back to Pasadena." No one said anything so I added, "To pick someone up."

"Who?" Zeus asked.

Taylor looked at me sympathetically.

"We're getting Nichelle."

For a moment everyone just looked at me like they were waiting for the punch line of a bad joke. Then they exploded.

"You gotta be kidding," Ian said.

"What?!" Zeus said. "What for?"

"She's coming with us."

"Tell me you're not talking about Hatch's wicked little pet, Nichelle," Tessa said.

"She's not his pet anymore," I said. "He abandoned her." The look of shock in their eyes didn't diminish. Or maybe it was pure revulsion. I was ticking badly. "Th-the council thought it would be a good idea to have her join the Electroclan," I stammered.

"Michael, I know Nichelle," Ian said, shaking his head. "Trust me, it's a bad idea."

"I've known Nichelle longer than all of you," Tessa said. "It's the worst idea I've ever heard. It's like concrete-parachute bad. The girl's creepy."

"And *mean*," McKenna added. "She's mean and she likes it."

"She's reptilian," Ian said. "You can't trust a reptile."

"They can't make us do this," Zeus said. "We can just say no. What are they going to do, fire us?"

"It was my decision to bring her with us," I said.

Everyone went quiet. Zeus and Ian both folded their arms. Even Ostin's forehead furrowed.

"Look, I know it sounds crazy. But something tells me we'll need her. Hatch's electric kids will be there to guard Jade Dragon. And if we have to fight them, the Elgen guard, *and* the Lung Li, having her powers will help."

"Help who?" Zeus said. "What if she turns on us?"

"If we get her close to them she'll just run back to them," Ian said. "You know she will."

"Maybe not," Taylor said. "Hatch left her to die. Even Nichelle must understand that."

"How will we even find her?" Zeus said. "It's been months since we left her. She could be anywhere."

"The resistance has been keeping track of her," I said. "After we left her she moved in with some guys she met. She's working at a taco stand in Pasadena. That's where we'll meet her today."

"What guys?" Zeus asked. "Elgen?"

"No. I don't know who they are. They just said they're some gangster guys she met on the street."

"What if she won't come?" McKenna said.

"Then you don't have anything to worry about—except the Elgen, the Lung Li, and Quentin, Torstyn, Tara, Bryan, and Kylee."

"And the Taiwanese army," Taylor added.

Everyone was quiet again. Then Ostin broke the silence. "Michael may be right. Maybe we should at least check her out."

"I'm telling you, it's a bad idea," Ian said.

Zeus was still upset. "If she turns on us, I'll fry her like bacon."

"Unless she gets you first," Tessa said.

"If she turns on us," Jack said, "I'll punch her out, then you can fry her."

"Fair enough," I said.

The flight to California took a little less than three hours, though it felt much longer. I think I was as anxious about picking up Nichelle as I was about rescuing Jade Dragon. After we'd landed and disembarked, the pilot came out on the tarmac to speak with me.

"Michael, we need to fly out of here by seven o'clock, so you need to be back no later than six. We're under the jurisdiction of the air traffic controllers, so we can't bend the rules."

"We'll be here," I said. "With or without her."

"Good luck."

I looked at the others. "I'm going to need it."

I wrote down the address of the taco stand where Nichelle was working and we split up into three taxis, Jack and Zeus taking charge of the other two.

"Let me do the talking with Nichelle," I said. "If you get there before me, don't let her see you. Don't do anything until we're all together."

Everyone was still upset, but at least no one spoke out.

As everyone walked to their cabs I said, "Jack, hold on a second."

He turned back. "Yeah?"

I walked up to him. "Back in the plane, you didn't say much about Nichelle. Do you think it's a dumb idea?"

He looked at me for a moment, then nodded. "Yes. But sometimes those are the kind that work."

22

Taco King

Our three cabs arrived simultaneously on the corner of Colorado Boulevard and Allen Avenue, just out of view of the Taco King. Once we were all out on the street I asked the drivers to wait; then we walked toward the restaurant.

"Is she there?" I asked Ian.

He looked a moment, then said, "Yeah. I think that's her."

"You think?"

"She's changed some."

"As long as we're here, can we get something to eat?" Ostin asked.

"I want something too," McKenna said.

"Sure," I said. "But let's take care of Nichelle first."

Even though there was a line of cars at the drive-through, the restaurant was mostly empty, with just two scary-looking, twenty-something-year-old men sitting across from each other at one of the side tables.

I walked up to the counter. I could understand why Ian wasn't sure if it was Nichelle because it took me a moment to recognize her too. She was turned away from me working the drive-through window. She had dyed her hair bright red with a single black streak and was wearing a black-and-purple cap and a Taco King shirt that looked several sizes too large. She had a tattoo sleeve on one arm.

Nichelle still hadn't noticed us when the boyish-faced kid at the counter asked, "May I help you?" (I swear he looked like he was twelve.)

"Uh, sure." I turned back. "Everyone want burritos?"

"I'll have a taco," Taylor said.

"Me too," McKenna said. "Two, please."

"Two beef chimichangas," Jack said.

"Okay, I think I've got this," I said, glancing first at Nichelle, then back at the kid. "I need eight bean burritos, two beef chimichangas, four hard-shell tacos, and eight large drinks."

"Add a couple deluxe nachos," Jack said. "And some churros. Eight of them."

"I don't want a churro," McKenna said.

"I'll eat yours," Jack said.

"Eight churros," the kid said, punching in our order. "And two deluxe nachos. That's sixty-one fifty."

While I was paying him, Nichelle turned around. It took her a moment to recognize me, but it was obvious when she did. She froze, her already pale countenance blanching still more. All she said was, "Vey."

"Hi, Nichelle."

She looked terrified. "What are you doing here?"

"We need to talk," I said.

She saw the rest of our group and looked even more frightened. She turned to an older Hispanic woman who was putting together orders. "Carlita, may I take my break now?"

"Not with that drive-through line," the woman replied. She glanced over at me. "May I help you?"

"I'm just an old friend," I said.

"Well, Miss Nikki is working, old friend."

"I'll wait," I said. "No problem. We'll just eat."

"I won't be long," Nichelle said anxiously. She glanced furtively at the others again, then went back to the drive-through window.

We found a table and sat down. A few minutes later the kid who had taken our order brought out our food on two trays. We were about halfway through our meal when Nichelle walked out from behind the counter. "I've got ten minutes," she said. "Let's go outside behind the building."

"Yo, Neesh," one of the men on the other side of the room said. "Where you goin'?" The man was tall and muscular with tattoos covering one side of his neck and both of his arms. The other man didn't speak. He was smaller than the first, Hispanic with a shaved head. He was wearing a sleeveless LA Clippers jersey exposing muscular arms and shoulders that were covered with tattoos.

"I just need to talk to these guys for a minute. I'll be back."

The second man looked at Jack, and there was palpable tension between them. "Whatcha lookin' at, 'Efe?" the man said, a dark smile crossing his face.

"Nothing much," Jack said coldly.

"Chill," Nichelle said, waving us on. "C'mon."

We followed her out the restaurant's side door and around to the back near a Dumpster. There was only one car in the drive-through, and it was at the window.

"How did you find me?" Nichelle asked.

"It wasn't hard," I said.

"What do you want?"

"We need your help."

"What kind of help?"

"I can't tell you," I said.

"You need my help, but you can't tell me why? What kind of proposition is that?"

"It's secret. But it involves the Elgen."

"You mean it involves Hatch."

"Yes. And probably the other electric kids."

"Which is why you want me."

"Right."

She looked down for a moment as if she was thinking. Then she looked up. "Do I get to hurt Hatch?"

"Maybe."

"You need to tell me more."

I shuffled my feet a little. "All right, but if you tell anyone, we'll come after you."

She lifted her hands. "Who am I gonna tell? Homeboys in there?"

"All right. We're rescuing someone they've kidnapped."

"Who?"

"I can't tell you."

She thought some more, then said, "You'll have to pay me. I'm broke."

"I'm good with that."

"How much can you pay me?"

"How much do you want?"

"Three thousand."

"Three thousand dollars?" Jack said in disbelief.

"It's what I need," she said, looking at him. "I work for a living."

"We can't trust her," Ian said to me. "A leopard doesn't change its spots."

"Yeah, lucky for you I'm not a leopard," Nichelle replied.

"I can give you three," I said. "But I'll have to pay you later."

"How much later?"

"I can give you a thousand now, and the rest after we're done. We'll pay for everything until then. Food and stuff."

"How long will this take?"

"It may take a while. We're leaving California."

"Then what?"

"After we're done, we'll take you wherever you want to go."

She hesitated for another moment, then said, "All right. I take it from those taxis over there that we're leaving now."

"Do you have a problem with that?"

"No. They'll fire me. But I was going to quit anyway. Do I have time to get my stuff?"

"No. We'll buy you whatever you need."

"That won't come out of my three thousand, right?"

"No. And one more thing," I said. "Taylor needs to read your mind to make sure you're not still with them."

"Still with who?"

"The Elgen."

"Do I look like I'm still with the Elgen?"

"It's the only way," I said.

Nichelle rolled her eyes. "Whatever."

Taylor walked up to her. "I'm going to touch your arms," she said.

"You have to touch me?" Nichelle said.

"Believe me, I don't want to touch you either."

"Just get it over with."

Taylor put her hands on Nichelle's forearms and closed her eyes. Less than a minute later she took her hands off and stepped back. She looked at me and nodded. "I think we're good."

"Did it really take a mind reader to tell you that I hate them?" Nichelle said angrily. "I hated them before they left me to die."

"We're just being careful," I said. I looked around at the others. No one looked happy. "All right, let's go."

Nichelle took off her hat and apron and threw them on the ground. As we walked around to the front of the restaurant Nichelle's two friends from inside approached us.

"Where you goin'?" the guy with the tattooed neck asked again. "Who are these losers?"

"Just some people I know. I'm going with them. I'll be a while."

He turned to me. "She ain't goin' nowhere with you."

"Yes, she is," I said.

He swaggered up to me, his face contracting into a sneer. "I say no she ain't."

"I wouldn't do that if I were you," Nichelle said to him.

"Who's gonna stop me?"

"He will," she said matter-of-factly.

He smiled, his eyes still locked on mine. "Him? Little dude?"

"Idiot," Nichelle said. "You have no idea who you're dealing with."

He looked at her. "What, little man knows kung fu?" He turned back to me with a cocky smile. "You know kung fu?" He pulled out a gun. "Never bring kung fu to a gunfight."

I looked at his gun, then said, "Want to see something cool?"

His eyes narrowed. "I wanna see you gone, dog."

"No, really, you'll like this." I held my hands in front of me and formed an electric ball about the size of a grapefruit.

He stared at it in disbelief; then looked at me. "What the . . ."

"Catch," I said, pushing the ball at him. It blew up on contact, shocking him so hard he actually left his feet. He landed unconscious and flat on his back on the pavement. The other man looked at me and turned to run but Zeus blasted him, knocking him down as well. He was still conscious but whimpering in pain.

Nichelle shook her head. "I told you, idiots," she said. "Don't wait up for me."

Zeus stepped over the man I'd shocked and lifted his gun. "He won't be needing this anymore."

"What are you going to do with that?" Tessa asked.

"Throw it away," he said.

"Let's go," I said. I turned to Nichelle. "You come with me."

Ian got in the front seat next to the driver while Taylor, Nichelle, and I climbed into the back. "Back to the airport," I said to the driver.

"We're flying somewhere?" Nichelle asked.

"Taiwan," I said.

"Where's Taiwan?"

"By China."

"For the record," she said, "I'm not a fan of Chinese food."

"That's too bad," I replied. "You're going to be eating a lot of it."

23

Swamp Eel and Fish Noodles

Even though we had hurried back to the airport, we still ended up sitting around for several hours before the pilots returned. Waiting wasn't awful since the private jet terminal was pretty nice. Not that I was any kind of expert on airports. Before I'd gotten involved with the voice, I'd never even flown on a plane, but Zeus and Tessa said this place was a lot better than regular airport terminals. It reminded me of an expensive mall. Tessa and McKenna even got massages.

Since no one had ended up eating much at the taco stand, we ate dinner at an expensive steak house—everyone except for Nichelle, who ate alone at an Italian restaurant at the opposite end of the terminal. After we ate we walked back out to the gate to wait. Ostin read his book while Jack found some cards and he, Taylor, Tessa, Ian, and I played Texas Hold'em. It was a pretty bizarre game since Ian could see through the cards and with Tessa so close Taylor could read our minds without touching us, so she always knew if someone had a good hand or was bluffing.

Nichelle sat away from the rest of us. I didn't really blame her. Everyone was treating her like she had a virus. Most of them wouldn't even look at her. I know they all had their reasons for hating her—so did I—but still something inside of me pitied her. She had been with the Elgen longer than any of us, and their world was all she knew. If Hatch had raised me I probably would have turned out like her as well.

I eventually gave up playing cards (since, no surprise, I was losing) and walked over to Nichelle. She was sitting on the ground with her back to the wall sketching something in a notebook she had bought at one of the terminal stores.

"Hey," I said.

She glanced up at me, then went back to drawing. "Hey."

"Mind if I sit here?"

She shook her head without looking up.

I sat down on the linoleum floor next to her. "What are you drawing?"

"Nothing." She took a few more strokes with her pencil, then held the notebook up so I could see. Her drawing was bizarre—a skeleton with lightning bolts coming out of its eyes and rosebushes growing inside its rib cage. Truthfully, she wasn't bad. She would probably make a good tattoo artist. "What do you think?" she asked.

"Cool," I said.

"Thanks," she said, going back to drawing.

"So what have you been up to since we left you?" I asked.

"Surviving."

"Us too," I said. "Hatch was holding my mother in Peru."

"Yeah. I knew that." We were both silent a moment. Then she said, "Did you save her?"

"Yes. But we had to take down an entire Starxource plant to do it."

She looked up. "You destroyed the Peruvian Starxource plant?"

I nodded. "Yes."

She looked happy to hear this. "That was Hatch's favorite. I bet he's crazy with rage."

"I doubt I'll be on his Christmas list this year."

"If Hatch *did* Christmas." She suddenly seemed a little calmer. "That electric bubble thing you do is new."

"Lightning balls," I said. "That's what Ostin calls them. I just figured out how to make them."

"You've gotten more electric since I last saw you."

"I know," I said. "I keep getting more electric."

"You're the only one of us that does that. What does it mean?"

"I have no idea."

"So now that I'm here, who is it that you're paying me to help rescue?"

"The Elgen kidnapped a little Chinese girl named Jade Dragon."

"Is she electric?"

"No. Just very smart. She figured out how to fix the MEI."

"That's big," Nichelle said. "Where are they keeping her?"

"I can't tell you yet."

"But Hatch and his stuck-up Glows are going to be there?"

"Yes."

"Who told you all this?"

"I can't tell you that either."

"So many secrets," she said, shaking her head. She went back to drawing.

As soon as the pilots returned we boarded the plane and took off. Our first flight was to Tokyo and took about eleven hours. Even though we landed just to refuel, we were on the ground for nearly four hours.

Taylor slept almost the whole way. In fact, almost everyone slept the whole way, except for me and Ostin. He was still memorizing *The Art of War*.

I was too anxious to sleep. The same thoughts kept running through my mind. *What if we fail to save Jade Dragon? What would an electric world be like? What if the Elgen capture us again? What have we gotten ourselves into?* Several times I reached into my pocket and brought out Gervaso's medal. For *valor* and *bravery*. I felt like a hypocrite even holding the medal. I didn't feel brave at all.

Our flight from Japan to Taiwan took about three and a half hours. As we prepared to land, I realized that my internal clock was all messed up—it felt like night but the sun was just rising.

"This isn't Kaohsiung," Ostin said.

"How do you know?"

"We came in from the east over the ocean. Kaohsiung's on the west side of the island. And Kaohsiung is a big city with millions of people. This airport is too small."

"Then where are we?"

Ostin scratched his neck. "That's what I want to know."

Taylor woke. "Where are we?"

"Not Idaho," I said.

"Didn't think so," she said sleepily, closing her eyes again.

After the plane had landed and come to a complete stop, one of the pilots emerged from the cockpit. "Welcome to Taiwan," he said. "This is where we say good-bye. You can pick up your bags at the bottom of the stairway. One of our associates will be meeting you on the tarmac. Good luck, Electroclan." He opened the door and we all got up and walked to the front of the plane.

Even though it was early morning, the air outside was already hot and more humid than anything I'd ever felt before. It was like walking fully dressed into a steam room.

"I'm not used to drinking my air," I said to Taylor.

"My hair is definitely going frizzy in this," she said.

"I'm going to melt," Ostin said. "I swear it."

Nichelle was the last one off the plane. She hadn't said a word to anyone the entire flight, which worried me. At the bottom of the jet's stairway she looked around and shook her head. "I should have asked for more money."

As we retrieved the last of our bags, a young Chinese man, probably in his early twenties, walked up to us. He was about my size, thin, and dressed simply in denim jeans and a light-blue sports shirt. He had short, spiky hair and a birthmark across his right cheek. He looked us over as if he was counting, then said with a light accent, "Welcome to Taitung. My Chinese name is Chen Jya Lung, but call me Ben."

"Why are we in Taitung?" Ostin asked. "I thought we were going to Kaohsiung."

"We are going to Kaohsiung," Ben said. "But it is far from here."

"That's my point," Ostin said. "Why are we so far?"

"For safety. The Elgen have spies everywhere. They will be watching the airports carefully. Taitung is small, so they will not be watching it. We are one hundred sixty kilometers from Kaohsiung. It will take us maybe three hours to reach our hotel. Do you all have your bags?"

I looked around. "We've got them."

"Good. We will go now. Follow me." He led us to a small service door a short distance from where we had landed. A Chinese man in a police uniform opened the door for us. Ben handed him a red envelope.

"Don't we have to go through customs?" Ostin asked.

"There are ways to not do things," Ben said. "Especially when you do not know who you can trust."

He opened the door and we entered the main terminal. As we walked through the crowded corridor, it felt like everyone was looking at us. We were the only non-Asians in the airport and, with the exception of McKenna, we stood out. I wondered if McKenna felt that way in America.

"I only have American money," I said to Ben.

"You will need to exchange it," he said. "I will do it. We do not want anyone to see your identification."

I handed him all the money Joel had given me except a thousand dollars.

"You have a lot of money," he said.

"It's not mine," I said.

He took the bills up to a currency exchange booth and returned a few minutes later with a stack of bills. I gave everyone the equivalent of a couple hundred dollars and kept the rest for our expenses.

"Can we get something to eat?" Ostin asked.

"Yes," Ben said. "We will get food; then we will drive to Kaohsiung. I know you are tired of travel, but it is a beautiful drive."

We followed Ben out to the airport parking lot and to a long white van covered with Chinese characters.

"Can you read what it says?" I asked Ostin.

"Something like Taiwan Excitement Travel Company."

"I'm sure it will be," Taylor said.

After we were all inside the vehicle Ben said, "I know a place in Taitung with good fish noodles."

"Lovely," Tessa said. "Nothing I like better for breakfast than a hot bowl of fish noodles."

"I am happy you like fish noodles," Ben said.

"I don't think he understands sarcasm," Zeus said.

"So it seems," Tessa replied.

I don't know what she was complaining about—after all the bugs and slimy creatures she'd been eating in the Amazon, fish noodles sounded normal.

We drove into the Taitung city center and Ben parked the van in front of an open restaurant. We all sat down at two round tables on the uneven concrete sidewalk in front of the restaurant. Christmas music was blaring from a CD player inside the restaurant, which seemed weird to us, but I figured was no different from any other American music to them. I lifted a menu. Not surprisingly, everything was in Chinese.

"At least the Chinese restaurants at home have pictures of the food," Taylor said.

"You're not at home," Ostin said.

"Really," Taylor replied, looking over her menu. "I thought this was Boise."

"This is my favorite restaurant in Taitung," Ben said. "I will make your life easy and order for you." He shouted something across the room to a woman standing behind a large serving table. A moment later she came out with a tray filled with glasses and bottles of amber liquid. "This is *pingwo sidra*," Ben said. "Apple soda. You like soda?"

"We like soda," Ostin said.

Tessa was the first to try it. "That's not bad. Kind of cidery."

"Cidery?" Ostin said. "Is that a word?"

Tessa ignored him.

The woman then brought out small plastic bowls of thin broth with chopped scallions. The soup was simple and salty but good. While we finished our soup they brought out chopsticks, soy sauce, and a shallow porcelain dish of red hot sauce, followed by bamboo baskets stacked on top of each other. They were filled with white steaming dumplings.

"What are these?" Taylor asked.

"There's meat inside," Ian said.

"I just thought of something," Taylor said, smiling. "If someone ever gives me a box of chocolates I'm bringing them to you."

"I don't like chocolate," Ian said.

"Not for you to *eat*," Taylor said. "So you could tell me what's inside them. That way I won't have to stick my fingernail in the bottom of each one." She looked at me. "That makes my mom so mad."

"These are called *syau lung bau*," Ben said. "That means 'little dragon dumplings.' They are very delicious."

I had trouble lifting one with my chopstick, so I finally just speared it. Something yellow and oily came out where I had pierced it.

"What's that?" I asked.

"There is soup inside," Ben said. "I do not think you have this in America."

"In America the dumplings are *in* the soup," Taylor said. "Not the other way around."

"Try it," Ben said. "You will like it."

I lifted a dumpling and bit half of it, and the other half fell to the table. I picked up the other half with my fingers and quickly put it in my mouth. Ben was right. I did like it.

"You may put them in the soy sauce or hot sauce," Ben said.

"What's the meat inside of these?" Taylor asked.

"Poke."

"Poke?"

"Pig meat," Ben said.

"You mean *pork*," Ostin said.

Ben looked distressed. "I am very sorry, my English is not always so good."

"Your English is very good," I said. "And a million times better than our Chinese."

"I can't use these things," McKenna said, setting down her chopsticks. "Can I have a fork?"

Ben's brow furrowed. "But you are Chinese."

"Only my genes," McKenna said.

Ben looked at her pants. "Your jeans are from China?"

McKenna shook her head. "Never mind."

Next they brought out bowls of noodles with broccoli and snap peas and pieces of some kind of filleted fish. The skin of the fish was thick and decorative, almost like snakeskin. The noodles were set in a yellow-brown mucus-like broth.

"I think I'm going to be sick," Taylor said, looking at the bowl.

"What is this?" I asked Ben.

"Fish."

"It looks like a snake," Zeus said.

"Eat," Ben said. "You will like it. It is famous in Taitung."

I ate a few bites. He was wrong this time. It was awful. "What kind of fish is this?"

"It is *shan yu*. I do not know how to say it in English." He took out his smartphone. "I will look it up on Wikipedia." He typed in some words, then handed me the phone.

"Swamp eel," I said.

"I'm going to throw up," Taylor said.

"You should see how gross it looks *in* your stomach," Ian said.

Taylor grimaced. "Now I'm definitely going to throw up."

"Generally speaking, I don't eat things from swamps," Tessa said.

"Me neither," I said, pushing the bowl away from me. I drank some of the apple soda to get the taste out of my mouth.

Ben looked at us all curiously. "You do not like noodles?"

"We like noodles," I said. "It's the eel."

"And the yellow mucus puss stuff," Tessa added.

"You do not like eel?" Ben asked.

"Only electric ones," I said.

"Do they taste good?"

"I have no idea," I said.

The woman brought out more bamboo baskets, which I was glad to see since I was still hungry and the dumplings were good. "What are these?" I asked.

"These are steamed buns with sweet meat."

"Barbecue," Ostin said.

They were as good as the dumplings, maybe better. Ostin clearly liked them because he ate like six of them, and Ben ordered more for the rest of us.

We finished eating, then boarded the van and headed off to Kaohsiung. We drove south along Taiwan's eastern coastline for more than an hour to a small city called Daren, west for another hour to another small town called Shihzih, then back north along the western coast to Kaohsiung, which was the largest and most crowded city I had ever seen. The streets were filled with cars, bicycles, motorcycles, and scooters.

Ben had booked us in a five-star hotel called the Grand Hi-Lai. It was the tallest building in that part of the city and overlooked the Kaohsiung bay. He parked across from the hotel's entrance, shut off the van, and turned back to speak to us. "This is where we will be staying. Please wait while I get your rooms." He went into the hotel and about ten minutes later returned with our room keys. We split up into four rooms: Ostin and me; Jack, Zeus, and Ian; Tessa and McKenna; and Taylor and Nichelle.

"I think we must walk in two or three at a time to avoid suspicion," Ben said. "It is best if you do not leave the hotel. There are many restaurants inside, but you should only be two or maybe four together. There is a nice mall with the hotel if you want to shop. Do you have any questions?"

"Where are you staying?" I asked.

"I am stay here too. I am in room 7011."

"Seven, zero, one, one," I memorized. "What's our schedule?"

"The Elgen boat *Volta* is still at least a week away. Tomorrow we will drive to look at the Starxource plant. I think you will be jet-lag, so we will not start too early. Maybe around ten." He looked around for confirmation.

"Ten's good," I said.

"Okay," he said. "We meet in the hotel lobby at ten. I will take you to breakfast. Do you need anything?"

"We're good," I said.

"Then we go."

Ben handed us our plastic room keys, and Jack, Zeus, and Ian went in first, followed by Tessa and McKenna, then Taylor and Nichelle. When it was just Ostin and me, I said to Ben, "Thank you. We'll see you in the morning."

"*Shr dyan,*" Ben said. "Ten o'clock. And welcome to Taiwan."

24

The Art of War

The Grand Hi-Lai Hotel was the nicest place I'd ever stayed. It had like five or six restaurants and a large fitness center with a yoga room and spa. Ostin and I had a room that faced west with a view of the Kaohsiung harbor. Across the street, twenty-two stories below us, was some kind of temple with green and blue dragons and tigers on its roof. It also had symbols that looked like swastikas.

"That's a Buddhist temple," Ostin said, looking over my shoulder. "The Buddhists and Hindus used the swastika symbol thousands of years before Hitler flipped it around and made it the symbol for the Nazi party. Ironically, the word 'swastika' is a Sanskrit word meaning 'well-being.' The Nazis kind of ruined that for the rest of the world."

There was a lot that I wanted to see, and I kept thinking what a shame it was that we weren't there on vacation.

Ostin and I ordered room service (something we'd never done before), and a waiter brought us Cokes in Chinese bottles, ham fried rice, and barbecue chicken. Even though it was just a little after two when we finished eating, we were both exhausted, and I drew the room's blinds and we went to sleep.

I woke early the next morning to the sound of classical music, like a symphony. I tried to turn off the radio, and then I realized it wasn't on. The music was coming from outside our window. I got up and looked out. On the street behind the hotel a garbage truck was playing music from a sound system.

"That's weird. It's a garbage truck," I said. "People are bringing out their garbage."

"They do that in Taiwan," Ostin said. "It's like the ice-cream trucks in America; they play music to let people know they're there. He's playing Beethoven's *Für Elise*."

There was something funny and happy about the combination of garbage and Beethoven.

"What time is it?" Ostin asked.

"Time to go back to bed," I replied, lying back down.

"I'm going to watch television."

"It's just going to be in Chinese," I said, hoping to deter him.

"I know. I can practice my Chinese."

"Practice softly," I said. I pulled the pillow over my head and tried to sleep, but couldn't. About forty-five minutes later I got up and looked out the window again. The harbor was filled with boats of myriad shapes and sizes. The sky was overcast and my view was slightly obscured by fog.

"I think it might rain," I said.

"Rain's never hurt anyone," Ostin said.

"Tell that to Zeus," I replied.

Ostin and I went down to the lobby a few minutes before ten. Everyone else was already there, though it took a while before I could tell since they weren't standing together. Zeus, Jack, and

Ian were sitting in the restaurant, and McKenna and Tessa were looking at jewelry in a display case on the far side of the lobby.

I could see everyone but Nichelle. Taylor had shared a room with her (in part because no one else was willing to, and also to keep an eye on her) and she was standing alone in the center of the lobby beside a massive display of flowers. I left Ostin next to the concierge desk and casually walked up to her. "Where's Nichelle?"

"She'll be down soon. She didn't want to wait around down here with everyone."

"I don't blame her," I said. "How was she last night?"

"Quiet. She went out to buy some clothes. She brought back some pastries from the bakery over there. She gave me one."

"She gave you a pastry?"

"I know, amazing, right?"

"Anything suspicious?"

"No. She just ate her pastry, then rolled over and went to sleep."

At that moment Nichelle came walking down the hall from the elevator. She glanced furtively at us, and then kept walking toward the front door and went outside.

Less than a minute later Ben walked into the lobby. He looked at me and nodded, then went back out. I looked around at everyone else to make sure they'd seen him; then we individually started toward the door. It took about five minutes before everyone was in the van. Tessa and McKenna were the last out.

"Do you really think this pretending we don't know one another is necessary?" Tessa asked as she climbed into the van.

"We don't want to find out," Ostin said.

"It is better to be careful," Ben said.

"I'm hungry," Taylor said.

"I have a breakfast surprise," Ben said, then added, "It is not fish noodles."

"Thank Buddha," Tessa said.

Ben drove out of the hotel's driveway, down the street toward the harbor, and then several miles up the coast before we turned off on a side street and parked outside a small open café. "We will eat breakfast here," Ben announced, shutting off the van.

An elderly man was sitting on a stool in front of the restaurant using the longest pair of chopsticks I had ever seen—at least twenty inches—to lift long bread sticks from a vat of boiling oil. We went inside the café and sat down.

"What's for breakfast?" Tessa asked. "Monkey-brain mush?"

Ben looked at her quizzically. "They do not make mush from monkey brains."

"Glad to know," Tessa said.

"We are eating *syau bing yo tyau*. It means 'little cookie oil stick.'"

The man brought over plates with sesame-seed-covered biscuits and a plastic basket with long golden sticks of deep-fried bread.

"How do you eat this?" Taylor asked.

"Fold the oil stick into the sesame cookie, then dip into *dou jiang*," Ben said.

"Dough what?" Taylor asked.

"Sorry," Ben said. "Soy milk. He has not bringed it yet."

"*Brought* it," Ostin corrected. "Brought it yet. 'Brought' is the past tense of 'bring.'"

"Sorry," Ben said. "My English is poor."

"Quit correcting his English," Taylor said. "It's embarrassing."

Ostin looked at her quizzically. "How else will he learn?"

The old man returned and set out a bowl of hot soy milk for each of us. Ben folded one of the oil sticks into a cookie, then dipped it into the milk. The rest of us followed his lead. I thought it was pretty good.

After we had eaten for a few minutes, I asked Ben, "What's our plan for today?"

He glanced around, then said, "I will take you up to the Starxource plant to prepare."

"Have you been there before?" Ostin asked.

"Many, many times."

"We were told the Taiwanese army is helping guard the plant," Jack said.

"This is true. There are many patrols of soldiers. We cannot go as close as I used to."

After breakfast we drove north along the coastal road, past flooded rice paddies and old concrete buildings, some surrounded by bamboo scaffolding. It began to rain and Ben turned on the windshield wipers.

"That takes me out," Zeus said.

"It rains a lot here," Ben said. "Especially now."

"Would have been good to know before I came," Zeus said.

A few minutes later Ostin asked Ben, "Have you ever seen the Lung Li?"

A shadow crossed Ben's face. He hesitated for a few moments before saying, "Yes, I have seen the Lung Li." From his tone I could tell that he didn't want to talk about them. It was maybe another twenty minutes before he said, "We are getting close now. We must be very careful. This is a public road, but the Elgen watch this area because it is near their plant."

Through the slapping windshield wipers we could see a fenced-in harbor with dozens of boats docked inside. "Is that it?" Jack asked.

"No. That is the *Xing zheng yuan Hui an Xun fang Shu*."

"I was just going to say that," Tessa said.

"What is that?" I asked.

"It is the Taiwanese coast guard," Ben said.

"They're not going to be helping us," Ian said.

Ben shook his head. "No, they will not. They will help protect the Elgen. The Elgen give them their electricity." He pointed off into the distance. "The Starxource plant is there."

The Elgen's Taiwan Starxource plant was made of concrete and surrounded by tall fences—though, from where we were, it was hard to tell how many. As I looked at it my stomach turned and I felt myself twitching. I hoped Taylor wasn't reading my mind because the only word that I could think of was "impossible."

Away from the coast the land rose slightly and Ben drove about a quarter mile past the plant, then up a dirt road that led into a bamboo forest, and doubled back toward the plant. A few minutes later he pulled over and said, "We will hike back through the forest so we can look at the plant. We must be very careful. This many Americans here is very suspicious. If we are found we will tell them we are a member of the American Animal Protection Society and we are here to help the civet. Do you understand?"

"What's the civet?" Zeus asked.

Instinctively we all turned to Ostin. He was obviously used to it because he immediately started talking. "A civet is a nocturnal mammal that is native to the tropical forests of Africa and Asia. It looks like a cross between a dog and a leopard, but its face looks like a raccoon."

"You're making this up, right?" Tessa said.

Ostin looked at her blankly. "No."

"That is right," Ben said, draping a pair of binoculars around his neck. "They are endangered and some have been found in this area. Recently some have been hit by cars. It is very upsetting to some people."

"Roadkill," Jack said.

"Which is what we'll be if the Elgen find us," Tessa said.

It was still raining, and everyone except Zeus climbed out of the van and followed Ben to a small, overgrown path surrounded by tall, junglelike foliage. Walking in single file it took us nearly ten minutes to reach a clearing in the forest that looked out over the plant.

"It is there," Ben said. "Be very quiet."

We looked out over the expansive compound spread out below us. The plant was situated at the end of a peninsula that extended out from the mainland about two hundred yards, the back and sides of the plant facing the ocean. The landscape outside the fence and concrete was tropical, with palm trees and thick vegetation.

There was only one road in and out of the facility and it passed through four twenty-foot-high electric fences topped with razor wire. The main wall around the facility was concrete with large V-beams supporting more lines of razor wire. The concrete walls had been painted to look like the surrounding foliage. About every hundred yards along the perimeter were concrete octagon-shaped watchtowers with a 360-degree exposure. This compound made the Peruvian plant look like an amusement park.

"They added two more fences in the last month," Ben said. "I think it is your fault. Because you broke the plant in Peru."

"It looks like a prison," Jack said.

"Yes, it was a prison," Ben said. "The Elgen buy the facility from the government four years ago. Then they added more electrified razor wire, motion-sensor devices, and cameras."

"Is that all?" Tessa said.

"What are those tents and buildings outside the fences?" I asked.

"They are new. I do not know."

"They look like army barracks," Ian said. "There are soldiers inside."

Ben looked out with his binoculars. After a few minutes he slowly lowered them. "It is the army. They must have decided to station around the plant."

"You're freaking kidding me," Tessa said. "We're supposed to pass through an army camp, climb over four twenty-foot electrified fences and a twenty-five-foot concrete wall, with cameras, watch towers, and motion detectors, and not be seen?"

Ben looked at her stoically. "Yes."

Jack shook his head. "That's impossible."

"It's even worse than that," Ian said.

"What's worse than impossible?" Jack said.

"There are landmines in the spaces between the fences."

"How many landmines?" I asked.

"Hundreds, maybe thousands. They're everywhere."

"There's no way to get in there," Taylor said.

"Not without a helicopter," I replied.

"This is a no-fly zone," Ben said. "They will shoot anything near." He pointed toward one of the turrets. "They have big guns."

"Anti-aircraft guns," Ostin said.

"Of course they do," I said.

"Maybe they'll have a public open house," Tessa said sardonically. "Or a tea."

Ostin scratched his chin. "I would doubt that. The security con—"

I put my hand on Ostin's shoulder to stop him. "She was kidding."

Ostin looked at Tessa, then said, "Oh."

"How can you be so smart and still be so *dumb*?" Tessa said.

"How can you be so *rude*?" McKenna said.

"Stop it," I said. "We've got enough to worry about."

"Look," Ben said, handing me his binoculars. "It is a food truck. You can see them enter."

"Maybe we could stow away in one of those trucks," Taylor said. "Isn't that how you got into the academy?"

"Just before we were captured," Jack said, grimacing.

I raised the binoculars. A small white van was moving slowly down the plant's long asphalt drive toward the building. The vehicle was stopped at every checkpoint and surrounded by guards and dogs before moving on to the next.

"They've got some kind of X-ray thing going there," Ian said. "They're scanning the truck."

I lowered my binoculars. "So much for stowing away. It looks like they've created the perfect defense."

We all stood there solemnly. Taylor put her hand on my back. After a few minutes she said to me, "What are you thinking?"

"Why do you ask when you've already read my mind?"

She exhaled. "All right, sometimes I just like to hear you say it. So you think it's impossible too."

"I *know* it's impossible. Even if we miraculously made it past the army, we would never make it past their checkpoints. And then we'd be captured. Houdini and David Copperfield combined couldn't pull that trick off."

"We made it out of the Peruvian prison," McKenna said.

"We had inside help," Ian said. "And it wasn't nearly that pro-tected."

"And we *still* almost got killed," Jack added.

"Small detail," I said. I turned to Ostin. "What do you think?"

"I think the odds are definitely not in our favor."

McKenna took his arm. "What if we shut down the plant? Then they wouldn't have electric fences or surveillance cameras."

"How would we do that?" Tessa asked.

"Same way we did in Peru," McKenna said. "We shut off the water supply."

"I don't see any pipes," Ostin said. "They probably have them running underground into the ocean. And after what we did in Peru, they probably have them guarded."

"They're difficult even for me to see," Ian said. "But it looks like there are pipes going deep into the ocean. Way too deep to reach."

"Could we clog them?" McKenna asked.

Ian shook his head. "How?"

"No," I said. "That still wouldn't get us in. And remember Joel said not to shut down the plant."

We were all quiet again. Then, for the first time since we'd arrived, Nichelle spoke. "If you think you can break into that place, you're crazy. They'll catch us."

"Thanks for the encouragement," I said. "Any ideas?" I asked Ostin.

Ostin thought for a moment, then said, "I think Nichelle's right. The only way to win this game is to not play it."

"What?" I said.

"Sun Tzu said, 'There are roads which must not be followed, towns which must not be besieged, positions which must not be contested.' This is precisely what he was talking about. If we attack this place we'll fail."

"Are you saying we should just give up?" Taylor asked.

"No, I'm saying that we should choose to fight on grounds favorable to us."

"I'm sure they'll agree to that," Jack said.

"What are you thinking?" I asked Ostin.

"They're going to be moving Jade Dragon out of the plant to the *Volta*. That's when they'll be most vulnerable. That's when we should attack. Instead of breaking into an impossibly guarded fortress, we attack them outside of the fortress."

"You can bet that will be some armed parade," Ian said.

"We stopped the Peruvian army to rescue you guys," Tessa said. "And that was just two of us."

"They'll be better prepared than the Peruvian army," Ostin said. He rubbed his chin, then said, "But we still have one advantage. Hatch probably expects us to be here, but he doesn't know for sure that we're here. We need to let them know that we're not."

"What do you mean?" Tessa said. "We *are* here."

"Sun Tzu said—"

"Wait," Jack said, raising his hand. "Who is this Sun guy you keep talking about?"

"Sun Tzu," I said. "He's an ancient Chinese general. He wrote a book about war strategy called *The Art of War*. Ostin's been studying it."

"Oh," Jack said. "That's legit."

Ostin continued, "Sun Tzu said, 'All warfare is based on deception. Hence, when able to attack, we must seem unable; when we are near, we must make the enemy believe we are far away; when far away, we must make him believe we are near.'"

"Your point?" Tessa said.

"Right now, Hatch and the Elgen are most likely focusing all their attention on this plant. The last thing they're expecting is for us to attack another plant."

"That's the last thing I'm expecting," Jack said. "Why would we attack someplace else? This place is bad enough."

"If we attack another plant, they'll think they've been tricked and that we had no intention of attacking them in Taiwan. Then their security will be down and we'll rescue Jade Dragon as they try to move her to the *Volta*."

I looked back out over the plant. "That makes a lot more sense."

"This part about attacking another plant," Taylor said, "we can't send all of us, or no one will be here to rescue the girl."

"Right," Ostin said.

"So you're talking about splitting us up?"

"Exactly."

Taylor looked at me. "Into what groups?"

"We can figure that out later," I said. "First we'll have to get the voice to approve of the plan, but it makes sense. When it comes right down to it, what other choice do we have?"

Ian shook his head as he gazed at the plant. "Not that one."

"We must leave," Ben said. "We have been here too long."

We headed back to the van. As we climbed in, Zeus looked at us all expectantly. When no one spoke he said, "So, how was it?"

I was ticking pretty badly and everyone was silent.

Zeus frowned. "That bad?"

"Worse," Tessa said. "Much worse."

We were quiet during the drive back to our hotel. After seeing the place, I wondered if they had purposely not told us more at the ranch. Our preparation hadn't begun to prepare us for what we were facing. Nothing could. Even with Ostin's plan, the chance of rescuing Jade Dragon seemed far less likely than us being caught trying. The idea of that sent chills through me. We'd escaped from the Elgen twice before. It was unrealistic to believe that we'd be that lucky again. I hadn't felt that discouraged since Cell 25. It didn't help that we were all so jet-lagged.

As we approached the hotel, I caught Zeus up on Ostin's idea about creating a diversion by attacking another power plant.

"Who do you think should go?" he asked.

"I'm thinking you and Tessa."

Tessa looked at me. "Us?"

"Your powers are perfect for attacking the plant," I said. "With your help, Zeus will able to ignite the explosives from a much greater distance." I turned back to Zeus. "Besides, if it rains here we won't be able to use you anyway. That is, if you're okay with the idea."

Zeus and Tessa looked at each other, then Zeus said, "I'm good with it. I just don't like the idea of leaving you guys here hanging."

"If the diversion works, it will do more to protect us than you could here."

"Then I'm in."

"I'm in too," Tessa said.

"Okay. Now we just need to see if the voice agrees."

When we got to the hotel Ben pulled the van up to the far side of the driveway. It had stopped raining. "There is no need to meet early tomorrow," he said. "I know you are tired, so we will talk after I hear back from the voice. Remember, do not be in a big group."

"We've got the routine," Tessa said.

"I will see you later."

Zeus and Jack went in first. We waited about a minute in between each group. Like before, Ostin and I were the last to leave. Before going to our room, we stopped at the bakery in the hotel lobby and got cream-filled pastries that looked a little like footballs with cream inside. Then we sat at one of the tables in the lobby restaurant. We weren't alone. Taylor and Nichelle were sitting on the other side of the restaurant. We both ordered a bowl of hot noodles and orange Fanta to go with our pastries. While we were eating, Nichelle walked over. She stood in front of me with her arms folded.

"Vey."

"Yeah?"

"You know this whole thing is insane, right? I said I'd help you, but I didn't say I'd commit suicide. If Hatch catches me helping you, he'll kill me. If I'm lucky."

"He'll kill all of us," I said. She didn't say anything and I looked at her anxiously. "So you're not going to help us?"

She took a deep breath, then slowly exhaled. "I think it's crazy."

"You've already said that. Are you in or out?"

For a moment she stood there looking uncomfortable, then she shook her head again. "All right, I'm still in. But if we somehow don't die, I want double the money."

She turned and walked alone to the elevator. Taylor glanced at me and frowned, then stood and walked after her.

"I told you we shouldn't have brought her," Ostin said.

"It's a little late for that," I said.

Ten minutes later Ostin and I went up to our room. Even though it was barely afternoon I drew the blinds and we both lay on our beds. As usual Ostin fell asleep immediately. In spite of my exhaustion, I was so anxious that I tossed and turned for nearly an hour before I gave up and went to see Taylor.

Taylor's room was just three down from mine on the same side of the hall. I knocked softly. She smiled when she saw me. "What's up?"

"I couldn't sleep. What are you doing?"

"I was about to check out that mall next door. Want to go with me?"

"Sure. What's Nichelle doing?"

"Nothing. She's just listening to her iPod," she said, shutting the door behind her.

We took the elevator to the lobby. There was an entrance to the mall at the east end of the lobby, past the bakery.

The mall was nicer than anything I'd seen in Idaho. It was four stories high and had a Tiffany and Cartier and other expensive stores I'd only seen in advertisements. We stopped to look at a diamond necklace in the showcase window outside Tiffany.

"Isn't that beautiful?" Taylor said, staring at the string of sparkling gems. She turned to me. "Did I ever tell you about the time Hatch offered to buy me a diamond necklace?"

"No."

"My second day at the academy I went shopping in Beverly Hills with Tara. Hatch met us for lunch; then he took me to a famous jewelry store called Harry Winston to try on necklaces. The one I liked was like a hundred and seventy thousand dollars. For about five seconds I thought I was the luckiest girl in the world."

"Then what happened?"

Her expression changed abruptly, revealing the pain she felt in remembering. "He *touched* me," she said. "After they put the necklace on me, Hatch put his hand on my arm and I read his mind. It was the darkest, ugliest thing I've ever seen. It was the first time I realized how much evil he was capable of."

I took her hand. "I can't imagine wandering through his brain. It would be like walking through one of those haunted houses they put up at Halloween time."

She nodded. "That's exactly what it was like, except it was real." We started to walk away from the window. "It's never left me. It's like once I go through someone's mind, I have a connection with them."

"What do you mean?"

"It's hard to explain. It's like I understand them." She looked at me sadly. "After I read his mind I felt dirty. In a way, I still do."

"He'll never touch you again," I said. "I won't let him."

She kissed my cheek. "I know."

We walked around the mall for another hour. Taylor tried on a few blouses but couldn't decide on anything. Joel had given me plenty of money so I could have bought her almost anything she wanted (except the diamond necklace), but I guess she wasn't in a buying mood as much as a looking mood. When she finally tired of looking, we walked back to the hotel to get some dinner.

We took the elevator to the tenth floor to the Shanghainese Dumpling Restaurant, which was exactly what the name said it was. A half dozen chefs behind a glass window rolled out dough into saucer-sized circles, added spiced meats or vegetable fillings, then crimped them into dumplings to steam in bamboo baskets. We ate chicken soup, ham fried rice, and three different types of dumplings. Halfway through our meal, Taylor dropped a dumpling into a bowl of soy sauce, splattering it on herself and the tablecloth.

"I give up," she said, picking the dumpling up with her fingers. "Forks are just better."

Once we'd finished our meal, our server brought us dessert, a little cake with sweet red bean filling. It wasn't my favorite, but it wasn't horrible either. Afterward I walked Taylor back to her room. As we got off the elevator she said, "You're really worried, aren't you?"

"You read my mind?"

"No. You're ticking."

"Sorry," I said, forcing myself to stop. Then I slowly shook my head. "I don't know if we can really do this."

She looked at me for a moment, then said, "Do you remember what you said to us in the Amazon jungle?"

"I said a lot of things."

"Just before we snuck into the Starxource plant you told us something your mother always said. 'If you remember the *why*, the *how* will work itself out.' Every time that I've been afraid or I've doubted,

I've thought about that. You know, we've been worried about what will happen if the Elgen get the information, but there's more to our mission than that."

"What's that?"

"Jade Dragon is not just a scientific formula. She's a little girl. And she's afraid. Could you imagine what it would be like to be unable to speak or hear and to be taken from your family and home by the Elgen?"

"No," I said. I looked back into her eyes. "You have a way of putting things in perspective."

"And you have a way of making me feel safe. I think I have a really great boyfriend." She leaned forward and kissed me. "Now try to get some sleep. It makes me tired just looking at you." She opened her door and went inside.

I walked back to my room. The television was on and Ostin was lying sideways on top of his covers snoring. I figured that he must have gotten up and started watching TV, then fallen back to sleep. I turned the television off and lay back on my bed. In spite of Taylor's encouragement, what we were up against frightened me more than anything I'd faced so far: more than the academy, more than the Peruvian army, more than the *Ampere*. Even more than the Peruvian Starxource plant with its two thousand guards. At least the Peruvian plant had been in the middle of a jungle. This one was completely out in the open with no place to hide.

I still couldn't sleep. It didn't help that Ostin had his snore going. I wanted to smother him with his pillow. A little after midnight I went down to the lobby lounge and ordered a hot chocolate. About a half hour later Ben walked into the restaurant as well. He looked surprised to see me.

"Michael, you are still awake."

"I couldn't sleep," I said.

He sat down across from me. "I think you are jet-lag."

"Probably." I said. "Why are you up?"

"I could not sleep too. I am nervous."

"I'm not nervous," I said. "I'm terrified."

He nodded. "Yes. I am also . . . terrified."

I exhaled slowly. "Do you want something to drink?"

"Maybe tea." He waved to a waitress, who came over to our table.

"May I help you?" she asked in English.

Ben answered in Chinese. *"Wo yau yidyan cha."*

"Ni yau hei cha, ma?"

"Heide hau."

She looked at me. "Do you want more chocolate milk?"

I shook my head. "No, thank you."

She nodded. "Okay." She turned back to Ben. *"Wo ma shang hwei lai,"* she said, then walked away.

Ben smiled at me. "She thought I was American."

"It's the company you keep," I said. I took a sip of my cocoa, then asked, "How did you get mixed up in all of this?"

"Mixed up?"

"I mean, how did you get involved with the resistance?"

"Oh," he said, nodding. "After I complete my military service, I work at a computer shop in Taipei. My mother was a reporter for the *Taipei Times*. When the government made the announcement about their agreement with the Elgen to take over Taiwan electricity production, everyone was very happy. There was much celebration. But my mother was not sure. She began writing a story about the Elgen. She traveled to other countries where there are Starxource plants to do research. She even found guards who had left the Elgen and were hiding. She learn about Dr. Hatch's plan to take over the economies of the countries they moved into. She wrote a long story about this, but it was never published. Her boss at the newspaper kill the story." His expression fell with his voice. "Then someone kill her."

I set down my cup. "Someone killed your mother?"

He nodded. "The Lung Li. The police said that it was an accident—she was electrocuted by dropping a radio into the bathtub. But my mother did not like baths because she had arthritis and had trouble getting into them. She only took showers. The day after she died a letter came to me from my mother. She wrote that a group called the Lung Li had been following her and she was afraid for her life. She told me that she was certain it had something to do with the story she wrote about the Elgen. She said if something happen to her, I should hide because they might kill me, too."

"I'm sorry," I said. "How did you find the resistance?"

"They find me. At my mother's funeral there was an American man. He introduced himself as a friend of my mother's. His name was Joel."

"I know Joel," I said.

"Yes, I have been working with Joel for three year now. He introduced me to the voice. Have you met the voice?"

"No," I said. "Have you?"

"No. We only talk on the telephone."

"I don't think anyone has met the voice."

"The Elgen now make almost all of Taiwan electricity. I fear that we are too late to stop them."

I took another sip of cocoa. "I don't understand how people can be so blind to what the Elgen are doing. Don't they care that someone will take their freedom?"

"The Elgen are very clever. People are busy with their lives. It is like people are watching a show on an airplane—they do not know where the airplane is going, they are just watching the show."

The waitress returned with Ben's tea and he stopped talking for a moment to drink. After he'd had a few sips I asked, "Did you ask the voice about our plan?"

"Yes. He will call us back in the morning. Until then, you should sleep."

"I keep trying," I said.

"You must get sleep. We have difficult things ahead."

"I should go back." I finished drinking my hot chocolate, then stood. "I'm glad we talked."

"Me too," Ben said. *"Wan an."*

"Good night," I said. *Difficult things indeed.*

25

A Second Look

I woke the next morning to Ostin shaking me.

"Ben just called," he said. "We need to go."

"Go where?" I said, rubbing my eyes.

"To the plant."

I sat up. "What time is it?"

"Late. It's almost eleven. Didn't you sleep last night?"

"Not like you did."

"I love to sleep. It's like being dead without the commitment."

I pulled on the same clothes from the day before, and we walked out of our room at the same time as Taylor, Nichelle, Tessa, McKenna, and Ian. The hallway was empty except for the housekeeping staff who were cleaning rooms.

"Where are Jack and Zeus?" I asked.

"They're already in the lobby," Ian said.

As we walked toward the elevator Taylor asked, "Should we split up?"

"We better," I said.

Ostin, Ian, and I waited as the four girls went down on two different elevators. We caught the next elevator that opened on our floor; then we walked out of the hotel to the idling van.

"*Dzau an*, good morning," Ben said as we climbed in. "Are you tired?"

We all looked as if we'd been woken in the middle of the night.

"*Lei szle*," Ostin replied.

Ben started laughing. "That is very good."

"What did you say?" I asked Ostin.

"He said he is tired to death," Ben said.

"He's the one who slept," I grumbled.

Ben weaved the van between several idling taxis, then pulled out of the hotel's driveway. The weather was better than it had been the day before, with only a few passive clouds blotting a beautiful blue sky. There was also less traffic, and we made it to our destination in less than a half hour.

As we neared the plant we veered off on a different road—one that led us to a coastal outcrop just south of the Elgen's peninsula and the coast guard station. Ben parked the van at the end of a vacant tree-lined street near a small temple, and we walked, single file, along a stone path to the water, staying behind the trees to conceal ourselves. We could see the silhouette of the Starxource plant from its southernmost exposure. It may have just been the contrast of the clear sky, but the plant seemed to be emitting more steam than the day before. There was a large white-and-red fishing boat docked on the south end of the compound.

"So that's it," Zeus said, his voice heavy with dread.

"Yeah, that's it."

Ben looked out through his binoculars for a moment, then pointed to a place about two hundred yards from the end of the peninsula. "I think that is where the *Volta* will anchor. I have found maps of the depth of the water in this bay. The water near the peninsula is shallow with reefs and sand bars. The size of the *Volta* will keep it from coming too close to the plant."

He handed me the binoculars and I looked out over the water, following the horizon to the end of the peninsula.

"What is that boat doing there?" I asked. "It doesn't look like an Elgen boat."

"It is a fishing boat. The local fishermen catch fish and bring them to the plant. They are there all the time, night and day, bringing tons of fish."

"Why do the Elgen need so much fish?" Taylor asked.

"For the rats," Ben said.

"Of course," Ostin said. "Remember in Peru the Elgen built their plant around a cattle ranch so they would have fresh meat to feed their rats. Here they're on the sea, so they bring in fish."

"That is correct," Ben said. "They have a very interesting process. They drop the fish in a large pool so the fish stay alive until they are fed to the rats."

"Is that the only pool?" I asked.

"No. There is a pool inside near the bowl."

"How do the fish get from the pool to the bowl?"

"There is an underwater pipe," Ben said.

"It's a huge pipe," Ian said. "Like ten feet in diameter. It's located on the bottom of the pool on the side next to the plant. It goes about sixty yards underground into another pool inside, near the bowl."

"Then what happens?" I asked.

"Hydraulic scoops lift the fish from the inner pool and drop them on the chutes that feed the rats," Ben said.

"How do they get rid of the water?" Ostin asked. "They can't get water in the bowl or it could electrocute the rats."

"The scoops are like cages. Lift the fish but not the water. Then they pass through fans. When they reach the chute, they are dry," Ben said.

"How many fish do their pools hold?" I asked.

"Maybe tens of thousands," Ben said. "The pools and the pipe that connects them are as crowded as a Taiwan subway train at rush hour."

"Could we enter through the pool and go through the pipe?" I asked.

"Not any easier than on land," Ian said. "There are soldiers and guards watching the outside pool, and the four fences extend down into the pool and the pipe. Breaking in would be the same as aboveground, except you would be underwater, which means you'd be slower and couldn't breathe."

"We could use scuba equipment," Jack said.

"We would still have to get into the pool without being seen," I said.

"What if we stowed away on a fishing boat and got dropped into the pool with the fish?" McKenna said.

"There's no way I'm going to get buried in fish," Taylor said. "I can hardly stand swimming in a lake knowing they're there."

Ian shook his head. "Even if it worked, you would still have to somehow cut through four fences underwater. There are guards on top and underwater cameras on each of the fences. It would not be easier."

I thought about it for a moment, then said, "Okay, then we stick with the original plan. We attack as they transport Jade Dragon to the *Volta*."

"Which they will have to do with a boat," Ostin said. "Since, if Ben is right, they cannot dock the *Volta* next to the plant."

"Yes," Ben said. "I am right."

Looking through the binoculars, I could see a floating aluminum-planked dock jutting out from the rock. There was a road coming out of the back of the plant that led to the dock. I handed the binoculars back to Ben. "There's a small dock there. Is it the only one they have?"

"They have the large dock for the fishing vessels, but for transport vessels there is only that one."

"So they'll be taking her from there."

"What if they use a helicopter?" Jack asked.

"They won't take the chance," I said. "They don't know if Tanner is with us."

"We wouldn't crash the helicopter with the girl on it," Taylor said.

"They don't know that," Ostin said. "In fact, we don't know that."

Taylor's forehead furrowed. "What are you saying?"

"If it was a question between killing the girl or letting the Elgen get information from her, we'd have to kill the girl."

"I can't believe you just said that," Taylor said.

"Don't look at me like I'm crazy," Ostin said. "Wouldn't you kill someone to save a hundred million lives?"

"I wouldn't kill anyone."

"But what if you don't kill someone, and they end up killing millions more?"

Taylor just looked at him.

Ostin turned to me for validation. "It's the logical choice."

"Let it go," I said.

"The *Volta* does not have a helipad," Ben said. "They will have to use a boat. That means there are two places the Elgen will be weak. We can attack the shuttle boat on the way to the *Volta*, or we can attack the shuttle boat at the dock."

"Three ways," Ostin said. "We could also wait until Jade Dragon's on board the *Volta* and kidnap her from there."

"There will be many guards on the *Volta*," Ben said.

"After the *Ampere* they'll be expecting that," I said. "The shuttle will be the weakest link." I looked at Ben. "How far out from shore will the *Volta* dock?"

"Maybe a hundred meters," Ben said.

"A hundred meters won't give us a lot of time to intercept the shuttle," I said. "Does the *Volta* have guns?"

"All the Elgen ships have guns," Ostin said. "And there are guns on land, too." He pointed at the towers at the back of the plant. "Fifty millimeter machine guns. The Elgen love those."

"Whatever shuttle they use will probably have a gun as well," Jack said. "As well as the guards."

"Which means they will be shooting at us from the shuttle, the *Volta*, and the shore."

"At least until we get on the shuttle. They probably won't shoot at the shuttle with the girl on it."

"What if they can't see us?" Taylor said.

"What do you mean?"

"If we could fill the area with smoke, then they won't know what to shoot at."

"Yeah, but then we can't see either," Zeus said.

"Ian could see," Taylor said.

"It will not work," Ben said. "It is too much area to create smoke and the winds are usually strong. It will blow any smoke away."

"So how do we get to the shuttle without them blowing us up?" I said.

We were all quiet a moment; then Ostin said, "I've got it." We all looked at him. "They wouldn't shoot at one of those coast guard boats. We'll use one of those to rescue her."

"I do not think they will let us use one," Ben said.

"Of course they won't," Ostin said. "We won't ask, we'll just take one."

"How do you *take* a coast guard boat?" Zeus asked.

"Easy," Ostin said. "We go out in a boat and send out a distress signal. When the coast guard arrives to rescue us, Taylor reboots everyone on board and we trade boats. It's like we did in Peru to get into the plant."

"That could work," I said.

"It's brilliant," Ostin said. "We take the coast guard boat, then patrol the waters around the *Volta* until we see the Elgen shuttle. Then we stop the shuttle, reboot everyone on board, rescue Jade Dragon, get back on our boat, and speed off to safety."

"But if the Elgen see a coast guard boat around, they won't leave the dock," Ian said. "They'll just wait until it leaves."

"Yes," Ben said. "If there is anything suspicious, the Elgen will think something is wrong."

"What we need," Ostin said, "is to have someone on the shore watching for the Elgen's transfer. That way the coast guard boat can stay out at sea. As soon as they put her on the boat we signal the coast guard boat. The Elgen won't even notice it, they'll just think it's coming back to dock, but then, at the last minute, we intercept them. We'll catch them in the water."

"That could work," I said.

"We need a boat to be rescued with," Taylor said.

"I can get a boat," Ben said.

"We'll have to time our boat-jacking with the arrival of the *Volta*," I said. "Assuming the Elgen want to get her on board as soon as possible."

"That's a logical assumption," Ostin said.

"But what if they don't?" Tessa said. "We're going to be floating around in a stolen coast guard boat."

"We should discuss this back at the hotel," Ben said. "We have been here too long."

I looked back out at the Starxource plant and then past it to the ocean. "I think this will work."

"Will we still need to attack the other plant?" Taylor asked.

I nodded. "The diversion will still take pressure off of us." I turned to Ben. "Any word from the voice?"

"I hope to hear from him this afternoon," he said.

"All right," I said. "Let's go back and wait for his call."

The drive back to the hotel was much more relaxed than it had been the day before. At least this time we had a workable plan. Not an easy one, but workable.

As I got out of the van Ben said, "I will call you when I hear from the voice. You will not hear from me until then."

As Ostin and I walked back into the hotel I said to him, "Good job. I think your idea could work."

He nodded. "It's no more difficult than attacking the *Ampere*."

I stopped and shook my head. "Yeah, because that was so easy."

Our room phone rang around two in the afternoon. Ostin and I were both sleeping. I answered the phone groggily. "Hello?"

"Michael, this is Ben. Please you and Ostin come to my room. The voice wants to talk to everyone except for Nichelle." He hung up.

I sat up. "Come on, Ostin. We've got to go."

"Go where?" Ostin asked sleepily.

"We need to go to Ben's room. The voice wants to talk to us."

Taylor was the last to arrive. "Sorry I'm late," she said as she walked into Ben's room. "Nichelle wanted to know why she wasn't invited. She wasn't real happy."

"Tell her it's because we don't trust her," Zeus said.

"That's direct," Taylor said.

"We're just being careful," I said. I looked at Ben. "Go ahead and call."

Ben dialed a number, then hung up. A moment later his phone rang. He put his phone on speaker and answered. *"Wei."*

A voice said, "Please confirm."

"This is white dragon to lightning rod," Ben said.

"White dragon, please confirm."

"Yi, ling, yi, yi, yi, jyou, lyou, er."

"White dragon confirmed. Just a moment please." There was a pause; then a familiar voice spoke. "Good afternoon, Electroclan. Ben. How is everyone?"

"We're fine," I said.

"Good. I have been discussing your request with the council, and we agree with your assessment that attacking the compound is too risky."

"Ask him if by 'risky' he means 'certain death'," Tessa whispered.

Taylor shushed her.

"We agree that intercepting Jade Dragon in transport is more logical. We also like your idea of creating a diversion. We have discussed our options and have concluded that the easiest plant to attack is in Samoa. It is a short flight from Taiwan and the Elgen have their smallest presence there—only twenty-seven guards. They also take their water from the sea, but they have an aboveground pump house and desalination plant. We have an agent there who can provide you with enough explosives to take it out."

"If it's that easy then why don't you guys just take it out?" Jack asked.

"That would defeat the purpose," Ostin said. "The Elgen need to think that we're there."

"That's right," the voice said. "Have you thought about who you want to send?"

"Zeus and Tessa," I said, glancing over at the two of them. "The plan is that they attack the plant just before the *Volta* arrives, and then fly back and meet us here to help rescue Jade Dragon."

"That will do," the voice said. "We've already contacted our Samoan agent, and he's making preparations. Right now the *Volta* is only a little more than a week out. Zeus and Tessa will have to leave immediately. Tomorrow afternoon Ben will drive them back to the Taitung airport. That will give them some time to meet with our operative and prepare."

"No sweat," Tessa said.

"Just as long as it's not raining," Zeus said.

"We've checked the weather. There is less than a five percent chance of precipitation. Is there anything else we should discuss?"

I looked around the room. No one said anything. "I don't think so," I said.

"Then good luck, Electroclan. We'll be waiting with great anticipation."

He hung up. For a moment we all just looked at one another. Then Ben turned to Zeus and Tessa and said, "We will leave tomorrow."

26

Dim Sum and Good-bye

That evening Taylor and I had dinner with Zeus and Tessa at the Japanese restaurant on the tenth floor of the hotel. The food was good, but Zeus and Tessa hardly spoke. Finally Taylor asked, "Are you guys okay?"

"We're anxious about leaving the group," Tessa said.

"I hate splitting the group up," I said. "But I still think it's the best move. Just remember, you're only a diversion. An attempt is as good as we need."

"You're saying that it doesn't matter if we shut the plant down?" Tessa said.

"I'm saying to come back safe," I replied. "Shutting down the plant is a bonus."

"I'm more worried about you guys than us," Zeus said. He glanced around to make sure no one could hear him; then he said, "I've got a bad feeling about Nichelle. She's a bad egg. I think she's up to something."

175

"If she is I can't tell," Taylor said. "I've read her thoughts a few times. She's afraid and she's not happy to be here, but her thoughts have been in line with the mission."

"Maybe she's purposely thinking things to throw you off," Tessa said.

"I don't think so," Taylor said. "I can usually tell when people do that, because part of their thoughts are about how they don't want to think about what they're hiding. Like, when Michael tries to hide something from me, I always know."

"Are you saying you knew about the prom?" I asked.

"Maybe."

I groaned. "At least you know I'll never throw you a surprise party."

Tessa looked at Zeus. "Why didn't you take me to the prom?"

"What prom?" he said. "There wasn't a prom at the academy."

"There wasn't a prom at the ranch either," she said.

I looked at Zeus sympathetically. "Sorry, man."

"Just be safe," Taylor said.

"I was about to say the same thing," Tessa replied.

The following afternoon we ordered some Chinese dim sum up to my room and everyone but Nichelle came to say good-bye to Zeus and Tessa. I wasn't surprised that Nichelle didn't show. She was probably glad to see them go. Neither Zeus nor Tessa had tried to hide how much they hated her. Not that I could blame them. I had no idea how many times Nichelle had been made to punish them, but living with her in the academy for all those years, I'm sure it was more times than either of them would forget. I'd been tortured by her and I still remembered every second of it.

We sat around eating and talking until Ben looked at his watch and said, "Okay, it is time for us to go."

"When will you be back?" I asked.

"I will come back with them," Ben said. "I have friends in Taitung so I will wait until they return."

I hugged Tessa, then Zeus. "Remember, dude," I said to him,

"you're just a diversion. Don't take any chances. We'll see you in a few days."

"All right," Zeus said. "You be safe. And remember what I said about N."

"I will."

"While I am gone it is best you stay in the hotel," Ben said. "Just to be safe."

"We'll be okay," I said.

"Please be careful. The Elgen are very smart."

"We know," I said. "We'll be careful. I promise."

He looked at me doubtfully, as if he was still unsure. "Okay," he finally said. "We go. *Dzai jyan.*"

The three of them walked out of the room. After the door shut Taylor said, "A full week cooped up in the hotel? Just shoot me now."

27

The Night Market

Over the next two days the six of us spent a lot of time together in my room, playing cards and watching whatever American television shows we could find, which consisted mostly of old Clint Eastwood movies. Nichelle never came over. She was still angry about being left out of the last meeting and kept to herself.

The evening of the second day Ostin, Jack, Ian, and I watched television in the dark while McKenna read in the corner, using her finger as a book light. Taylor was just staring out the window when she suddenly broke. "I've got to get out of here," she said, turning back. "I'm going."

"You're going where?" I said.

"*Out,*" she replied. "I heard someone in the lobby say there's a night market only a few miles from here."

McKenna put down her book. "I want to go."

"Ben said not to leave the hotel," Ostin said.

"It's not going to hurt anyone if we go out for an hour," Taylor said. "No one will know."

"Everyone will know," Ostin said. "We stand out. Except McKenna."

"They won't know who we are," Taylor said. "It's not like we're the only foreigners in this city." She crossed her arms. "I'm going." She looked at McKenna. "You with me?"

McKenna glanced apologetically at Ostin. "Sorry. I've got to get out too."

Taylor looked at me. "Will you come? Please?"

I turned to Ian. "What do you think?"

He shrugged. "I don't think it's a big deal. I think Taylor's right. There will probably be a lot of foreigners at the night market."

I looked at Jack. "What do you think?"

"I don't think it matters."

I knew Taylor well enough to know that she wasn't going to back down, and I wasn't about to let her go without me. "All right," I said. "But only for an hour. And we stick together."

"Will you come?" McKenna asked Ostin.

"If everyone else does," he said.

"How about you?" she asked Jack.

"I'll go."

"I'm not going," Ian said.

"Why not?" McKenna asked.

"I'm not into shopping."

"It's not about the shopping," Taylor said. "It's the looking."

"I can look from here."

"I would feel better if you came with us," I said. "If there's a problem, you'll see it before the rest of us."

He didn't look too happy about it, but he said, "All right."

"What about Nichelle?" McKenna asked.

"We'd better at least ask her," I said. "She's still mad that we left her out last time."

"I'll ask her," Taylor said.

"We'll meet you by the elevator," I said.

While Taylor walked back to her room, I turned off the television and the rest of us went out into the hall. A moment later Taylor walked out of her room followed by Nichelle.

"You're coming," I said to Nichelle.

"Thanks for the invite," she said. I couldn't tell from her tone if she was being snarky or sincere.

As we stepped into the elevator Taylor handed me her room key. "Would you mind holding this for me? I don't have any front pockets."

I took the key from her.

"And my lip gloss?"

"Sure." I just looked at her.

"What?"

"Anything else?"

She smiled. "Nope."

The seven of us took the elevator down together. Ostin stopped at the concierge desk for directions, then met up with us near the front doors.

"She says we'll have to take a taxi. She wrote down the address." He held up a paper covered with Chinese characters.

We showed the paper to one of the hotel's attendants, who signaled for two taxis and told each of them the address. Taylor, Nichelle, and I got in one of the cabs, while Jack, McKenna, Ostin, and Ian got in the other. We rode with the windows down, and the cool night air combined with the sounds and smells of the city to create a dizzying panorama.

"Man, we're not in Idaho," I said.

"*Definitely* not Idaho," Taylor said.

Nichelle glanced over at us but said nothing.

Our cabs let us off near the corner of a crowded city block. The night market was a bright pulsating beast of electric lights, music, and throngs of humanity. The pungent smells of food from sidewalk vendors filled the air. Some of the scents were definitely more pleasant than others.

The market took up at least eight city blocks, and the inner streets were blocked off to cars. People flowed between the buildings like a river flooding its banks. Most of those around us were Chinese but, as Taylor had guessed, there were also many tourists and foreigners, which made me feel more relaxed.

"Aren't you glad we came?" Taylor said, taking in the ambience. "This is a lot funner than sitting in our rooms."

"'Funner' isn't a word," Ostin said.

"Did you understand me?" Taylor asked.

Ostin blinked. "Yes."

"Then it's a word," she replied.

We joined in with the crowd's flow, letting it pull us through the labyrinth of the market. In addition to the stores that lined both sides of the streets, merchants spread blankets down in the middle of the road to display their wares: knockoff Chanel and Louis Vuitton purses, sunglasses, T-shirts, and a million other knickknacks.

As we passed a booth a man shouted something to McKenna in Chinese.

"What did he say?" she asked Ostin.

"He asked if you want a tattoo."

"Why would I want a tattoo?" she said.

"They're not permanent," Ostin said. "They're hemp. They'll wash off in a few days."

"Why don't *you* get one?" McKenna said.

Ostin glanced at Jack's tattoo, then back at her. "Maybe I will."

"Do it," she said, making it sound like a dare.

"Okay, I will." He walked into the man's booth. The walls were covered with black-and-white paper displays of art ranging from Chinese characters to American cartoon characters. "Check this one out," Ostin said, pointing to a drawing of a dragon. "I want that."

"You're getting a tattoo?" I asked.

"Yes. This one is really cool. It's kind of like Jack's."

"Go for it, wild boy," Taylor said.

"Why are you encouraging him?" I said.

"It might be good for him," she said. "It's probably the most rebellious thing he's ever done."

"I'm doing it," Ostin said resolutely. He said to the man, "*Wo yau jei ge*." He pointed to the tattoo.

"*Hau, hau,*" the man said. He gestured to a stool. "*Ching dzwo.*"

Ostin sat. The man rolled Ostin's sleeve up to his shoulder, then wiped his arm with an alcohol towelette. He fished a plastic stencil out of a large box and put it up against Ostin's upper arm.

"*Jeli, hau?*"

"*Hau,*" Ostin said. He looked at me. "He just wants to know if this is where I want it."

The man taped the stencil to Ostin's arm, then turned on a small air compressor. He adjusted the spray on an airbrush, and then, holding it a few inches from Ostin's arm, began making swiping motions, spraying the stencil with blackish-brown ink. A crowd of Taiwanese gathered around the booth to watch. Ostin smiled at his audience. I think he felt pretty cool.

After the man finished, he peeled back the stencil, then dusted it with some kind of powder.

"How does it look?" he asked McKenna, bulging what little bicep he had.

"Cool," she said, hiding a grin.

Ostin asked Nichelle, "What do you think?"

"It's cool," she said, though she wasn't even looking at it. I was glad Ostin had asked her. It was the first time someone, other than Taylor or me, had included her in something.

We continued walking deeper into the market. A few minutes later we walked by a booth where a man was selling leather shoes. He was sitting on the ground next to his wares applying MADE IN ITALY stamps to the inner soles of his shoes.

"Look," I said to Taylor, pointing at the man.

She shook her head. "That's just wrong."

"Look at these," Jack said, holding up a pair of leather sneakers. "They're only twelve bucks. And they're Adidas."

"Look again," Ian said.

Jack examined the shoes, then laughed. "Abibas. I don't care, I'm still buying them."

"These clothes around here are pretty fashion forward," McKenna said.

"That's because Taiwan produces so many of the world's clothes that they have the new fashions before they hit Europe or the U.S.," Ostin said.

At the end of the fourth street, a few yards from the corner, an oily-faced man was standing behind a vinyl-topped card table with a crowd gathered around him. On the table were three walnut shells.

"What's this?" Taylor asked.

"It's a shell game," Ostin said. "One of the shells has a pea underneath it. You pay him something; then he shuffles the shells around. Then, if you choose the shell with the pea, they have to pay you. It's a scam."

Just then the man pointed at me. "You, Mr. American. You pay five hundred Taiwanese dollar. If you tell which nut has pea, I give you thousand back. You double your money." Then he lifted all three walnuts, exposing a pea under the middle one. The people standing around him were all looking at me.

"What is that, like twenty dollars?" I said.

"Don't do it," Ostin said. "It's a scam."

"I can't lose," I said. "Ian can tell me where the pea is."

"Ostin's right," Taylor said. "You shouldn't do it."

More people gathered around us.

"If he's ripping people off he deserves to lose," I said.

"Let's do it," Ian said.

Taylor rolled her eyes. "It's a bad idea."

"No, it's not." I handed the man five hundred yuan. "Okay. Double my money."

"Sank you," he said. He lifted the shell again to show me the pea; then he quickly shuffled the shells and stopped. "Where the pea?" he said.

"Which one is it under?" I asked Ian.

"It's on the right."

I pointed at the right shell. "It's under that one."

The man lifted the walnut. The pea was gone.

"He has it in his hand," Ian said. "He pulled it out as he was lifting the shell."

"I told you it was a scam," Ostin said.

I pointed at his hand. "It's in your hand," I said. "You cheated."

"No." He put his hands on the two other shells.

"He just slid it into the shell on the left," Ian said.

I pointed at it. "You just put it there. You cheated."

"Of course he cheated," Ostin said. "That's why it's a scam."

"Give me my money back," I said.

"You lose," the man said.

"No, you cheated," I said. "Give me my money back."

The man's eyes narrowed. "You lose."

The crowd sensed a confrontation and pressed in on us.

"Come on," Taylor said. "It's not worth it. Let's go."

"I'm not letting this thief get away with this."

Suddenly a muscular Taiwanese man grabbed my arm. "You, America, go."

"Don't touch me," I said. I pulled my arm away from him.

He grabbed me again. I spun around on him. "I said don't touch me."

Jack grabbed the guy's arm. "Get away from him."

The man reached into his pocket.

"He has a knife," Ian said.

At Ian's warning I surged and the man dropped to the ground like a bowling ball. His head made a dull thud against the asphalt. I turned back to the man with the shells. He looked terrified. "Give me my money. Now."

"Yes, Mr. American, sir." He handed me back the bill I'd given him. I snatched it from him. "You owe me a thousand," I said.

"Okay," he said. "There is no problem." Before I had the other bill Taylor grabbed me by the arm and pulled me away from the man. The crowd parted around us as if everyone was afraid of touching me.

"That was stupid," Taylor said. "Do you know how many people just saw that?"

"The guy was a thief," I said.

"You just called all that attention to us for twenty dollars."

"It's the principle," I said.

"The *principle* is that you just endangered all of our lives."

I groaned. "You're right. I just lost my temper."

"You don't have the luxury of losing your temper," Taylor said. "Save it for Hatch."

Just then McKenna said, "My wallet's missing."

"Oh great," Ostin said. "That's part of the scam. While everyone was focused on the shell game, they were pickpocketing everyone."

"I'll find it," Ian said.

"I'll go with you," Jack said. "I'm going to pound that guy."

"No, wait," I said. "Taylor's right, we need to get things under control." I turned to McKenna. "Just let it go. I'll get you more money."

She breathed out slowly. "All right."

"Let's go," I said.

"Wait," Taylor said, looking around. "Where's Nichelle?"

"She's over there," Ian said, pointing.

Nichelle was standing in the middle of the street while crowds of people walked around her. She had a peculiar look on her face. "Nichelle," I said.

She just looked around.

I shouted louder. "Nichelle!"

She turned and looked at me. She wore a strange expression.

"Are you okay?" I asked.

She hesitated before answering. "I don't know."

"What do you mean?" I said.

She looked around again, then said, "I don't know."

Taylor said, "C'mon, let's get out of here."

"Let's go," I said to Nichelle.

We all started walking again.

"What's up with her?" Ostin whispered.

"I don't know," I said.

We walked farther down the street until McKenna pointed to sign in front of a well-lit building. "Shaved ice. I want one."

"It's called a *bing* or *bau bing*," Ostin said. "In Chinese, *bing* means ice."

"I want a *bing* too," Taylor said.

All of us, including Nichelle, who was still acting a little spacey, walked inside the shop. The front counter was lined with bins of brightly colored fruit: mango, guava, bananas, papayas, and many I'd never seen before.

"What's this?" I asked Ostin, pointing to a hairy brown-and-white fruit.

"*Lung yen*," he said. "Dragon eyes. They're good."

The shop's proprietor assumed that McKenna was our translator. "*Nimen yau shemma?*"

She turned to Ostin. "What did he say?"

"He wants to know what we want."

"I want a *bing* with mango."

"*Lyang ge mangwo nyounai*," Ostin said.

"*Hau, hau, hau*," the man said so quickly that it sounded like he was laughing. He held two plastic bowls under the spinning blade of an ice shaver until the bowls were heaped with finely shaved ice. He took two mangoes from a bin, cut the fruit from them, and carefully placed them on the ice. Then he poured sugarcane juice over the concoction, followed by sweetened condensed milk. He pressed a plastic spoon into each one of the bowls, then set them on the counter in front of Ostin. Ostin handed him some money.

"What kind do you want?" I asked Taylor.

"One with bananas and chocolate. And that milk stuff on top." She suddenly smiled. "Look, that shirt over there makes me happy."

"What?" I said.

"That shirt in the window," she said. "I'm going in that clothing store for a minute. I'll be right back." She headed toward the store.

I turned back. "Ostin, how do you say banana?"

"*Syang jyau*," he said.

"*Syang jyau*," I repeated. "And chocolate?"

"It sounds like chocolate. *Chow-ke-li*."

The man at the counter looked at me. "You want bananas and chocolate?" he said in English.

I flushed. "Yes, two of them, please."

He made two more *bing*s.

While Ian, Jack, and Nichelle ordered their *bing*s, I carried mine and Taylor's over to the table where Ostin and McKenna were already eating. I sat down next to Ostin.

"Where's Taylor?" McKenna asked.

"She went in that store right there. She liked that shirt. How's your *bing*?"

"Delicious. Try it."

I took a bite—it was delicious—but decided to wait for Taylor to come out before eating any more. After five minutes Ostin said, "Dude, your *bing* is melting."

"I know. I'm waiting for Taylor."

"I'll go get her," McKenna said.

"That's all right," I said. "I'll do it."

Just as I stood, Taylor walked out of the store. She looked around for us, then came over. "Sorry that took so long. They didn't speak any English."

"Did you buy something?" McKenna asked.

"No. I didn't like how anything looked on me."

"I got your *bing*," I said.

She looked at me. "What?"

"Your *bing*," I said, looking at her bowl. "It's melting."

"Oh, I'm sorry." She suddenly rubbed her face. "I don't think I could eat it. My head hurts."

"You have a headache?" McKenna asked.

"Yes. It's weird. It just came on." She glanced over at Nichelle, who was sitting alone at the table next to ours, then back at me. She leaned close to me and whispered, "You don't feel anything from her, do you? It feels like . . . you know."

I glanced over at Nichelle. Something was definitely going on with her. She looked spooked. "She better not be using her power," I said.

Nichelle noticed us looking at her. For a moment she stared at Taylor with a dark, peculiar expression.

"Wait, close your eyes, guys," McKenna said. "Taylor, your blouse is undone."

Taylor looked down. "Oh, thanks. I must have missed a button when I was trying on that blouse."

I took a few more bites of my *bing*; then Taylor said, "I still don't feel well. Can we go back?"

"No problem," I said, standing. "Guys, we're going back."

"We'll come with you," McKenna said.

"Ian and I want to check out some throwing stars," Jack said. "We'll meet you back at the hotel."

"You better ask your roomie if she's coming," I said to Taylor.

Taylor just looked at me. "What?"

"Your roommate."

She still looked at me blankly.

"Nichelle?" I said.

She blushed. "Oh, sorry," she said. "I just feel so spacey. Will you ask her? I can't deal with her right now."

"Sure." I walked over to Nichelle. "We're going back. Do you want to come with us?"

She hesitated for a moment, then said, "No. I'm going to stay a little longer."

Something about the way she said it made me feel uneasy. "All right. Just don't stay out too late. We need to be careful."

"Yeah," she said.

The four of us walked back to the main road and hailed a cab. On the way back to the hotel Taylor leaned forward against the driver's seat holding her head.

"Still hurts?" I asked.

"It feels like a migraine," she said.

"Have you ever had a migraine before?" I asked.

"No," she said.

At the hotel I walked her to her room. "I don't have a key," she said. "Nichelle must have it."

"No, you gave it to me," I said, handing it to her.

"Sorry, it's just this headache. I can't think straight."

"Do you still think it's Nichelle?"

"I don't know. Not from this distance. But I don't feel like myself. Maybe she learned a new trick." She forced a smile. "Or maybe I just need some rest."

"You'll feel better in the morning," I said. "Good night." I leaned forward to kiss her, which, oddly, seemed to surprise her. She smiled apologetically, then quickly kissed me back. "Sorry. Good night." She opened her door and disappeared inside her room.

I walked back to my room, undressed, and climbed into bed. Something didn't feel right. I couldn't figure out what it was, but I felt a growing sense of dread, as if something bad was about to happen. I wondered what Nichelle was up to.

PART SIX

28

The Betrayal

Admiral's Quarters
Taiwan Starxource Plant

It was a few minutes past midnight when one of the Taiwanese guards stationed outside Hatch's door knocked. "Admiral, sir."

In spite of the hour, Hatch was awake. He was reclined in his bed, reading. "Come in," he said.

The guard opened the door and poked his head in. "Forgive me for interrupting, Admiral. But there's a young woman here to see you."

"She'd better be my masseuse," Hatch said.

"She claims to be one of the electric children. She says her name is Nichelle."

Hatch set down his book. "Is that right? Has she been searched for weapons?"

"Of course, sir. She's accompanied by two guards."

Hatch sat up, turning his body toward the door. "Go ahead and send her in. Alone."

A moment later Nichelle walked into the room. When she saw Hatch she stopped, nervously standing at attention. The last time she'd seen him was at the academy in Pasadena when he'd abandoned her in his escape from Jack and the revolting GPs.

"Nichelle," Hatch said in a low voice that sent shivers up her spine. "What are you doing in Taiwan?"

"I came with Michael Vey."

"Did you?" he said, leaning forward. "That's bold of you, to stand in front of me and admit you're with Vey."

Nichelle blanched. "I'm not *with* Vey, sir. He just thinks I am. He wanted me to help them kidnap someone from you. A Chinese girl. I came because it was my only way to get back to you."

Hatch studied her carefully. "Do you know where Vey is?"

"Yes. I can lead you to him. And the others."

Hatch was quiet for another moment, then said, "Why did you really come, Nichelle?"

Nichelle swallowed. "I want to be part of the family again." She stopped and her eyes welled up. "It's hard out there. In the Nonel world I'm nothing special. I'm just another chicken."

"And you want to be an Eagle again," Hatch said. "Do Vey and his fellow terrorists know you're gone?"

"They think I'm still at the night market. But they hate me anyway, so they don't care."

"Do you think they suspect you would come here?"

"No."

"Why not?"

"They think I hate you."

Hatch drummed his fingers on his desk. "Why would they think that?"

"After you left me at the academy . . ." She took a deep breath. "They just do."

Hatch's eyes narrowed. "Do you hate me, Nichelle?"

Nichelle hesitated, frightened by his stern gaze. "I felt betrayed. I was hurt."

"But do you hate me?"

"I did."

"But you don't now?"

"I want to come back. Please, sir."

He looked her over a moment more, then said, "Where is Vey?"

"He's with the others at the Grand Hi-Lai Hotel in Kaohsiung. They're in suite numbers 2273, 2275, 2285, and 2287."

"Who is with Vey?"

"Taylor, Ostin, Ian, McKenna, and Jack."

"No Zeus?"

"He was with us. But he and Tesla left."

"Tesla? My deserter. Where did she come from?"

"I don't know. She was with them when they came for me, sir."

"They must have found her in Peru. I look forward to seeing her again. And Frank," he said, curling his lip. "I'm especially looking forward to reuniting with Frank. Are there any members of the resistance with them?"

Nichelle looked at him, perplexed. "I don't know what you mean."

"How did you get here?"

"Vey came for me in California. I don't know how he found me. I was working at a taco stand. He had a private plane. I don't know where he got it."

"He didn't mention any organization?"

Nichelle's forehead furrowed. "You mean the Electroclan?"

"No. The organization that is flying him around the world."

"He said someone was helping him but he didn't tell me who. I didn't ask. I didn't want to raise suspicion."

Hatch stood, his eyes locked on her. "All right. I'll send guards over to the hotel. If what you're telling me is true, I will let you back in the family with full privileges."

"Thank you, sir."

"I want you there with my guards, to help keep Vey and his friends under control."

"I'll do my best, sir."

"That's all for now. Wait out front and someone will come for you."

"Thank you, sir."

"You can go."

She took a few steps toward the door; then Hatch said, "Nichelle."

She turned back. "Yes, sir?"

"Welcome back, Eagle."

PART SEVEN

29

A Rude Awakening

Grand Hi-Lai Hotel
Kaohsiung, Taiwan

It was almost three in the morning when I was woken by a knock at my door. I stumbled to it. "Who's there?"

Ostin rolled over and mumbled something but didn't wake.

"Michael," Ian said. "It's me."

I walked to the door and opened it. Jack and Ian were both standing in the hallway. "What is it?"

"Nichelle just got back to her room," Ian said. "She's been out all night."

"All right," I said. "Let's see where she's been."

I put on some pants, and we walked over to Taylor and Nichelle's room. I knocked on the door and Nichelle answered. She looked afraid.

"Where have you been?" Ian asked.

"None of your business," she said.

"Your business *is* our business," he replied.

"Where have you been, Nichelle?" I asked.

"Out," she said.

We all just stared at her.

"Look, I know you guys hate me, all right? It's not exactly a secret. I didn't want to hang out with any of you either. You okay with that?"

I glanced over at Ian.

"I don't trust her," he said. "She looks like we caught her doing something. Her heart is beating faster than usual."

"It's been beating faster than usual since I saw your suicide plan to attack the Starxource plant. If Hatch catches me, he's going to torture me for helping you. Am I supposed to be calm?"

"Maybe we should have Taylor read her mind," Jack said. "Ask where she's been."

"Fine," she said. "Have your girlfriend read my mind. Like I care what any of you dorks think."

I looked over. Taylor stirred. "We'll do it in the morning," I said.

Ian pointed at Nichelle. "You watch yourself."

"I don't need to," she said. "You watch everything, you pervert."

Ian's face hardened. I thought he might punch her.

"Let's go," I said, taking Ian by the arm.

"She's bad," he said. "To the core."

We went back to our rooms to get some sleep.

30

A Leopard's Spots

The sun still hadn't risen when I was woken again by pounding on our door. "Michael, open up!" a voice shouted.

"Who is it?"

"It's Ian. Open now!"

I stumbled to the door and opened. Jack and Ian pushed past me into the room and slammed the door behind them. "The Elgen found us."

The words sent chills through me. "Where are the girls?"

"They've already captured them. The guards have them down the hall with RESATs on."

"What about Nichelle?"

"She's with them," Jack said. "She's the one who led them to us."

"What's going on?" Ostin said.

"Get up," I said. "The Elgen are here."

"Crap. Where?"

"They're right outside," Ian said.

"Let's block the door," Jack said.

Jack and Ian slid our dresser lengthwise up against the door.

Then a voice from the hallway shouted, "Open up!"

"Yeah, right," Jack said.

"We'll blow a hole through the wall if we need to," the voice said.

"They've got explosives," Ian said. "They've strapped explosives to McKenna."

"No," Ostin said.

"So if she flares she kills herself," I said. "They're getting smarter. How many guards are there?"

"At least thirty." He paused. "Some of them are dressed differently. They're wearing all black."

There was suddenly a high-pitched metallic sound.

"What's that?" I asked.

"They're drilling," Ian said.

Within seconds a drill bit poked through the middle of the door. The bit was removed and replaced by a miniature camera lens.

"They can see us," Ian said.

"The ones in black," Ostin said. "Is there a patch on their uniform?"

"Yes. It's a dragon head."

Ostin shook his head. "Looks like we're going to meet the Lung Li after all."

"Come out of the room," Nichelle said, "and no one will be hurt. They promise."

"The Elgen don't make promises!" I shouted. "And if they do they don't keep them. Just like you."

"Your plan was a suicide mission from the beginning," Nichelle said. "They would have caught you and executed you. This way they'll let you live."

"No, they won't," I said.

"She's telling the truth!" Taylor shouted through the door.

Ian suddenly grabbed his eyes, groaning. "Ah!" He fell back. "It's Nichelle."

I could feel her too. For a moment there was a struggle between us. I began pulsing and pushing against Nichelle until I heard her scream. The pain stopped. Ian staggered to his feet. He was soaked with sweat.

An amplified voice said through the doorway, "Admiral Hatch has authorized us to kill you all. Starting with this one. I am counting down."

I looked at Ian. "Who is he talking about?"

"He's holding a gun to McKenna's head."

I glanced at Ostin. He looked terrified. "Can you deflect their bullets?"

"I don't know," I said. "Not if he has the gun to her head."

"Ten, nine, eight . . ."

"All right!" I shouted. "I'll come out."

"You'll all come out, or we'll shoot her, then open fire on you. We'll shred the entire room."

"They've got machine guns," Ian said. "Big ones."

"We're dead either way," I said.

"Seven, six, five, four . . ."

"Stop!" I shouted. "We're coming."

"Hold your fire," the voice said.

"What are they doing?" I asked Ian.

"They still have the gun to McKenna's head."

"Michael Vey, before we open the door, let me be very clear. If you don't do exactly what we say, there will be no warning. We'll kill the girls first, then we'll blow the rest of you away."

"We'll do what you say," I said.

"Move the furniture from the door."

I looked at Jack. "Do it," I said.

Ian and Jack pulled the dresser back.

"Now open the door," the voice said. "I want you in front, followed by Ian, Jack, and Ostin, in that order. All of you put your hands on your head. Do you understand?"

"We understand," I said.

I opened the door. An Elgen captain in the requisite black-and-purple uniform was standing in front of the door.

"Vey, come forward and kneel. Put your hands behind your back." I walked into the hallway, then knelt down in front of six guards holding guns and RESAT guns. Through my peripheral vision I could see the Lung Li in their solid black uniforms and helmets. Something about them sent shivers through me. They seemed almost nonhuman. Taylor was kneeling on the ground next to them. I hoped she would look at me, but she didn't.

A guard holding carbon handcuffs said to the guards next to me, "If he shocks us, shoot him, then the girls."

"I won't," I said.

A guard grabbed my wrists and pulled them up while another guard handcuffed me, then strapped a RESAT over my chest and turned it on. So much pain shot through my body that I fell to my side, unable to breathe.

"Stand up!" the first guard shouted. He might as well have commanded me to fly. The pain was so intense that I couldn't even answer him. He and the other guard lifted me and pushed me against the wall, but as soon as they released me I collapsed again.

"Stand up!" the guard shouted again.

I somehow forced out, "It's . . . too . . . much."

They looked at each other; then the second guard pulled out a remote and adjusted my RESAT. The pain lessened. It was still high but not so much that I couldn't stand.

They followed the same routine with the others, strapping boxes on Ian, Jack, and Ostin. This time the boxes they put on Jack and Ostin looked different. They looked like RESATs but they were black and red. Ostin groaned when they turned his on.

"They figured it out," he gasped.

A door across the hall opened and a middle-aged Chinese man looked out.

"*Ni gan shemma?*" he shouted.

One of the Lung Li fired something at the man, and he fell

forward unconscious at their feet. Two of them dragged him back into his room, disappearing for a few minutes before emerging back out into the hall.

The captain spoke into his radio, saying that the enemy had been secured, and then, with the Lung Li guards at the front and back of our procession, the guards marched us down the hall to a utility elevator. As we walked past Nichelle, Jack lunged at her. One of the guards caught him and slugged him in the stomach. He fell to his knees, gasping for breath.

"Get up!" the guard shouted. "Or we'll throw you out one of these windows."

Jack struggled to his feet. He looked at Nichelle. "How could you do this?"

Nichelle's eyes narrowed. "Ian said it. 'A leopard doesn't change its spots.'"

As I walked by her I looked her in the eyes. "I believed in you."

"Then you're an idiot, Vey. I don't even believe in me."

"Shut up and keep moving," the guard behind me said.

They were in a hurry to get us out of the hotel, so they crowded us into two elevators, with two guards holding each of us. Ostin was in front of me and Taylor was in front of him. I noticed she was leaning against the elevator's sheet metal wall. I leaned against the side wall and thought, *Taylor, nod your head if you can hear me.* She didn't move. *We're going to get out of this. Move your head against the wall.* Still nothing. The RESAT must have been sucking everything out of her.

The doors opened below ground level into a room with concrete walls, electrical panels, and thick floor-to-ceiling pipes. "Move with your guards," the captain ordered. The Elgen took us out a back door to where four large vans were idling. The vans were tall and black with the sky-blue Elgen logo and the words STARXOURCE POWER written out in English below Chinese characters.

Ostin and I were taken in the first van, Ian and Jack in the second, and McKenna, Nichelle, and Taylor in the third. I hoped that Nichelle wouldn't torture them, but she didn't need to—the RESATs were doing it automatically.

They strapped me to the wall, then pushed some buttons on my RESAT, and the machine hummed louder as more pain shot through my body. I gasped in agony.

Ostin was strapped to the opposite wall. His shirt was soaked in sweat. "I liked the old RESATs better," he said.

They slammed the van's back doors and the vehicle immediately lurched forward, rocking us from side to side. The only light in the back of the van came from the green and amber LEDs on our RESATs and from my glow, which was dimmer than usual, affected by the RESAT.

"Something's not right," Ostin groaned.

"No kidding," I said.

In spite of his pain, he continued to puzzle. "If Nichelle led them to us, she would have told them who was with us."

"She did," I said.

"Then they would have known Taylor was with us. Why weren't they wearing those mind helmets?"

"Because they had guns," I said. "And they outnumbered us five to one."

"That's never stopped them before. And the light on her RESAT wasn't even on."

I had no answer.

"Remember at the night market when you asked Taylor about her roommate, and she acted like she didn't know who it was? After we left did she do anything else out of the ordinary?"

I thought about how strangely she had acted when I went to kiss her. "Yes, but she had that headache. She said she wasn't feeling like herself."

Sweat was dripping down Ostin's face and he groaned out in pain. Then he said, "Maybe that's because she *wasn't* herself."

"What are you saying?"

"I don't think that was Taylor."

PART EIGHT

31

Jade Dragon

The only thing Taylor remembered about being captured at the night market was seeing Tara, her twin sister. For a second she thought she was looking at her own reflection in a mirror until Tara squinted, and paralyzing horror filled her so completely that she collapsed. Then someone powerful, someone she never saw except for the black material of their shirtsleeve, held a cloth over her nose and mouth. When she woke she was lying on the floor of a dim concrete cell, wearing different clothes, her head throbbing. She was wearing a RESAT, but it didn't seem to be on. The whole situation was like a nightmare except she wasn't asleep. *Where am I?*

As she lay there, something moved in the shadows on the opposite side of the room. It took her a moment to realize that it was a child. *What is a child doing in my cell?* Then the thought came to her—the girl was Jade Dragon. She looked even younger than nine years old. Her black hair was cut in bangs, cropped short above eyes that were so dark her pupils were invisible. She had full, pouty lips and her nose was slightly turned up.

Taylor stood, steadied herself against the wall, then slowly walked over to her. The little girl watched her curiously, but avoided eye contact.

Taylor crouched down in front of the child so they were about the same height. "You're very pretty," she said.

The girl said nothing.

"You should meet my friend McKenna. She looks like you."

The girl stood as still as a statue.

"You can't hear me, can you? Can you read my lips?" She thought of what Chinese she had picked up in the few days she'd been in Taiwan. *"Ni hau."* The child looked at her and blinked. Taylor walked closer and reached out her hand. "I heard your name in Chinese. I think it's Yoo Loong." The girl stared curiously at Taylor's glowing skin. "It's okay. It won't hurt you."

The girl reached out and touched her, then retracted her hand. Taylor nodded. "It's okay. You can touch me. I came to help you." Taylor moved forward and started to put her arms around the girl, but Jade Dragon stiffened and groaned.

Taylor immediately released her. "I'm sorry. You don't like that." She tried to remember what she knew about autism. For several weeks they had studied autism in her health class. She remembered learning that some autistic children were hypersensitive to touch.

"I'm sorry," Taylor said. "This whole thing must be so awful for you."

The little girl looked at her for a moment, then, to Taylor's surprise, stepped forward and touched Taylor's arm again. This time she grabbed on to it and something peculiar happened. Taylor was drawn into the girl's mind, as if the girl had hijacked her power. It was unlike anything she had experienced before. She couldn't understand the Chinese words in the child's head but she could understand the meanings and feelings that accompanied the language. It was the difference between the letters *A-P-P-L-E*, and biting into the crisp, red fruit. She was communicating better than she ever had before, understanding without words—something Taylor had not even known was possible.

She now knew, without a doubt, that this was the child they called Jade Dragon. She was inside the child's brain, a participant of her past and present, in a way she'd never experienced with anyone before. Usually when she read someone's mind she caught glimpses of their thoughts—language and symbols appearing in her brain like text messages. But now she felt as if she were standing in the middle of a theater and seeing the child's thoughts and memories on screens around her. Was it the autism? Or was it the power of the child's mind?

She could see the Elgen guards, the Lung Li, dressed all in black, grabbing Jade Dragon, taking her from her home accompanied by feelings of fear and confusion and curiosity. She saw her parents on the ground. Motionless. She could feel the prick as the Lung Li put a needle into her arm, then the mind-numbing drug spreading through her body as everything went dark. She could see, on another screen, thoughts poured out in numbers.

Suddenly math problems she hadn't understood made sense. Except now they weren't just numbers and equations, they were patterns and colors. Calculus, geometry, and trigonometry were easy to understand, simple as a game, like shooting balls at a basketball hoop that was a hundred feet wide. Then a specific sequence of numbers, letters, and symbols started running through her mind.

$$s(t; t_y) = k \frac{Q}{r^2} \hat{r} \int_{R^2} m(x,y) e^{-2\pi i 7 (\frac{G_x xt + 7G_y yt_y}{2\pi})} dydx$$

She almost said the equation when a powerful thought came over her not to speak it out loud—that she must not ever divulge it. Somehow she knew that what she was receiving was something of great importance, even if she had no idea what it meant.

$$s(t; t_y) = k \frac{Q}{r^2} \hat{r} \int_{R^2} m(x,y) e^{-2\pi i 7 (\frac{G_x xt + 7G_y yt_y}{2\pi})} dydx$$

Taylor looked at the girl. "Are you trying to tell me something?"

The child just stared at her. She saw a glimpse again of the Elgen soldiers, then suddenly all the screens turned to white and the girl's thoughts flashed into blinding fear. Anger and fear. Then Taylor left Jade Dragon's mind, or, more accurately, Jade Dragon let go of her.

"What's happening?" Taylor asked.

The girl was looking over Taylor's shoulder. Taylor turned back to see what she was looking at, but saw nothing. Then she heard the hiss and click of a pneumatic lock. The cell door swung open and a Caucasian Elgen captain dressed in black and purple walked in flanked by two other guards. All the men wore mindwave helmets. *How did she know they were coming?* Taylor thought.

"It's good to see you again, Ms. Ridley."

"I don't know you," Taylor said.

"You don't remember me from Idaho?"

"You're an *Elgen*. That's all I need to know."

"You make that sound so . . . *repulsive*."

"It is."

The captain smiled darkly. "If you want repulsive, you should see feeding time in the bowl. Especially when the meal is human flesh."

"I've heard about it."

"Hearing and seeing are not the same thing. Until you actually see someone fed to the rats, you can't fathom the horror of thousands of tiny pointed teeth tearing the flesh away from live muscle, muscle away from bone, the little beasts seeking the tender meat inside, burrowing under skin."

Taylor turned white.

"What I find most remarkable about the human feedings is the perseverance of the human body. You'd be surprised at how long people actually stay alive while it happens. Sometimes we make bets on it. Of course, lowering our victims feetfirst into the bowl does make a difference. It adds at least a full twenty seconds to the misery."

Taylor felt as if she might throw up.

"Do you believe in reincarnation?"

"No."

"You should." He reached into his pocket and pulled out a small brown biscuit. "Have you ever seen one of these?"

Taylor shook her head.

"They're called Rabisk. Along with fresh meat, it's the primary food we feed our rats. These tasty little biscuits are made from the bodies of the dead rats we collect from the bowl. So follow me here: Our enemies are eaten by the rats; the rats eventually die and are made into Rabisk, which are then again fed to the rats; the rats die and are again made into Rabisk. So, if you think about it, our enemies are fed to the rats over and over and over again. It's reincarnation. They'll spend all eternity as rat food. It's a horrific thought, isn't it?"

"You're sick," Taylor said. "All of you."

The man smiled. "I shouldn't waste your time telling you about it. You have so little time left before you experience it yourself."

"I don't want to see it," Taylor said.

"You won't just see it," he said. "You're going to feel it. Smell it. You're going to hear the high-pitched shrieks of ten thousand ravenous rats as they swarm over your body like bees on honeycomb, seeking the moist meat under your skin." Taylor froze. "Yes, dear. We're going to feed you to them. Both of you."

Taylor's knees gave out and she fell to the concrete floor.

"Good. I see you're finally comprehending the predicament you're in."

Jade Dragon walked over and knelt down next to her. When Taylor could speak she said, "Please, no."

He threw the biscuit on the floor next to her. It broke into several pieces. "Whether you're an eternal rat meal or not is completely up to you. There's only one way you can spare yourself that fate. You do this one thing and I'll escort you out of here myself, *with* the child, and put you on a plane home."

"What do you want?"

"We need a scientific formula that's in this little girl's head. You get the girl to give you the formula and we let you go." He put out his hand and one of the guards handed him a pad of paper and a pen. "We don't care how she gives it to us. Just write it down here."

"I'm not a scientist. How would I know what the formula is?"

"We'll know," he said. "And so does she. She just needs to dictate it to you. So if I were you, I'd keep chumming up to this little genius until she spills her secrets. Because you've got eighteen hours until feeding time."

"My friends will rescue me before then."

The other two guards who had stood quietly at attention suddenly laughed. The captain smiled, then said, "Sorry, you're not in on the joke. The question is, who's going to rescue them?" He threw the pad and pen to her. "Get the formula, write it down. Or spend eternity as Rabisk."

He spun on his heels, and he and his guards left the room, the heavy, metal door slamming shut behind them. Taylor looked down at the pad, then back at Jade Dragon. The formula was still in her head. All she needed to do was write it down. She might save her own life, but she would doom the lives of thousands of others. Taylor's eyes filled with tears. "We'll get out of here. I don't know how, but we will."

She turned away and wiped her eyes. When she looked back, Michael was standing where Jade Dragon had been. "Michael . . ." She stood. "How did you get in here? Where's Jade Dragon?"

Michael just looked at her.

"Never mind, I don't care how you got here." She threw her arms around him. He stiffened, squirming beneath her embrace. "Michael, what's wrong?" She stepped back. It wasn't Michael in her arms, it was Dr. Hatch. She screamed as she fell back. Hatch started laughing.

The pneumatic door lock again hissed and clicked; then the door opened. Tara walked into the room.

"Hello again, Sis."

"Tara." She turned back to see Jade Dragon standing against the wall where Hatch had just been. "What are you doing?"

Tara smiled. "I was just having a little fun. Like my new trick?"

"You're psychotic," Taylor said.

Tara smiled. "Now, Sis, don't be so judgmental." She turned into Taylor's mom. "I mean, you're the one having delusions."

"Stop it!" Taylor shouted.

Tara laughed as she changed back to herself. "Have you figured it out yet, Sis?"

"Figured what out?"

"That you're on the losing team. While you were destroying one Starxource plant, we built five more." She stepped toward Taylor, and Jade Dragon looked curiously back and forth at the girls' identical faces. "And soon you won't be special. There will be thousands of people with powers just like yours."

"And yours," Taylor said.

"Real power comes from position," she said. "That's what I have. Someday we're going to run this place."

"Real power comes from someplace else," Taylor said.

Tara smiled. "What are you going to say next, that power comes from the heart?"

"And mind," Taylor said, rebooting her sister. While Tara was still confused, Taylor lunged at her, pushing her up against the wall. Then they both fell to the floor, wrestling.

A voice came over the cell audio system. "Occupants of Cell 19, stop your fighting immediately." The voice was followed by a loud, high-pitched squeal, and Taylor suddenly screamed as she fell back from Tara. Her RESAT was squealing and the lights were flashing in rapid succession.

"It's too much!" Taylor shouted. "Stop! Stop!"

Tara stood, wiping her face. There was blood on her hand.

"You made me bleed."

Taylor was writhing in pain. "Tell them to stop."

"Yeah, I'm going to do that," she said. "I can't believe we came from the same egg." She crouched down next to her. "They *will* feed you to the rats. I've seen them do it. So you'd better grow a brain and get them the information they want." She walked to the door. "I told you, Sis. You can't win."

She walked out of the cell, leaving Taylor screaming in pain.

PART NINE

32

An Unexpected Visitor

It may have been pain altering my perception, but passing through the four Elgen checkpoints into the Starxource compound seemed to take even longer than the drive from Kaohsiung.

Ostin had stopped talking long before we reached the first gate. Probably before we had even left Kaohsiung. I was afraid for him. I wasn't sure how much more he could take. I wasn't sure how much more I could take either.

When the van finally reached the inside of the plant, the back doors were unlocked and they swung open. Through my blurred vision I could see three Elgen guards waiting to take us. One of them climbed inside and unlatched my restraints. I fell to the van's floor, unable to move. The RESAT had drained all of my power.

Then six of the Lung Li appeared. One of them grabbed me by the leg, his powerful hand digging into my calf as he dragged me to the edge of the van while the others huddled around me, like demons. They wore black-mirrored goggles, but I was close enough to them to see through the lenses to the darkness of their eyes.

Four of the Lung Li lifted me and carried me to a stainless-steel gurney and strapped me down. I had seen these gurneys before. I had been strapped to one at the Peruvian plant just before Hatch had tried to feed me to the rats.

With the Lung Li surrounding me, they began to roll me away. I tried to lift my head to see what they were doing to Ostin but couldn't. Then I passed out.

I don't know how long I was unconscious. I thought it was ten or fifteen minutes, but it could just as easily have been hours. Or days, for that matter. My mind was spinning and I had no grasp of time. I didn't know where I was other than that I was in a strange place—a small, dark room with symbols on the wall; some looked like Chinese characters and others looked like ancient runes or the markings of alchemists. The room was lit by flickering candles that glowed red and smelled of incense. There was no sound except the repetitious, peaceful dripping of water. Oddly, the place had a calming effect.

I was still strapped down but not to the metal gurney. I was on some type of hard leather pad. The RESAT was gone. When I lifted my head I saw that I had no shirt or shoes and I was wearing peculiar tight black pants made of a thin, cottonlike material—almost like long johns—except they only came down to my knees.

I was held fast by thick leather straps at my wrists, waist, chest, arms, thighs, and ankles. I tried to pull against them, but it was like lifting an elephant. I'm certain each of the straps could have supported more than a ton. My body ached. My insides felt bruised or burned, damaged from the RESAT.

Then I realized there was a man sitting quietly next to me. He wore the Lung Li uniform with the dragon head patch. He had no helmet or goggles and his eyes were locked on to mine with an intense stare. His expression was emotionless, neither sympathetic nor cruel.

"You are back, Michael," he said with a thick Asian accent. "I am pleased you are back. Now we can get to work." He reached over and pulled a metal cart next to me. I could hear the squeaking of the cart's wheels, but I could not see what was on it.

"We don't know where acupuncture began. But it is ancient. Very ancient. Much older than Western medicine—even older than your gods. There are records of it being used for more than three thousand years. Some attribute it to Shennong, the emperor of the five grains. But that sounds like superstition. Unlike many of my order, I am not a superstitious man. I am a man of science.

"A more reasonable explanation is that the Chinese doctors of the Han dynasty observed that soldiers wounded by arrows were sometimes cured of illnesses.

"I do not know why acupuncture was never accepted in Western culture. Maybe they were afraid of the unfamiliar." He lifted something from the cart and held it above me so I could see it. It was a simple steel needle about six inches long. I closed my eyes.

"Yes, you prove my point," he said. "You Westerners are squeamish about needles. You act as if this fascinating art were barbaric. It's not. Acupuncture isn't about pain. In truth, if done properly, most patients report feeling a pleasurable sensation." He moved his face closer to mine and looked into my eyes. "*Most*. But that would not be true for you. You see, acupuncture is about directing the electricity in your body. But where there is an abnormal amount of electricity, it tends to cause pain. Sometimes great pain.

"We have observed that you have more electricity than the others, so your pain might be especially exquisite." He held the needle a few inches above my chest. "There are three hundred and sixty acupuncture points. This one is called the *Wuyi*." With a slight twisting motion he inserted the needle about an inch into my skin. Immediately, electricity shot through my body toward the needle. I yelled out.

"Yes, you see, I was right." He lifted another needle from the tray. "Now, if we place a needle here, it will create a circuit between the two points." He poked another needle into the skin between my neck and clavicle. It felt as if a live high-voltage electric wire had been inserted through my body. I screamed. "Stop!"

The man seemed intrigued by my reaction. "The challenge is to keep the pain as high as possible while still keeping you conscious."

"Please, stop," I cried.

"We are only beginning," he said clinically. He inserted another needle near my groin. The electricity created a triangular current that contracted my stomach muscles. Involuntarily my body heaved forward as if I were trying to do a sit-up, but the leather restraints held me down. I felt as if I was going to vomit. Sweat streamed down the sides of my face, and already my hair and skin were completely drenched. My eyes felt locked shut.

"*Hen you yisz,*" he said. "Very interesting."

I forced my eyes open as he lifted another needle. His eyes scanned my body like it was a map and he was searching for a destination.

"What do you want from me?" I cried.

His eyes settled on mine in a curious gaze. "Nothing. What would I want from you?"

"Then why are you doing this?"

"I told you, I am a man of science. For thousands of years we have believed there were three hundred and sixty acupuncture points. I believe the number is closer to five hundred. With your hypersensitivity to the needles, I believe, together, we can find them all."

The thought of hundreds of more needles stuck into me paralyzed me with fear. "That will kill me," I said.

The man was quiet for a moment, then said, "That is a possibility." He breathed out slowly. "But there is a cost for all knowledge."

He looked back at my body. "Now, we continue. If I place a needle here . . ."

I shut my eyes as I felt the cold tip of the needle against my neck. He began to slide it into my skin when someone shouted, "Stop!"

"Sir . . ."

"Take those out, now! Or I'll have you fed to the rats."

"Yes, sir."

He immediately pulled the needles out. The pain stopped.

"Now get out of here. *Ma shang, ba*!"

"*Bau chyan*," the man said. "*Bau chyan*."

I could hear him running from the room, his soft footfalls echoing down the corridor. There was a moment of silence; then whoever had entered the room sat down next to me. "Barbarian," he grumbled. I was still too weak to open my eyes. I could feel a dry cloth being dabbed on my head and face. "I'm sorry, Michael. I had no idea they were doing this to you. Trust me, they will pay for this atrocity."

The voice sounded oddly familiar. I forced my eyes open. Though my vision was blurry I could make out the visage of a man, not too old, maybe a few years younger than my mother. His hair was light brown, almost the same color as mine, and he had thick eyebrows.

When I could speak I said, "Who are you?"

He didn't answer but continued to wipe the sweat from my neck and face. Then he said, "Are you sure you don't know who I am?"

"No."

"I know your vision must still be blurry, but look more carefully."

As my vision cleared I could make out the details of his face. He looked so familiar. Then I remembered. I knew who he was.

"No," I said. "I'm hallucinating."

"It must seem . . . odd," he said. He ticked, his face contracting in a grimace. "Or maybe impossible. But I am who you think I am."

My eyes welled up with tears, but this time not from pain. "Dad?"

33

A Father's Story

"You have no idea how much I've missed you," my father said as he unlatched the straps that held me down. I slowly rubbed my wrists, then tried to sit up.

"Not too fast," he said. "I'm sure you're still dizzy. Is the ice helping?" My father had set ice packs where the needles had been used.

"Yes. Thank you."

"You must be thirsty. Let me get you some water." He reached down and brought up a plastic bottle. I drained the whole thing.

"Thank you."

"You're welcome." One of his eyes twitched and he gulped like I sometimes did. "How are you feeling?"

"I don't know. Confused."

"I'm not surprised, after what they've done to you. You'll feel better in a few hours."

"I mean about you," I said.

He hesitated a moment, then said, "I understand."

"How are you . . ." I couldn't think of the right word.

"Alive?" he said. "It's simple. I never died."

"But I went to your funeral. I remember it."

"How was that?" he said, sounding slightly amused. "I would have liked to have been there. I even considered going in disguise, but it was too risky."

I didn't find what he was telling me amusing. "Was Mom in on this?"

He was quiet a moment; then his voice softened. "No. She believes I'm dead."

"But you had a death certificate. I saw it."

"That's not hard to get when you work at a hospital."

Suddenly anger welled up inside of me. "I cried every day for a year. How could you do this to us?"

"Not *to*," he said calmly. "*For*. It's a big difference. And I had my reasons. After we discovered that the MEI had malfunctioned, we had reason to fear for our lives. Not just mine and James Hatch's, but yours and your mother's as well.

"We were working with unsavory people, like Giacomo Schema, who had lost hundreds of millions of dollars. We had board members who could potentially lose millions of dollars more in lawsuits. You have to understand that these were ruthless men and women who were willing to kill not only my colleagues and me but even my wife and newborn child. In fact, they openly threatened me that if the deaths the MEI caused were discovered, they would take you from me. That, I couldn't risk. So James Hatch and I—"

"Hatch is a demon," I blurted out. "He tried to kill me."

My father seemed disturbed by my outburst. "No, he just pretended to, or you wouldn't still be alive." He let the words settle. "Michael, sometimes things aren't as they seem. James Hatch did what he had to do. He pled with the board not to use the MEI until it could be safely tested. We both did. So did Dr. Coonradt. But they wouldn't listen. They forced us to use the machine before it was ready.

"The MEI could have saved millions of lives a year. It would have allowed us to detect and treat cancer months, even years, before it was a threat. And that's just the tip of the iceberg. The three of us doctors—Hatch, Coonradt, and I—were certain that we could make the MEI work if we had the time. But the Elgen board wouldn't wait. And when things went wrong, they blamed us for doing what they forced us to."

He took a deep breath. "I could have resigned. I should have. But hindsight is always twenty-twenty. I was young and employed in a good job. Your mother's and my dreams were coming true. Your mother was pregnant and we were about to start our family. It wasn't the time to quit my job—especially when there was a chance that the MEI might have worked.

"Had I known what the machine would do, I would have quit. But there was no way of knowing." He breathed out slowly. "The weight of that decision has been crushing. You might say that I was one of the lucky ones, because you could have been one of those babies killed. But I had to lose you just like those other parents did." His eyes welled up. "But now that we've stopped Schema and his jackals, it doesn't matter. No one can take you or my wife away from me. That's why we came looking for you. Not because you're electric, but because you're my son and I couldn't bear not having you."

"Hatch told me I killed you."

"I wasn't happy about that. But he said what he thought he needed to in order to protect us. And you."

"What about Mom? Why would Hatch kidnap her?"

My father frowned, then his jaw began ticking. "Things got a little out of hand," he said.

"A little?"

"A lot." He put his hand on my arm. "Michael, never forget that what I did, I did for you and your mother. I sacrificed everything I knew and loved to protect the ones I loved most."

We looked at each other for a moment; then my father said, "Oh, before I forget." He held up my watch. I hadn't seen it since I'd been captured in Peru by Hatch. "I thought you'd want this back."

I took it from him. I looked at it for a moment, then handed it back. "You should keep it. It's yours."

My father seemed a little taken aback. "No, I want you to have it."

I put it on my wrist, which was still red and indented from the leather strap I'd been tied down with. "It got kind of beaten up," I said.

"Like you?"

"Yeah," I said.

We were quiet for a moment. As I looked at him, he ticked a few more times.

"You have Tourette's too?" I asked.

He nodded. "You know it's genetic. You had to suspect that I had it, since your mother doesn't."

"I never thought about it."

"I'm sorry I gave that to you." He lightly grinned. "But I also gave you your good looks. You've got to take the bad with the good."

"I think Mom helped."

"Helped," he said, laughing. "She was ninety-nine percent of your good looks."

As I looked at him I suddenly broke down crying. My father looked at me for a moment, then he put his arms around me and held me. I wept for a long time before we parted. When I could speak I asked, "Now what?"

He shook his head. "Things have gotten a little . . . sorry, *a lot* out of hand. Now this whole crazy resistance thing has started. . . ."

"They said *you* started it."

He looked at me. "Why would I start a resistance against myself? Who told you that?"

"Simon."

"Simon? I don't know any Simon."

"He said he worked with you."

He looked down to think. "Right. It's been a long time, but I think I know who it is. Simon Kay. He worked at the hospital." He looked back at me. "It's time we rescued your mother. Now that we've taken back our company from Schema, we can all be together again. We can fulfill the dream that started all of this, and save millions of lives."

My eyes filled with tears again. "I've done such bad things."

"You can't blame yourself, Son. You're only fifteen. You've done what you were told to do by Simon."

"It wasn't Simon," I said. "It was the voice."

He looked at me quizzically "What's the voice?"

"I don't know. It's just a voice that talks to us."

He looked at me quizzically then said, "We need to save your mother before they hurt her. Where is she?"

I didn't answer.

"I appreciate your hesitation," he said. "You're trying to protect her. So am I. That's why I need to know where she is."

"She's at a ranch."

"Where?"

"I don't know. They wouldn't tell us, in case we were captured."

"Do you remember any details?"

"My friend Ostin figured that we were around Texas or Mexico. It was a three-hour flight to Los Angeles."

"Exactly three hours?"

"Maybe a little less. Like two hours and forty-five minutes."

"When were you there?"

"Like, eight days ago."

"Exactly eight days?"

"Yes."

"Do you remember the weather? Was it cloudy or raining?"

"It was pretty warm. I remember someone saying it had gotten up to ninety-seven degrees."

"Ninety-seven," he said. "Thank you, Son. This will definitely help. We've got to save her before they find out you finally know the truth."

"What truth?"

"That the Elgen are the good guys."

34

Another Unexpected Visitor

That night I couldn't sleep. The room they gave me was locked, which my father apologized for. "Corporate protocol," he called it. He explained that since the plant was a federal facility and a national security risk there were federal regulations that not even he or Hatch could waive. "Stupid bureaucrats," he grumbled, shaking his head. "Every country has them. Until you are certified as a non–security risk you cannot have free access to the plant."

From a comfort level, my room was nice. It had a cupboard stocked with snacks and a small refrigerator with all kinds of drinks, both Chinese and American. There was a television with a library of DVDs, and the bed was soft with fresh-smelling silk sheets. But comfortable or not, it was still a prison, and I knew that I was being watched. In one corner of the room there was the constant blinking of a camera's red LED.

I asked my father where Taylor and the others were. He assured me that they were being kept in rooms as nice as mine, but when I asked to see them he apologized again and said he would have to get approval, which might take a few days. I couldn't understand why seeing my friends would pose a national security risk, but he just said, "I know it sounds ridiculous. Trust me, it is. But that's Chinese bureaucracy for you."

In spite of my father's assurances, I still had an ocean of questions. Hatch had fired a gun at me at the academy. He certainly wasn't faking that bullet that Zeus had shot out of the air. Or what about when he tried to feed me to the rats? It wasn't adding up. Maybe my father had been deceived. Maybe Hatch wasn't really who my father thought he was.

Soft as my bed was, I tossed and turned for several hours. In the middle of the night I heard a key in my door. I looked over as my heart pounded wildly. *Who would be coming into my room at this hour?* Maybe my father was breaking the rules after all. As the door slowly opened I noticed that the light on the surveillance camera went out.

"Michael."

Contrasted against the radiance from the corridor's dim lighting, I could see the partial silhouette of a form standing in the doorway. When my eyes adjusted I couldn't believe who it was. It was the only Glow who didn't glow.

35

The Prodigal

"Nichelle," I growled. I stood, balling my hands into fists. "What are you doing here?"

"We've got to go. We don't have much time before they realize your camera's out."

I grabbed her by her neck and threw her up against the wall. "I should fry you right now, you traitor."

"I didn't betray you," she said. "Things aren't what they seem."

"You think I'm that stupid?"

Nichelle grimaced with pain. "If I betrayed you, why am I here?"

"No idea," I said, my electricity sparking with my anger. "But I know you led the Elgen to us."

"I only pretended to. The Elgen had already found us. That night at the street market . . . that wasn't Taylor who came back with us."

I remembered what Ostin had said in the back of the van. "What?"

"I can smell different electricity," she said. "It was Tara who came out of the store. That's why I was acting strange. And that's why she wanted to leave so fast. They must have captured Taylor when she went into that store."

Her explanation flustered me. "Why should I believe you?"

"Because I'm telling the truth! Remember how different Taylor was acting? How she suddenly had a headache?"

I just glared at her.

"Michael, you have to believe me or we'll all die."

"I *don't* believe you."

"Remember, Tara's blouse was unbuttoned? She must have traded clothes with Taylor so we wouldn't know."

"Why didn't you tell us then? We could have held Tara hostage."

"Because they would have just killed Taylor *and* us. You couldn't have held Tara hostage. Hatch doesn't care what happens to any of us. I know that better than anyone."

I just looked at her.

"Please, Michael. I'm not lying. I know you think I'm evil and worthless, but right now, at this moment, I'm not lying. And if we don't hurry the Lung Li are going to kill the real Taylor. They're going to feed her to the rats." Then Nichelle did something I'd never seen her do before. Her eyes welled up with tears. "You've got to believe me. If not for us, then for Taylor's sake."

I slowly relaxed my grip on her. "How do you know they're going to feed her to the rats?"

Nichelle slid back against the wall, clutching her throat. "I heard the guards talking about it. The Elgen feed people to rats."

I knew this better than anyone. The memory of my time in the bowl filled my mind with terror. "Why did you lead the Elgen to us?"

"It was our only chance. They already knew where we were, and they'd already captured Taylor. I had to make Hatch believe that I was betraying you."

Everything she said made sense except for one thing. "You could have just run away. Why didn't you?"

"I know," she said softly. "I almost did." She looked me in the eyes. "But I didn't, okay? I promised I'd help you."

I didn't know what to say.

She breathed out in exasperation. "We've already wasted too much time. We need to go. *Now.*"

"Where are we going?"

She took a piece of paper out of her pocket and unfolded it. "We need some light," she said.

I held my hand close enough to the paper that my glow illuminated it.

"I drew this map. I think it's pretty accurate." She pointed to a square she'd drawn. "We're right here. The Lung Li are stationed where I put the Ls. The regular guards are where I put the Xs. If we can get into the air duct through the mechanical closet across the hall, I think we can crawl through the duct out to here." She touched the other end of her map. "That's the hallway where they're holding everyone except Taylor. We'll need Ian to find her. She's probably being held somewhere near the bowl."

"Do you have keys to the other rooms?"

"No, I could only get this one. But you have more electricity than Bryan. I think if you focus, you could burn through the bars."

I didn't know if I could or not, but at this point I didn't have much of a choice. "All right, let's go."

Nichelle slowly opened the door, then stopped. "The camera is sweeping our way," she said. "Come closer. When I say 'go' we'll run to the closet across the hall."

I stepped in close behind her.

"Ready . . . Go."

We stole across the hall to a mechanical closet and quickly ducked in, shutting the door behind us.

"There should be an air vent in the ceiling," Nichelle said.

My glow wasn't bright enough to illuminate the ceiling, so I created a small lightning ball, which lit the closet. "Right there," I said, looking up. The vent cover was mounted with screws. "It's screwed in."

"I got this," Nichelle said, holding up a screwdriver.

I looked at the vent, then back at the tool. "It's the wrong kind of screwdriver."

"It's all I could find."

"Maybe we can pry it off," I said. "Give me the screwdriver."

She handed it to me.

"Now help me up."

I climbed up a pipe while Nichelle pushed against me. I slid the flat tip of the screwdriver under the vent cover and pulled on it but couldn't pry it loose.

Suddenly we could see the light under the closet door brighten.

"They must know you've escaped," Nichelle said. "This is our only way out. Focus your electricity in your fingertip and melt the heads off the screws."

I had never tried melting anything before. I held up my index finger and concentrated on it. It began to glow brighter and brighter until it was bright enough to light up the room. It was fortunate that they had turned on the hall lights when they did, otherwise they would have seen my light from under the door. I touched my finger to one of the tops of the screws. It took just a few seconds before the head turned bright red, then melted. "It worked," I said, starting on the next.

"Hurry," she said. "I can't hold you much longer."

There were four screws. I melted them all, then slid the vent cover out of its brackets and handed it down to Nichelle before climbing back down. "I'll help you up first," I said.

I crouched down to my haunches. Nichelle climbed up onto my back, then shoulders. She didn't weigh very much, and I stood so she could get her elbows into the open vent. She pulled herself up into the duct. We could hear footsteps walking toward us.

"Hurry," she whispered.

I handed her the vent cover, then climbed up the pipe and pulled myself into the duct. "Quick, give me the vent cover," I said. "I need to cover this back up." She handed it to me. As I reached out to slide it into its frame it slipped from my fingers. I clenched my teeth as it hit against the pipe, then the floor with a loud clang.

I glanced back. Nichelle's eyes were wide with fear.

"Maybe they didn't hear it," I whispered.

Suddenly there were footsteps approaching the door. If they saw the open vent we were as good as dead.

As the door handle moved, I reached down toward the cover and magnetized. It flew up to my hand. As the door opened I maneuvered the cover into place, then backed my hand off magnetically, holding it over the opening.

Someone stepped inside the closet. He coughed, and then there was nothing, which was more unnerving than his noise. I didn't dare look through the vent but I listened carefully for the unholstering of his pistol. It would be easy for him to shoot us through the tin ductwork. The beam of a flashlight shone through the cover to the top of the vent. The guard hesitated just a moment more; then he walked out of the closet and shut the door. We waited a moment longer; then, still magnetically holding the vent cover with one hand, I reached out and grabbed it with my other hand and slid it into place. "Let's go," I whispered.

The duct we were crawling through was as large as the one in Peru, about thirty inches high and three feet wide, and pitch black except for my glow. We crawled on our elbows and knees as fast as we could.

The air duct passed by both Ostin's and Jack's rooms. We came to Ostin's first. The vent covering in his room wasn't an ordinary screen but made of the same reinforced steel bars that were on the room's windows.

"How are we going to get through *that?*" I said.

"Just like you did with those screws," Nichelle replied. "You can melt through it. Just focus."

Nichelle made the room's surveillance camera go dark; then I heated up, focusing all my energy into my right palm. As the light from my hand grew brighter, Ostin woke. He curiously sat up in bed, watching. "Michael?"

I burned through two of the bars, leaving a space big enough for him to fit through.

He stood. "Michael? Is that you?"

"Yes," I said. "Drag your bed over and climb up."

He pushed his bed over to the vent, leaving one end of it propped up against the door to slow the guards if they entered. I reached down and grabbed his hand and pulled him in to his waist. He climbed the rest of the way in. It wasn't until after he was completely inside the duct that he saw Nichelle.

"What's she doing here?"

"She's helping us escape."

"She's the one who got us captured."

"It's not her fault. Remember what you said about Taylor not being Taylor?"

"Yeah."

"You were right. That was Tara who came back to the hotel with us."

"I knew it," he said. "And Nichelle knew it was Tara, so she went to Hatch and turned us in so he'd think she was on his side."

Nichelle looked at him in amazement. "That's exactly what I did."

"Brilliant," he said.

I suppose that was one of the benefits of being friends with Ostin. You didn't always have to explain things. We made our way to the next vent, which was Jack's room. Jack was lying in his bed, facing away from us. Nichelle killed the camera; then I whispered, "Jack."

He didn't move.

"Jack!" I said louder.

Still nothing.

"He must be asleep," Ostin said.

I melted through the bars and let myself down into the room. As I neared I saw that he was tied up in a white canvas straitjacket. I gently shook him. "Jack, it's me."

He slowly rolled over. "Michael?"

I was horrified. From my glow I could see that the Elgen guards had severely beaten him. Both of his eyes were swollen and he had a huge contusion under his left eye. "I'm so sorry, buddy," I said.

The jacket he was tied up in was fastened with simple buckles.

"Roll onto your stomach," I said. "I'll get this thing off."

Jack groaned with pain as he rolled over. I quickly released the buckles, then Jack took off the jacket and slowly stretched out his arms, grimacing with the movement.

"Are you okay?" I asked.

"I think they broke my ribs," he said.

"I wish Abi was here to help you."

"I'm glad she's not," he said.

We pushed his bed to the wall beneath the vent.

"Can you lift yourself up?" I asked.

"I'll try."

Jack stood on the bed and grabbed ahold of the vent's outer bars but, probably for the first time in his life, struggled to do a single pull-up. "I can't do it."

"Yes, you can." I got down on all fours. "Step up on my back."

He looked at me doubtfully but did as I said. He weighed more than I thought he did, but now that he was two feet closer he was able to pull himself the rest of the way up. It was not until I began to climb back up myself that I realized I had forgotten to tell him about Nichelle. I heard his voice echo from the vent. "You!"

Fortunately Ostin was positioned between Jack and Nichelle.

"Take it easy," Nichelle said.

"I'm going to rip your head off, you—"

"Jack, stop," I said, pulling my upper body into the duct. "She's on our side."

"You can beat me up later," Nichelle said dully. "But now's not really the time."

I pulled myself the rest of the way in.

"Jack, she's cool," Ostin said.

"Have you guys lost your minds?"

"Trust me," I said. "Things aren't the way we thought they were."

"Here," Nichelle said, handing Jack the screwdriver. "You can use this as a weapon." He looked surprised at the offer, but reached out and took it. "Just don't kill me with it," she said, turning back around.

"How much time do we have?" I asked Nichelle.

"About an hour."

"We need to go faster," I said.

"What's going on?" Jack asked.

"They're going to put Taylor in the bowl," I said. "We need to get Ian and McKenna, then go for her."

"Taylor was with McKenna," Jack said.

"No, she wasn't," Ostin said.

We crawled farther down the duct, though Jack did so with great difficulty. Crawling on his stomach with broken ribs was like walking barefoot on broken glass.

Five minutes later Nichelle said, "There's a Glow coming up. I can feel him. I think it's Ian."

"Let me get in front," I said. I crawled past everyone. As I approached the opening, I heard someone shouting. I looked through the vent. Ian was sitting on his bed yelling at the two guards in the room with him. It took me a second to figure out why—he must have seen us coming and was keeping the guards from looking at us. As I peered out of the vent, Ian glanced up at me for a millisecond, then, turning away, slowly shook his head.

"Two guards," I whispered to the others. Normally I could take them, but I couldn't pulse that far and I couldn't throw an electric ball through the bars. I wished Zeus were with us. They'd already be on the ground.

"We're going to have to go in through the hall," I said. "We need to back up."

We had crawled over a mechanical closet about sixty feet back and we crawled backward until we reached the vent. I lit a single finger and pushed it through the metal, then dragged it around the edges until I'd cut through three sides.

"You're getting good at that," Nichelle said.

"Thanks." I bent the grate back with my foot.

There wasn't enough room in the closet for all of us, so only Nichelle and I climbed down. Nichelle put her ear against the door. I looked at her in anticipation. "Anything?"

She shook her head. "I'm going to look out. Be ready." She slowly turned the doorknob and opened the door just enough to look down the hall. Then she raised her hand and turned off all the cameras and stepped out.

"You there! What are you doing?" someone shouted.

"What do I do?" Nichelle asked without looking back. "It's a guard."

"Try to get him close," I said.

"Put your hands up," the guard said.

Nichelle laughed. "In your dreams."

"I said put them up. Now!"

"Since when do Eagles take orders from captains?"

There was a pause; then he said, "I'm sorry, miss. I didn't realize it was you."

"No worries," she said. "I knew it was *you*."

"What are you doing here?" He was coming closer.

She lowered her voice. "Looking for you, Captain."

"May I help you with something?"

"I was just hoping to get to know you a little better."

The man seemed rattled. "You know, it's against the Elgen code to—"

Nichelle interrupted him. "Do you always follow the code?"

"Not always," he said softly. He was getting close.

"Good. Because that code could definitely get in the way, if you know what I mean."

There was a pause.

"What time is your shift over, handsome?"

"I'm done at—"

Nichelle raised her hand. "Wait, did you hear that?"

"What?"

"Hatch is looking for me. If he finds me with you, who knows what he'll think." She reached out her hand. "Hurry. In the closet."

"But . . ."

"Hurry!"

The captain ducked inside the closet, and Nichelle pulled the door shut behind them. I was crouched on the opposite side of a heating unit just a few feet from the guard. He was facing the opposite direction, so he didn't see my glow.

It was quiet for a moment; then the captain said, "I didn't hear anything."

"I thought I saw Michael Vey."

"Vey?"

"You've heard of him?"

"Of course I've heard of him."

"Have you ever met him?"

"I really shouldn't be in here."

"That's for sure," I said.

"What?" As he swung back, I put my hand on his leg and pulsed. He dropped to the ground.

"You're good," I said to Nichelle. "You could be an actress."

"I lived with Hatch for ten years. I was." She looked down at the guard. "Let's get his keys."

Ostin stuck his head through the open vent. "Hey, he's about Jack's size. He could wear his uniform."

"Good idea," I said. It wasn't easy undressing the guard in the closet, but we got his clothes off and handed them up to Jack. Then we handcuffed the guard to a pipe with his hands behind his back and stuffed his T-shirt in his mouth to keep him from shouting for help. I helped Ostin down from the vent, then Jack climbed down by himself, even though he was still in a lot of pain. We gave Jack the guard's keys.

"What's the plan?" Jack asked.

"You've got the uniform, Captain," I said. "Ian is in the second door on the left. There should still be two guards in there. Get them to the door and I'll take care of them."

"Got it," Jack said.

Jack stepped out of the closet and looked around. "All clear," he said.

The four of us walked to the room. Jack looked in through the one-way window, then unlocked the door. Nichelle, Ostin, and I pressed up behind him. We could hear the guards yelling at Ian.

Jack glanced back at us and pushed open the door. "What's going on?" Jack said to the guards. "What's all this shouting?"

"Captain," one of the guards replied. "We were questioning the prisoner."

"We don't have time for that. There's been a breach of security. Two of the prisoners have escaped. We've been ordered to lock down our hall and join the hunt. Come with me."

"Yes, sir," two voices said in unison.

As they got to the door, I stepped in around Jack and pulsed, knocking them both back into the room. Nichelle knocked out the camera while I released Ian.

"That was some trick getting in here," Ian said.

"You watched the whole thing?" I asked.

"From the second Nichelle walked into your room." He looked at Nichelle. "You can explain later."

"Happy to," she replied.

"Where's McKenna?" Ostin asked.

"Just two cells down from this one. No guards with her."

"We'll grab her on the way. Have you seen Taylor?"

"They've got her locked up in a cell by the bowl. She's with the girl."

"Jade Dragon?"

He nodded. "Yes. And we'd better hurry. The guards are on their way to get her. It looks like it's feeding time in the bowl."

"Come on, Taylor," I said. "You just need to buy us some time."

PART TEN

36

Feeding Time

Taylor and Jade Dragon were still awake, huddled in one corner of the cell as the door opened. The same three guards from before walked in accompanied by two Lung Li.

"It's feeding time, sweetie," the captain said. "Do you have the information?"

"It's about time you got here," Taylor said.

The captain looked at her dully. "What?"

"I'm not Taylor, Captain. I'm Tara. I came down to see if I could persuade Taylor to help us and she did something to me. She's out there pretending to be me."

"And I'm Admiral Hatch," the captain said.

The other two guards laughed. The Lung Li stood motionless.

"Take the child," the captain said.

The two Lung Li grabbed Jade Dragon. She started screaming.

"Leave her alone!" Taylor shouted. "You're hurting her!"

"Take her," the captain repeated.

One of the Lung Li shoved a needle into the child's thigh and she immediately slumped over. The other guard slung her over his shoulder, then the two Lung Li took her out.

"Now for you," the captain said.

"I'm not Taylor!" Taylor screamed. "Just look at me!"

"I just saw Tara," the captain said. He leaned close. "Do you have our information?"

"I told you, I'm Tara!"

The captain's eyes narrowed to angry slits. "You're playing with your life."

"And you're playing with yours," Taylor said.

"Enough of this," the captain growled. "Take her."

Taylor pressed back against the wall. "I can prove I'm Tara. If you touch me, you'll pay."

The guards hesitated. Disobeying one of "Hatch's kids" was like disrespecting an EGG. Or worse.

"Don't listen to her," the captain ordered.

Taylor looked up at the camera. "Dr. Hatch, they're going to kill the wrong girl. Taylor switched places with me. I can prove it and this fool of a captain won't listen." She turned to the captain. "We both know they record everything. If something happens to me, Dr. Hatch will feed you to the rats next. I guarantee it."

This time the captain hesitated.

"Just give me five minutes to prove who I am. Your life is worth at least five minutes, isn't it?"

"How will you prove it?"

"Get Quentin and Taylor. Q will know the difference between the two of us. He can verify who I am."

The captain looked at her for a moment, then turned to the guard on his left. "Get Quentin. And Tara. Bring them both. Hurry. We have a feeding schedule."

* * *

Five minutes later Quentin stormed into the cell, with Tara and the guard following behind him. It was clear he'd been woken up. "What is it?" Quentin asked angrily.

"This girl claims to be Tara."

"You interrupted my sleep for that?" Quentin snarled.

"She says she can prove it and that you would know."

Quentin looked at her. "What do you want, *Taylor*?"

"I'm not Taylor," Taylor said. "Taylor is standing next to you."

"Oh, please," Tara said. "That's just lame. You really are desperate."

"Quentin, ask her something only *we* would know," Taylor said. "Like what we had for dinner at the mall. You know, before we came to Taiwan."

Quentin suddenly looked confused.

"Just ask her," Taylor said.

He turned to Tara. "How did she know about the mall?"

Tara looked confused. "I don't know."

"What did we have for dinner?"

Tara paled. "Oh, come on, you're not really going to play her game. You know me."

"You didn't answer," Taylor said. "So what was it? What did you have for dinner? Easy question."

Tara looked panicked. "I . . . I had . . . we had . . ."

Taylor lifted one eyebrow. "Yes?"

"I'm not doing this," Tara answered.

"It's a simple question," Quentin said. After a moment he pressed her. "Well?"

"I . . . I don't remember."

"Really?" Taylor said. "Because I remember that the calzone we all had was pretty good for a food court. And the capellini that Q ordered on the side was just as good." Taylor looked at Quentin. "Ask her what 'calzone' means."

He looked at her. "What does 'calzone' mean?"

Again Tara couldn't recall. "C'mon, this is a trick. She's doing something to me."

"Yes, it is a trick," Quentin said. He turned to the guards. "Take her." They grabbed Tara.

"Quentin! Stop it!"

Taylor breathed out in relief. "Finally."

Quentin stepped up to her. "How did this happen?"

"I went to visit her alone to see if I could talk some sense into her. But apparently she's learned some new trick. The next thing I remembered I was lying on the ground next to the little girl."

"She's lying!" Tara shouted.

"That was stupid to come alone," Quentin said. "Don't do it again."

"Believe me, I won't. I thought I could save us some time. I thought you'd be proud of me."

"I am proud of you." Quentin turned to the guards. "Take her to the bowl. You're already late for feeding time."

Tara turned white. "Quentin, I'm Tara!"

"Yeah, and I'm Michael Vey."

The guards began dragging Tara away. Tara screamed. "No! Stop! Stop!"

"She was right about one thing," Taylor said. "That was lame."

"You have to be careful," Quentin said. "These Electrodorks are clever little monkeys." He put his arm around her. "Are you okay?"

"Yeah. For almost dying."

"That was too close," he said. He went to kiss her when, from down the hall, Tara shouted, "Quentin, my tattoo. Look at my tattoo."

He stopped.

"My tattoo!" she shouted again.

"Hold up," Quentin said to the guards. He looked at Taylor. "Show me your tattoo."

"You just want to see my ballerina," she said coyly.

He didn't smile. "Yes, I do."

Taylor forced a smile. "I'll show you later. In private." She rebooted him. "Shall we go?"

Quentin blinked a few times, then said, "Of course. I'm tired."

They started to walk away when the captain said, "Sir, did you want to check the tattoo?"

"My tattoo!" Tara shouted. "You're the one who chose it. Look at my tattoo."

Quentin looked at Taylor uneasily; then he walked over and pulled the collar of Tara's blouse down over her shoulder, revealing a tattoo of a ballerina.

"It's me," Tara sobbed. "I'm Tara."

He turned back to Taylor. "Show me your tattoo."

Taylor folded her arms at her chest and grinned. "Like you said, we *Electrodorks* are clever little monkeys."

Just then there was a blast of electricity and all three guards hit the floor. Then Tara and Quentin fell to the ground, doubled over in pain.

Taylor looked at Michael and smiled. "It's about time you got here."

PART ELEVEN

PART ELEVEN

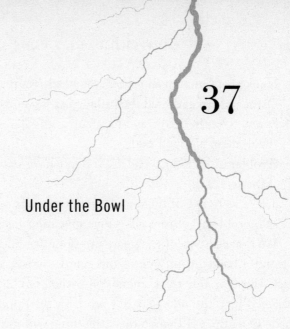

37

Under the Bowl

I could tell we were near the bowl because I was feeling more electric. Sparks snapped uncontrollably between my fingers and legs and underneath my arms. I'm certain the three guards sprawled out on the ground had noticed how electric I was too. They were all still unconscious.

"Nichelle, stop this," Quentin shouted from his knees. "That's an order."

"*You're* giving *me* an order?" Nichelle said. "I think you've got that backward, Q-bert." She crouched down until her face was inches from his and her eyes narrowed in anger. "You were the only family I had. And when things went bad you all left me to die. Michael Vey was my enemy, and he showed more mercy than all of you creeps combined."

"You and Vey?" Quentin said. "That's pathetic. You're going to be sorry."

"I was born sorry," Nichelle replied.

I looked at Quentin and shook my head. "Karma sucks, doesn't it?"

Ostin and Ian gathered the prone guards' weapons while Jack and McKenna took their keys and handcuffs.

"Lock them all up," I said.

"Problem," McKenna said. "We don't have enough handcuffs for all of them."

There were five of them and only three pairs of handcuffs.

"No problem," Ostin said. "Guys, give me a hand."

We dragged two of the guards to opposite sides of the metal toilet, put a handcuff on one of the guard's wrists, threaded it around back through the thick metal pipe that fed into the toilet, and attached it to the other guard's wrist on the opposite side. We then made Quentin and Tara do the same thing with the second pair. With the last pair of handcuffs, we slid the guard up the base of the toilet and handcuffed his hands around it. By the time we were done they definitely weren't going anywhere. And they looked pretty silly.

Nichelle smirked at Quentin and Tara. "You look like some weird monument to toilets."

"You're a loser, Nichelle," Tara said. "You always were. That's why everyone always hated you."

"I'm so hurt," she said. Nichelle put her hand out toward them and Tara and Quentin began to shake from the pain. "Who's losing now?"

Tara screamed out in pain.

"Nichelle," I said.

She turned toward me. "What?"

"That's enough."

"I've just started."

"We're not like them."

She looked at me with a peculiar expression, then I saw a look I hadn't seen on her before. She put her hand down. "No. *We're* not like *them*."

"Where's Jade Dragon?" I asked Taylor.

"I don't know," Taylor said. "The Lung Li guards took her."

I turned to Ian. "Do you see her?"

"No. Just a lot of armed guards looking for us."

"We can worry about her later," Ostin said. "We need to get out of here before the plant goes on full alert."

As we stepped out into the hall a siren went off.

"Too late," I said.

"We can't leave without Jade Dragon," Taylor said.

"We haven't given up on her," I said. "But for now, Ostin's right. We need to get out of here if we can." I turned around. "Ian, what's going on?"

"Chaos," he said. "This place looks like an angry beehive."

"Can you see any way out?"

"No. But we've got to move. There are guards coming from both sides of this hall."

I pointed to a large set of double doors. "What's through there?"

"It's the underside of the bowl," he said. "It's where they bring the fish in."

"How many guards?"

"None. Just the feeders. All the guards are outside."

Jack swiped one of the guards' magnetic keys across the door pad and the door unlocked. We hurried inside and the door automatically locked behind us.

With the exception of a massive steel-plated pool in the center of the room, the space was similar to the Peruvian feeding room, rectangular with a resin-coated concrete floor and forty-foot-high ceilings that curved on one side with the exterior of the bowl. The room was humid and smelled like a fish market.

It stinks in here. I hate fish.

I looked over at Taylor. It was her voice, but she wasn't talking. There was so much electricity in the air that I could read her thoughts.

"Ian, where do the wires from the lock run?"

He ran a finger down the wall. "Right here."

"Tell me what this does." I put my hand against the wall and pulsed. The intensity of the surge surprised me. Being directly under the bowl enhanced my powers to extreme levels.

"Dude, you melted the pad. You even melted some of the nails in the wall."

"That should at least slow them down," I said.

"Michael . . . ," Taylor said. "Look."

"*Bu dung!*" someone shouted. I turned around. There were now a half dozen men standing on the other side of the pool in bright orange jumpsuits with rubber waders and gloves. One of them was pointing a shotgun at us. "*Da jya, syou chilai.*"

"He said, 'Don't move,'" Ostin said. "And put our hands up."

"Are there any others with weapons?" I asked Ian.

"Not that I can see."

"I'm going to reboot him," Taylor said. She looked at the man intensely. At first he looked confused and lowered his gun as if he'd forgotten why he was holding it. Then he fell over unconscious. The other men turned and ran to a door in the back.

"I think you melted his brain," Ostin said.

I walked over to the man and checked him. He was out but still breathing. I picked up his gun and threw it into the pool.

"Look at all those fish," McKenna said, staring into the water. "There's, like, a million of them."

The pool was easily as large as the Olympic-sized one we had at Meridian High School, though much deeper. The water was dark and rough and the pool itself was steel-plated and riveted. There was a car-size, cagelike apparatus that hung from chains from the ceiling a few yards above the center of the pool, and a twelve-foot metal boat was tied to a cleat at the pool's far edge.

"Ian, how do we get out of here?" I asked.

"I still don't see a way out."

"What about that door those guys ran through?"

"It's just a freezer."

"No pipes out?"

"No Weekend Express," he said.

"We should use the pool," Ostin said. "The tunnel leads out."

"We can't hold our breath that long," Taylor said. "And there are fish."

"Maybe there are scuba tanks in the back room," Jack said.

"I don't see any," Ian said. "And there are still bars in the pipe."

"Michael can cut through them," Nichelle said.

"We still can't hold our breath that long," Taylor repeated.

"We can improvise a diving bell," Ostin said.

"A what?" Taylor said.

"A diving bell. It's how people centuries ago used to explore underwater. If we turn the boat upside down, there's enough air in the boat to get us through the pipe."

"Yeah, but the pipe is underwater," Taylor said. "And the air keeps the boat from going underwater."

"It's a metal boat," Ostin said. "And a metal pool. If Michael can magnetize enough he could pull the boat to the bottom, then we'll walk along the bottom to the pipe."

"It could work," I said.

Something heavy started pounding against the door. "We've got to go," Ian said. "A bunch of guards are trying to break in."

"Let's do this," I said.

We ran over to the far side of the pool. Jack untied the boat, but it took all of us to flip it over.

"Everyone in the water," I said.

"With the fish?" Taylor said.

"Or stay with the Elgen," Jack said.

"They both stink," Nichelle said.

"I'll take the fish," Taylor said.

We all jumped into the pool, then swam underneath the overturned boat. The inside of the boat was faintly lit by our glows. McKenna lit up her face to brighten it.

"Now what?" Taylor asked.

"I magnetize," I said. I put one hand on the top of the boat, then reached the other toward the floor and pulsed. It took us a moment to realize that the boat was gradually descending.

"It's working," Ostin said.

I could see the floor of the pool coming closer. Every now and then Taylor would scream when a fish swam up against her. It took us about a minute to reach the bottom.

"How long will this air last?" Jack asked.

"Long enough," Ostin said. "My worry is, how long will Michael last?"

258 RICHARD PAUL EVANS

Sweat was already pouring down my face. If it wasn't for the extra power the bowl gave me I couldn't have done it. "Which way to the pipe?" I asked.

"We spun a little on our way down," Ian said. "It's that way. Ten o'clock."

"Everyone start walking," Ostin said. "Start to the left."

Everyone grabbed onto some part of the boat and pushed forward—everyone except for me. Holding the boat down was not only taking all of my strength, but it was also a difficult balancing act keeping the right amount of magnetism. Too much would crush us to the floor; not enough and we floated up and were unable to touch the bottom and push forward.

Ian kept us moving in the right direction, occasionally looking up to the feeding room. We had traveled about twenty feet when Ian said, "The Elgen are in. They're looking for us."

"They'll never look down here," Ostin said.

"They just did," Ian said. "They're pointing at us." He paused. "Now they're pointing guns at us."

"Faster!" Ostin shouted. "We just need to make it to the pipe."

A bullet struck the side of the boat next to me, ricocheting with a loud clang. "That was too close."

"Thirty-five more feet to the pipe," Ian said.

Just then a bullet burst through the center of the boat, grazing Nichelle. "Ah!" she cried. She fell down into the water. Water gushed in through the hole. Jack grabbed her and lifted her as the water around us began to darken with her blood. "Where are you hit?"

"Shoulder," she said, grimacing in pain.

"Don't worry about pushing," he said. "Just walk."

The water level in the boat rose as air escaped through the bullet hole.

"Someone plug the hole!" I shouted.

Ian shoved his finger into it, stopping the flow. "Got it."

"How far to the pipe?" I asked.

"Thirty feet," Ian said.

Another bullet struck the boat, puncturing another hole through the metal. No one was hit but more water sprayed in. Ian stuck a finger in that hole as well. "They're setting up a machine gun," he said.

"We're not going to make it," Jack said. "It's like shooting fish in a barrel."

"That's it," Ostin said. "Michael, can you pulse hard?"

"I am pulsing hard!" I said.

"I mean electric, not magnetic."

"Why?"

Another bullet pierced the bow of the boat and more water sprayed in. McKenna stuck her finger in the hole to stop it.

"They've got the machine gun up!" Ian shouted.

"Just pulse!" Ostin shouted.

"I'll shock everyone."

"They're aiming," Ian said.

"Do it!" Ostin shouted. "Everyone prepare to be Tasered. Go!"

I pulsed. Everyone screamed and Ostin, Jack, and Taylor fell into the water, then stood back up.

"Man, that hurt," Ostin said.

Then Taylor screamed as paralyzed fish floated up all around us. "What did you do?"

"Electric fishing," Ostin said. "Michael just stunned all the fish and they floated to the top of the pool. The Elgen won't be able to see us or shoot us through them."

"He's right," Ian said. "It's like a six-foot barrier of fish."

We reached the corrugated pipe floor without being hit by any more bullets, but the pipe brought another problem. The farther we got from the bowl, the more difficult it was for me. I felt like I went from carrying a hundred pounds to two hundred. I groaned beneath the strain.

"Are you okay?" Taylor asked.

"How much farther?" I asked.

"We're getting close," Ian replied.

Suddenly there was a huge surge of water, pushing us forward and up against the first set of bars. My head hit the side of the boat hard enough that, for a second, I lost magnetism and the boat started to flip over. Jack threw himself against it, holding it for a few seconds before I regained control.

"Michael, are you okay?" Taylor said.

"Yes," I replied, my head aching. "Sorry."

"They threw a grenade," Ian said. "It's like fish stew out there."

"At least we're at the bars," I said.

"Can you cut through them?" Ostin asked.

I moved to the front of the boat and grabbed onto a bar. It was thicker than anything I had cut through so far. As I began to heat up, the back of the boat began to rise. I stopped to pull it back down. I looked at Ostin. "I can't magnetize the boat and cut through the bars at the same time."

"It's okay," Ostin said. "We're in the pipe. Just let the boat float to the top."

"Let it up easy," Jack said. "If it flips, we drown."

I slowly let the boat rise until it knocked against the top of the pipe. Everyone was now treading water.

I grabbed the bar again and began to cut. It took me nearly five minutes to burn through the first bar, the water boiling next to my hand. I'd have to cut through at least five bars to get the boat through. We were still losing air and the water level was rising in the boat at about an inch a minute. At that rate we would be out of air before I cut through the pipes, and I was already exhausted. I don't think I could have pulled us back down to the bottom if I wanted to.

"Ian, how far is it from these bars to the end of the pipe?" I asked.

"About twenty yards."

"Are there any more bars before the end of the pipe?"

"No. The next bars are at the first fence, about twenty-five yards past the end of the pipe."

"So if we make it to the end of the pipe, we can swim up."

"Yes. We'll still have the fences, but we'll be outside the plant."

"Are there guards up there?"

"Not yet," he said. "Why?"

"I don't think I can make the cuts with the air we have left. And even if I did, I can't make it much farther magnetizing the boat. The farther we get from the bowls the harder it gets."

Taylor put her hand on my arm. "What do we do?"

"If I take out one more bar we can swim for it."

"I don't think I can swim it," Nichelle said. "I'm not a good swimmer."

"Can you hold your breath for thirty seconds?" Jack asked.

She looked at him. "I think so."

"Then you can do it. If you can't swim, I'll carry you out."

Nichelle looked at him quizzically. "Why?"

"We don't leave family behind."

For a moment Nichelle was speechless. "Thank you."

"Okay," I said. "Let's do this." I went back to cutting. By the time I cut through the second bar there was only six inches of air left in the boat. The gap between the bars was at least twenty-four inches wide. "We can fit through that," Ian said.

"Can we see which way to swim?" McKenna asked.

"It's a little lighter toward the end of the pipe," Ian said.

"Any guards yet?"

"Not before the first fence. If we stay close to the building they might not see us. There's some kind of concrete retaining wall I think we can hide behind."

"Maybe I should go first," Taylor said. "I'm a good swimmer. And that way I can reboot anyone on top."

Ostin looked at me. "Are you strong enough?"

"I can make it," I said.

"I'll go after Taylor," McKenna said. "I can help fight if someone's up there."

"Who's next?" Ian asked.

"Ostin, Nichelle, and Jack," I said.

"What about you?" Ian asked.

"I'll go last," I said. "I need a minute to rest."

"You know as soon as we unplug these holes you'll only have a minute of air."

"Yeah," I said. "I'm okay."

Taylor swam up to the front next to me. "Are you sure you're strong enough?" she asked.

"Yes," I said. "Be careful."

She kissed me. "I'll see you outside." She grabbed the bars, took a deep breath, then disappeared under the water.

"I'm ready," McKenna said. "But someone's going to have to plug this hole."

"I'll get it," I said.

Water gushed in as McKenna pulled her finger out of the bullet hole. I reached up past her and pushed my finger into the hole. "Got it."

"Go," Ian said.

McKenna inhaled, then ducked under, leaving the boat dim with just Ian's and my glow.

Ostin looked at me nervously. He had never been much of a swimmer.

"You can do it," I said. "Remember summer camp."

"Right." He took a deep breath, then went.

Jack helped Nichelle to the front. "Are you ready?"

"I think so."

"I'll be right behind you."

To my surprise, Nichelle kissed Jack on the cheek. "Thank you." She took a deep breath, ducked under the boat, and swam through the bars. Jack swam after her.

"Just us," I said to Ian.

"Are you ready?" he asked.

"Let's do it."

He pulled his fingers out of the holes and water shot in like two high-pressure water hoses. He inhaled once, then dove under.

I tried to take a deep breath, but what was left of the air was pretty thin.

"You can do this," I said to myself. I grabbed onto the bars and pulled myself underwater, then swam as fast as I could toward the end of the pipe.

38

Out of the Frying Pan

I must have run into a hundred fish on the way up. I broke the pool's surface gasping for air. Someone grabbed me by the back of my shirt and lifted me out of the water. I almost pulsed before I saw it was Jack. Somehow, in spite of his injuries, he had found the strength to lift me to shore.

The shrill, ear-piercing sound of alarms filled the air. Everyone was sitting on the ground in puddles, soaked and out of breath, partially shielded behind a concrete retaining wall about four feet high. When I caught my breath I said, "We made it."

"Thanks to you," Taylor said.

"Are you okay?" I asked Nichelle.

"I'll make it. The bleeding's not too bad, it just stings."

"It's the salt water," Ostin said.

"Let me see," Jack said. He rolled her sleeve up over her shoulder to examine the wound, then he ripped a piece of cloth from his undershirt and wrapped it around Nichelle's shoulder as a bandage.

"Thank you," she said. "Again."

I looked at Ian. "Any guards?"

"Just ahead at the fences."

"What's this wall?"

"It's a storm wall," Ostin said. "It keeps water from the plant. In the last fifty years Taiwan's been hit by more than two hundred typhoons."

We were fortunate to have something to hide behind; otherwise the Elgen would have already been shooting at us. The sun hadn't risen yet, but the compound was lit by flood lamps and was as bright as a nighttime football game. I could see the Elgen guards at the closest fence, which was less than a hundred feet from where we were. There was little movement outside other than the constant panning motion of surveillance cameras.

"There's too many cameras out here," I said.

"I'll try to put some out," Nichelle replied. She reached out and several of the closest cameras stopped moving.

As I surveyed our surroundings, everything seemed even more hopeless than it had inside the plant. I realized that getting out of the plant might have been the easy part.

"Does anyone have any ideas on how to get out of here?" I asked.

Ostin shook his head. "This place used to be a prison. It was made to keep people in."

"If we try to climb the fences they'll shoot us," Jack said.

"Michael's the only one who can climb them anyway," Taylor said. "They're electrified."

"And don't forget the landmines," Ian added.

"There's no way out of here," Taylor said.

Suddenly the alarms stopped, which should have made things less stressful, but it didn't. The Elgen must have turned them off for a reason. I wondered if they had found us. I looked over at Ostin. His head was down and he looked like he was lost in thought.

"What have you got, Ostin?"

Without looking up he said, "Ian, what do the landmines look like?"

"I don't know. They look like landmines."

"What shape?"

"They're round, mostly."

"Mostly?"

"There are different kinds," he said, sounding annoyed.

"Are some big?"

"Define *big*."

"Bigger than a car tire?"

"Yes. Some of them."

"Are the big ones made of metal or plastic?"

He looked back out. "Looks like metal."

"Can you see wires inside of them?"

Ian shook his head. "I'm not sure."

"What are you thinking?" I asked.

Ostin was quiet a moment, then shook his head. "After the Korean War, the Chinese farmers used to clear fields of landmines by starting fires. I was thinking that maybe McKenna could melt the triggering devices. But it won't work. McKenna would be too bright a target for them. They'd just shoot her."

"Not a good plan," McKenna said.

"I could stand in front of her and deflect the bullets."

"No you couldn't," Ostin said. "Or you would be *on* the landmine."

"And we'd still have to get over the fences," Taylor said.

Ostin bowed his head again. Then suddenly his expression changed as if he'd had an idea. "Ian, can you see any balls in the mines?"

His brow furrowed. "Balls?"

"Little ones. Like ball bearings. Just look."

He looked back out. "Yes. In the big ones."

"How about the small ones?"

"No."

"Awesome," Ostin said. "How close are the mines to one another?"

"Depends. Some are, like, three feet."

"Sympathetic detonation," Ostin said to himself. "Is there a pattern? Like a small one next to a big one?"

"The way they're arranged looks like a flower," Ian said. "There's one large surrounded by one, two, three . . . six little ones around it like petals."

"How close are the flowers to one another?"

"Close. Less than six feet."

"Do you have an idea?" I asked.

Ostin was still formulating. "Are the mines near the fences?"

"They're everywhere," Ian said.

"But how close to the fences?"

"In some places just a few feet. Some are right under the fence."

"Yes," Ostin said. "I think they might have given us a way out." He turned to me. "The big mines in the center of the clusters are anti-tank mines. They're there to stop vehicles from just running through the fences. The smaller mines surrounding them are antipersonnel mines—they're triggered by light pressure; if someone steps on them, they blow up. The antitank mines have a magnetic switch. When the metal ball moves around inside of it, it detonates the explosive. But because it's so close to the other mines, it will probably detonate all six of them with it."

"Why would they put them so close to one another?"

"To maximize the blast radius. But the clusters are so close to one another that it might set off multiple clusters. It might even cause a chain reaction."

"So what's the plan?" I asked.

"You need to create a magnetic force powerful enough to trigger as many of the switches as possible. The antitank mines can blow through a tank, so they can easily shred the fence. If we can blow them all up at the same time, the guards won't know what hit them."

"I don't know if I can magnetize that far," I said.

"Not without a boost." He thought for a moment, then turned to Nichelle. "Can you do the opposite of what you normally do?"

Nichelle was sitting on the ground holding her shoulder, her makeshift bandage soaked with blood. I wondered if she would even be able to walk. "What do you mean?" she asked.

"Can you *give* power instead of taking it?"

"You mean like Tessa?"

"Exactly."

"I might. Not as powerfully as Tessa, but maybe some."

"We need to test it," Ostin said. He turned to me. "Make a small spark."

I held my thumb and index finger about an inch apart and a thin bolt of electricity began to spark between them. Nichelle looked at the spark. She held her hand out toward me, but nothing happened.

"Try touching him," Ostin said.

She reached over and touched me on the shoulder. The spark snapped between my fingers. I looked at her and she was smiling. "It worked."

"It did," I said. "I could feel it." I looked back at everyone. "If this works, we're going to have to run. I'll go in front in case the guards start shooting. Nichelle, you stay with me, touching me. Taylor, create as much mental confusion as you can."

"There will probably be some of the smaller landmines that don't go off," Ostin said. "Ian needs to watch in front of us for undetonated landmines."

"We should move in a single-file line," I said.

"Got it," Ian said.

"No one steps out of line," I said. "Ready?"

I looked at Taylor and she nodded.

"Cover your ears," Ostin said. "If this works it's going to be *loud*."

"All right, Nichelle," I said. "Power me up."

She put her hand on my shoulder. I could feel her energy coursing through me. I stood up and stretched my hand out toward the yard. Someone shouted out in Chinese, but if they had seen us it was too late. *Way* too late. The yard exploded. The shock wave knocked us all back. It was as if the entire compound lifted ten feet into the air. I don't know if I managed to pull all the triggers at once or, as Ostin predicted, the proximity of the bombs to one another caused a split-second chain reaction throughout the entire compound, but regardless, it was impossible to tell where the explosion started. The flash from delayed explosions reflected off massive columns of smoke that rose hundreds of feet into the sky, shrouding the entire compound in an impenetrable cloud. The peninsula was so thick with black smoke it was impossible to see anything, even one another.

When the explosions finally stopped there was no sound but the ringing in our ears. Then a distant machine gun started firing.

"It's coming from one of the towers," Ian said. "He's firing blind. He just shot his own guys. He has no idea where we are."

"Are the fences down?" I asked.

"Shredded," Ian said.

"Then let's go. Which way?"

"Move straight ahead. Be careful as you walk, the ground is mostly craters."

"Nichelle?" I asked.

"Right here," she said. She put her hand on my shoulder. I covered my mouth with my arm and held my hand out, pulsing to deflect bullets.

"You're clear for sixty feet, Michael. Straight ahead," Ian said, before breaking out coughing. I started forward with Nichelle holding on to me. We moved slowly and blindly. As Ian had warned, the ground was broken up, and my nostrils were filled with the pungent smell of fresh earth mixed with smoke and the acrid stink of explosives.

"The fourth fence is still partially up," Ian said. "I can see some undetonated landmines."

I froze. "In front of me?"

"Not yet. Keep walking."

"Should I magnetize again?"

"No!" Ostin shouted. "If there are any undetonated landmines around us we're dead."

"I'll keep watching for them," Ian said. "Duck a little, Michael. You're about to pass through the first fence."

I reached out and touched pieces of twisted wire. "Careful!" I shouted back.

"The second fence is thirty feet straight ahead. After the third fence we'll need to go twenty yards to the right."

"What are the soldiers doing?"

"Their commander is trying to gather them, but they still can't see anything."

"Neither can I," Taylor said, erupting in a fit of coughing.

"Let's hope the smoke remains," Ian said. "We'll have to pass right through the middle of their camp."

I continued forward another twelve feet when Ian shouted, "Stop!"

I froze, my foot in the air.

"Don't move, Michael. You're right above a mine."

"Where?"

"Right where your foot is about to go."

Nichelle pulled me back.

"Step to your left twice, walk ahead five feet, then two steps back to this same path."

"All right, left two feet." I stepped over. "Ahead five feet." I walked forward. "Ian, keep your eyes on that mine."

"Sorry I missed that. I'm going to stand next to it," Ian said. "Taylor, you're too close. Step more to the left."

"Thank you," she said.

I walked about twenty feet past it, then stopped.

After Jack had passed the mine, Ian walked back up behind Nichelle. "Okay, let's go."

We began to move forward again. We passed through the second fence. It was still sparking where the electrical wires had been separated, and I reached over and grabbed the wire, letting it spark in my hand. "This fence is still live," I said.

"Why are you doing that?" Nichelle asked.

"I like it," I said. "It's like an energy drink." I paused for just a moment, then continued on. We had moved another forty feet when I heard Jack shout, "Stop!"

We all turned back.

"I think I stepped on something," Jack said.

Ian groaned. "You're on a mine."

"Why didn't it blow?" I asked.

"I don't know."

"It's either bad," Ostin said, "or it's the kind that blows up as soon as you release pressure."

"Jack, don't move," I said.

"Just get out of here," he replied. "The smoke's already starting to clear."

"We're not leaving you," I said.

"You don't have a choice," he said.

"Yes, we do," Nichelle said. "We don't leave family behind."

"Didn't you say that heat could melt the trigger?" McKenna asked Ostin.

Ostin looked anxious. "Yes, but you would have to be right next to it."

McKenna turned back. "Then let's do this. Ian, tell me when it's melted." She felt her way back to Jack, then knelt down on the ground next to him.

"What are you doing?" Jack said. "Get out of here."

"We're getting you out," she said.

"It's too dangerous," Jack said.

"Tell me about it," McKenna replied. She leaned over his foot, and her hand began to lightly glow.

"McKenna, they'll see your fire," Ostin said.

"Not if we stand around her," I said. "Ian, are there any undetonated mines around this one?"

"No, it's an outlier."

The smoke had cleared enough that we could see one another's shadows. I walked over to Jack's side, followed by Taylor, Ian, and Nichelle. Ostin got down on his knees next to McKenna. "If this thing goes, we're all going with you."

Nichelle knelt down next to McKenna. "I can help," she said. "I'm going to touch you." She laid her hand on McKenna's back. "You're trembling."

"I know," McKenna said. She set her hand flat on the ground next to Jack's foot and her hand began glowing again, orange at first, then brighter, until it was white-hot.

"Not too hot!" Ostin said. "The heat could set it off."

She quickly backed off.

"I think she did it," Ian said. "Everything is melted inside. The wires look . . . wilted."

"Wilted?" Ostin said.

Ian shrugged. "Yeah."

"You ready, Jack?" I said.

"I'm not taking my foot off until you're all gone. I mean it."

"We've got to go, Jack," I said.

"So go!" he said. *"I mean it."*

I exhaled. "Come on." Everyone walked forward, stopping about thirty steps ahead. "Now, Jack!" I shouted.

Even though we couldn't see him, we didn't need to. If McKenna's work had failed we'd all know soon enough. We all held our breath. A moment later Ian said, "He's off."

I breathed out in relief. "All right, let's keep going."

The smoke was beginning to dissipate and as we neared the Taiwanese army at the perimeter of the compound the sound of shouting intensified. I passed through the shredded remains of the third fence, then turned back. "Ian, where to?"

"Sixty feet to the right. But stay in the middle of the strip—there's undetonated antipersonnel mines on each side. The fence isn't down, there's just a hole. We'll have to crawl through it."

"Then what?"

"We'll come out next to one of the army tents. There's no one in it. When we get there I'll come up front and lead everyone through the army camp."

"Got it."

Carefully keeping my distance from either fence, Nichelle and I took about thirty steps before Ian said, "You're there." The spotlights were especially intense around the army camp and I could make out the silhouettes of several tents just past the fence, which meant that if we got too close, the soldiers would be able to see us too. The hole in the mangled fence was about the diameter of a bike tire and I got down on my knees and began to crawl through. A stray piece of razor wire caught above my elbow, ripping my skin and stinging like crazy. Blood streamed down my arm. "Agh," I said.

"Are you okay?" Nichelle asked.

"I'm great," I said. I bent the wire back, then Nichelle and I crawled the rest of the way through, stopping just a few yards from the fence to wait for everyone else. As Ian came through he said, "You're bleeding."

"I know," I said. "We'll deal with it later. Where to now?"

"There's a trail about fifty yards southeast that leads up into the hills."

"Go ahead and take the lead," I said. "Nichelle and I will protect the rear."

We waited until everyone else passed, then crouched down and followed Ian through the center of the army's camp. We could hear soldiers shouting around us in Chinese, but everything was in such chaos that even if someone had seen us I'm not sure they would have known who we were. As we neared the trail leading up the hill Nichelle froze. "Stop," she said.

"Are you okay?" I asked.

"There are Glows around," she said.

"Are you sure?"

"I'm always sure."

"Can you tell who it is?"

"Not yet."

"Stay alert," I said to everyone.

We crossed a dirt road to a line of trees, then began climbing a steep wooded incline. The camp's lights were no longer on us, and we hiked in darkness with Ian carefully choosing our path. We were about a hundred yards away from the compound when bolts of lightning began striking the camp, followed by more shouting and chaos. Occasionally a strike was followed by an explosion.

"Zeus?" I asked.

"Sure is," Ian said. "I think he's trying to distract them from us."
We continued hiking up the hill until we were above the line of
smoke but still well secluded in the darkness of the forest.

"Now what?" Jack asked.

"We get out of here," I said. "Hopefully Zeus brought something
to drive. Ian, we need to somehow get Zeus's attention."

"We're okay," Ian said. "Ben's here."

I looked over as Ben walked out from between some trees.

"Where'd you come from?" I asked.

He held up a pair of night-vision binoculars. "I have been watching you. It was very smoky." He lifted his radio. "Zeus, they are here.
Go now to meeting place." He turned back to me. "We were trying to
figure out how to rescue you when the alarms went off."

"How did you know we were captured?" Taylor asked.

"You left everything in your hotel room." He looked around. "Is
everyone here?"

"Yes."

There was one last storm of lightning bolts striking the camp, followed by a massive explosion. The display reminded me of the finale
of a fireworks show.

"What was that?" I asked.

"We brought bombs to blow up the road in case they tried to follow us," Ben said. "We must go now. Come."

"I see the car," Ian said.

It was another five minutes before the rest of us saw it. Concealed
in dense forest was an all-black Range Rover. "It will be crowded,"
Ben said. "But we will fit."

Everyone had gotten in except for me when Zeus and Tessa came
running up. They were both out of breath.

"Hurry!" Ben shouted.

"Good to see you two," I said, holding the door for them.

"Looks like you've had some fun," Zeus said, helping Tessa in.

He got in and I jumped in after him, holding my arm. Ben hit the
gas and the car lurched forward, its wheels spinning in the dirt before
intersecting with an asphalt road.

"Hey, guys," Zeus said, still panting, "I thought we weren't going to try to break in."

"Wasn't our plan," I said. "We were captured."

"Where's Jade Dragon?" Tessa asked.

"She's still inside," Taylor said, hurt evident in her voice. She looked at me. "Michael, you're really bleeding."

"I cut myself on some wire."

"Here," Jack said. He ripped another piece from his undershirt.

"I'll do it," Taylor said. She leaned over the back of my seat and wrapped the cloth around my throbbing arm. The cloth slowly turned red with blood. "I hope you don't need stitches," Taylor said.

We drove past three police cars with flashing lights, followed by a fire truck and some military vehicles. Within five minutes we were back on a major thoroughfare with traffic. Ben drove past the Kaohsiung off-ramp.

"I think you missed the exit," Jack said. "The hotel's back there."

"We are going someplace else," Ben said. About ten minutes past Kaohsiung, Ben exited the highway into the shipping district. We drove past a long harbor filled with cargo ships, freighters, and barges.

"Where are we going?" I asked.

"To a safe house," Ben said.

The safe house wasn't really a house—it was a large, abandoned-looking warehouse just two blocks from the waterfront. The building was surrounded by a tall chain-link fence with razor wire and security cameras.

Ben unlocked the gate, then drove the SUV inside and got back out to lock the gate behind us. Then he pushed a remote and a large overhead door in the warehouse opened. He drove inside, then shut the overhead door after us. A light went on, exposing a large open garage with several different vehicles and stacks of crates on wooden pallets. Ben shut off the engine and turned around.

"This is where we will stay until the *Volta* arrives."

"How many days is that?" I asked.

"The boat is still two thousand kilometers out," he said. "Maybe three days." He looked us over. "Do you know you escaped from an inescapable prison?"

"What do you mean?" Taylor asked.

"The Zuoying prison is famous like your Alcatraz prison in America. No one has ever escaped. And the Elgen made it even more strong."

"Not to mention the Taiwanese army camped around it," Jack said.

"Yes, with an army around it, you still escaped. You should be very proud of what you have done."

"We owe our escape to Nichelle," I said. "If it wasn't for her we wouldn't have gotten out. And if she hadn't gotten us in there, we never would have gotten Taylor out." I looked Nichelle in the eyes. "I'm sorry I doubted you."

"Me too," Ian said.

"Yeah," Jack said. "We owe you."

Nichelle looked at the wall, then shrugged. "It's okay. I wouldn't have trusted me either."

"We need to get you bandaged up," Jack said to her.

"And Michael," Taylor said.

"Upstairs we have medicine. and a wrap."

We got out of the car. As we walked over to the stairwell Jack asked Ben, "Do you have anything for pain?" He must have been in a lot of pain because I'd never heard him ask for as much as an aspirin.

"Yes," he said, opening the stairwell door. "Also upstairs."

"I hope it's good," Jack said.

"I am," Abigail said. She stood at the foot of the steps.

Jack looked as if he'd seen a ghost. "What are you doing here?"

"I missed you, so they let me come."

They hugged and the pain left Jack's face. He sighed with relief.

"Let's get you wrapped up," she said.

As we climbed the stairs Ben said, "I know you must be very tired and hungry. We have food and beds."

"Thank goodness," Ostin said. "I'm starving."

"We'll make something to eat," Tessa said to Ben. "You take care of the wounded."

The stairwell opened into a kitchen, and Nichelle, Jack, and I sat around the kitchen table. Ben walked out of the room, then returned with a plastic case with a large red cross on it.

"Nichelle first," I said.

Nichelle pulled her sleeve up over her shoulder and unwound the makeshift bandage Jack had made for her. The bullet had grazed her, leaving a four-inch red trough across her shoulder. The wound was deep but wasn't bleeding anymore. The biggest casualty was her full-shoulder tattoo of the grim reaper.

"I didn't like that tattoo much anyway," she said.

"This will hurt," Ben said, lifting a brown bottle with Chinese markings.

"Hold on," Jack said. "Abi, help Nichelle."

Abi stepped back. "I'm not taking her pain away."

For a moment there was silent tension, then Nichelle said, "It's okay. After all the pain I caused her, I deserve it."

"No," Jack said. "It's not right." He looked Abigail in the eyes. "She's changed. You need to help her."

Abigail looked at Jack incredulously. "No, I *don't*."

"It's okay," Nichelle said.

The tension in the room was palpable. Abigail looked at us, then angrily shook her head. "Fine." She reached over and touched Nichelle. "Do it."

Ben poured the liquid over Nichelle's shoulder and it foamed up around the wound. He patted it dry, then taped a large piece of gauze over it.

"Thank you," Nichelle said. She turned to Abigail, who had already stepped back from her. "You're right. I didn't deserve it, but thank you anyway."

Abigail didn't reply.

"Your turn, Michael," Ben said. "Let me see your arm now."

I took off my shirt, which was more painful than I expected because the fabric had stuck to the wound. It started bleeding again. The cut was about three inches long and deep enough to reveal yellow tissue and muscle. The entire area was covered with dirt. "We must clean it first," Ben said. He led me over to the kitchen counter, and I held my arm over the sink. He turned the water on and waited until it was warm, then lifted the sink sprayer and rinsed my wound until the dirt had all run off into the sink. I grimaced with pain.

"Sorry," Ben said.

Taylor was drying my wound off with a terry cloth towel when she suddenly exclaimed, "You got your watch back."

"I thought Hatch took it," Ostin said.

I looked around the room. Everyone was looking at me. "He did," I said. "They gave it back."

Ostin stared at me incredulously. "Hatch gave you your watch back?"

"I didn't say Hatch," I said.

"Then who?" he asked.

I wasn't ready to tell them about my father. "Just one of the Elgen," I said. I noticed that Ian was looking at me with a curious expression. "Can we get back to my arm?"

"Sorry," Taylor said. "I was just glad to see it again."

"Let me look at your arm," Ben said. His forehead furrowed. "We have a needle and thread for stitches, but we do not have a doctor."

"Maybe we could just bandage it tight," Taylor said.

"It's a laceration," Ostin said. "It needs to be stitched."

"I can stitch it," Nichelle said.

"You can stitch?" I asked.

"I like to sew. After I got out on the street I sewed up a few guys after fights." She frowned. "It's going to hurt."

"I'll be your anesthetic," Abigail said. She took my arm. Even though I could still feel it throbbing, the pain immediately went away.

Nichelle took a needle and thread from the first aid kit while Ben poured liquid from the brown bottle over my wound.

Nichelle walked up next to me with the needle. "Are you ready?"

"Yes."

"I don't think you should watch," she said.

I turned away. I could feel the needle tug at my skin, but, thanks to Abigail, the pain was as minor as someone pinching my cheek. It took Nichelle about five minutes to finish stitching up my arm. Finally she said, "That should do."

I looked over. The stitching looked professional.

"You're good."

"It's just like stitching a pillow," Nichelle said. "Except there's a lot of blood and tissue and puss."

"That's graphic," Ostin said.

"I'm going to put a bandage over it," Taylor said. She wrapped a piece of gauze around my arm and taped it.

"You can let go," I said to Abigail.

"Are you sure?"

"Yes. Thank you."

As she let go of me, pain shot through my arm as if the needle was just going in. Abigail saw me blanch and grabbed my arm. "Sometimes it hurts more than you think it will."

"It's okay," I said. "I've got to get used to it."

She slowly released my arm again. The pain came back but at least this time I was expecting it.

"Not to interrupt all the fun you're having over there, but the food is ready," Tessa said.

Zeus and Tessa had made a large pot of ramen noodles with shrimp and eggs, along with a dozen peanut butter sandwiches. Taylor got bowls for both of us. I was hungrier than I realized, and I gulped down a bowl of noodles and two sandwiches.

After eating, everyone went to the sleeping quarters to rest, leaving Taylor, Ben, and me sitting alone at the table.

"What time do you think it is?" I asked.

"You are wearing a watch," Ben said.

"I forgot." I looked at it. "I think it's still on Peru time."

"I think maybe nine o'clock," Ben said. "It was a long night."

I looked over at Taylor, who was staring off into space. It was one of those times that I wished I could read her mind. "Are you okay?"

"I was just thinking," she said softly.

"About what?"

She looked at me. "When we decided to come here it was to stop the Elgen from getting information that could threaten the world. I never thought about Jade Dragon being a real person. But now I know her, and she's really scared." Her eyes welled up. "We have to save her. Not just to save the world, but to save *her*."

"We'll save her," I said. "Our plan will work. It's just a few days more." I looked at Ben. "Are we safe here?"

"We have alarms and sentries that can fire six guns." He looked at us, then breathed out slowly. "But the Elgen are powerful. I do not know if we are ever safe."

We fell silent. After a few minutes Taylor said, "I think I'll go to sleep."

"Me too," I said, rising.

The upstairs of the warehouse was divided into a kitchen, two bathrooms (connected to the sleeping quarters), a television area, a radio room, and two long, rectangular rooms for sleeping, each with six cots. After Taylor had gone to bed I walked over to the men's side.

The sleeping quarters reminded me of pictures I had seen in a history textbook of a World War II army hospital. It wasn't the Grand Hi-Lai Hotel, but I wasn't complaining either. I'd sleep on dirt as long as it didn't belong to the Elgen. Still, less than an hour later I woke thinking about my father. Even after all we had done to escape, a part of me wanted to go back to see him.

After a half hour I walked out to the kitchen. I found some tea bags and put a kettle on the stove. As the kettle started to whistle, Ian walked into the kitchen.

"Did I wake you?" I asked.

"No. I couldn't sleep. Too much on my mind."

I turned off the flame, then lifted the kettle from the stove. "Want some tea?"

"Sure."

I poured two cups to the brim, then carried them both to the table. For a moment we both just sipped our drinks in silence. Then Ian said, "Something's bothering you."

"You can see my thoughts now too?"

He smiled. "No. That's Taylor's gig. Am I right?"

I paused a moment, then said, "Yeah."

"What's up?"

"I don't know if I should tell you."

"Does it have to do with your watch?"

I wondered how he knew that. "Yes." I looked down at my cup, then back at him. "You need to keep this a secret. I don't know how the others will take this."

"I'm always keeping secrets," he said. "That's what happens when you see everything."

I hesitated a moment then said, "I saw my father back at the Starxource plant."

Ian looked as if he wasn't sure how to respond. "I thought your father was dead."

"I thought he was, but he's not. He's part of the Elgen."

"When did you see him?"

"Right after we were brought into the plant. One of the Lung Li was torturing me and my father came in and stopped them. He took care of me. That's when he gave me back my watch."

Ian was quiet a moment, then said, "No, he didn't."

His response annoyed me. "What do you mean, 'No, he didn't'? I was there."

"That wasn't your father who gave you back your watch."

For a moment I was speechless. "Then who was it?"

"Hatch. And Tara."

"What?"

"Hatch was sitting right next to you and Tara was standing near the door. She must have a new trick."

My head spun with confusion. I began to tick.

Ian leaned toward me. "Think about it. Hatch tortured you. He's caged and tortured your mother. Would your father have allowed that?"

After a moment I shook my head. "No."

"I was waiting until everyone was asleep to talk to you about this. I saw Hatch give you the watch. I also saw you put your arms around him. I knew there had to be something strange going on."

My mind boiled with emotion. The anger and hurt I understood, but there was disappointment too.

After a few minutes Ian said, "Aren't you relieved that your father's not part of the Elgen?"

"I should be."

Ian frowned. "But you aren't?"

"I feel like I just lost my father again."

"I'm sorry," he said.

Suddenly I remembered all I had told Hatch. I lowered my head into my hands. "Oh no."

"What?"

"I told him about the voice."

"You what?"

I looked up. "I didn't mean to. It just came out."

Ian looked at me anxiously. "Did you tell him anything else?"

"He asked me where my mother was. I told him about the ranch. I told him where it was."

"You couldn't have told him where the ranch was. We didn't even know where it was."

I hung my head, covering my eyes with my hands. "He asked me how long the flight was from the ranch to Pasadena. Then he asked me about the weather. I told him the temperature." I felt sick to my stomach. "I thought it was my father." I looked up at him. "He couldn't find them from that, could he?"

Ian shook his head. "I don't know. Let's hope not." He breathed out slowly. "We need to tell Ben."

I buried my head in my hands again. "What have I done?"

39

Waffles and Maps

When I woke up the next morning, Ostin was standing next to my cot.

"What's up?" I said groggily.

"Not you."

"What time is it?"

"It's like noon," he said. "Can you smell that?"

I breathed in. "Yeah. It smells good."

"Good? Dude, Ben's making waffles."

I sat up. "There aren't waffles in Taiwan."

"Do not be too sure of it," Ben said. I looked up to see Ben standing in the doorway. "Get up. I have made American-style breakfast."

"Give me a minute," I said.

After Ostin and Ben had left the room I pulled on my pants and shirt, then walked barefoot out to the kitchen. There was a plate stacked tall with waffles. Taylor was standing at the stove making omelets with ham and peppers. "Good morning, sleepy-head," she said.

I walked over to her side. "Omelets?"

She pecked me on the cheek. "Yes, but without cheese. Apparently the Chinese aren't into cheese."

"Nearly ninety percent of people of Asian descent are lactose intolerant," Ostin said. "That means they can't digest milk."

"I'm not," McKenna said.

"That's because you're special."

"I know," she said, smiling.

"Would you like an omelet?" Taylor asked.

"Yes. Thank you."

She scooped up an omelet and put it on a plate. "There you go. Waffles are on the table."

Nichelle was sitting at the end of the table next to Ian and McKenna. Jack was sitting on the opposite end next to Abigail. She was rubbing his back.

"How are you feeling?" I asked Jack.

"Better. Now it only hurts when I breathe," he said wryly.

"I think they broke every rib he has," Abigail said.

"Not all of them," Ian said.

"I forgot we had a human X-ray," Jack said. "So how many are broken?"

"Eleven."

"How many ribs does he have?" Abigail asked.

"The human body has twenty-four ribs," Ostin said. "Though ten of them are called false ribs since they aren't connected to the sternum."

"Another lesson," Abigail sighed.

"How are you feeling?" Jack asked me.

"Better. I think Nichelle did a good job with those stitches."

Nichelle smiled. "Anytime."

"I hope not," I replied. I took a waffle from a stack on the table, then sat down next to Nichelle. "Where're Zeus and Tessa?"

"They're on the roof," Jack said.

"What are they doing on the roof?"

"They're on lookout."

"When did we start doing that?"

"This morning."

"There's syrup," Taylor said. "At least a version of it. It's made from boiled sugar." She pointed to a saucepan on the table. "It might be cold."

"I can take care of that," McKenna said. She put her hand above the pan and it heated up. Within seconds the syrup started to boil. She handed me the pan.

"Thank you," I said. I poured a little on top. It didn't taste like maple syrup, but it wasn't bad.

"Does the waffle taste correct?" Ben asked. "I learned the recipe from the Internet."

"They taste great," I said. "Where did you get a waffle iron?"

"From the same place I got my weapons," he replied.

"I'm glad they're thinking of us," I said. I ate for a few minutes, then asked Ben, "What's on the agenda today?"

He looked at me blankly.

"What are we doing today?"

"We wait inside," he said. "Everyone is looking for us. The Elgen, the Taiwan army, and the police. There has been much on the television about the attack. They say the terrorists tried to shut down the Elgen plant but the Taiwan army stopped them."

"Yeah, right," Ostin said. "We walked through the middle of their camp, and they didn't even see us."

"Public relations," Ben said.

I looked at Taylor. "I guess that means no night markets."

"I'm heartbroken," Taylor replied. She put an omelet on her plate, then came over and sat next to me.

"No going outside at all," Ben said. "They will be looking for Americans. And you look like Americans." He looked at Abigail. "Especially you. Your hair is *very* light."

Jack ran his fingers through it. "And *very* pretty."

"Thank you," Abigail said.

I noticed Nichelle staring at Jack. She saw me looking at her and turned away.

Ben said, "We need to go over our plans."

"We need Zeus and Tessa," I said.

"I'll get them," Ian said.

We cleared off the table and Ben laid out a map he'd drawn of the Taiwanese coastline near the Starxource plant.

"We're back," Ian said, walking toward us with Zeus and Tessa.

"What's up?" Zeus asked.

"We're going through our rescue plan," I said.

We all gathered around the table. Ben leaned over his map. "This is the plant," he said, touching a pen to the paper. "The *Volta* will likely anchor here." He drew a small rectangle to represent the boat. "That means the Elgen will transport YuLong maybe about here." He ran the pen in a straight line between the plant's dock and the *Volta*. "If the sea is calm, to go that distance will take only two or three minutes. If we wait until they leave the dock, we can catch their boat halfway." He drew an X between the *Volta* and the shore. "That means we need to be about ninety seconds away from the middle point. I think we should wait with our boat here." He touched a spot on the shore opposite the plant.

"That's by the coast guard base," Ostin said.

"Yes," Ben replied. "Very close."

"That won't work. We're going to be in one of their boats. They'll see us," Ostin said.

"He's right," I said. "We'll have to capture the coast guard boat before the *Volta* docks, but we don't know how long the Elgen will wait to transport Jade Dragon. If the Elgen delay, the coast guard will know something is wrong and send their boats out looking for us."

Ostin looked at the map. He ran his finger in a circle around the *Volta*. "Assuming the coast guard boat can do at least forty knots, to intercept in ninety seconds, we could be anywhere in this radius."

"Yes," Ben said.

"Then how about here?" He drew an X in the ocean behind the *Volta*.

"Hide behind the *Volta*?" Zeus said.

"Why not? Neither the Elgen nor the coast guard will be able to see us."

"But the *Volta* will."

"The *Volta* won't think anything of it. They'll be taking orders from the Elgen inside the plant."

I looked at the map. "That would allow us to stay out longer." I turned to Ostin. "But if they can't see us, how will we see them?"

"Ian could see them," Abigail said.

"I should be closer," Ian said. "I get some electrical interference from the plant. I could miss something."

"What if some of us hike up to where we were the last time Ben took us?" Ostin said. "When the Elgen are ready to move, we'll radio the boat. Then they'll speed in and intercept the transport halfway between the shore and the *Volta*, where it's most vulnerable."

"That could work," Jack said.

"Who will be on the boat?" Taylor asked. "And who will be on land?"

I thought about it a moment, then said, "Taylor, Ben, Zeus, Tessa, Nichelle, and Jack should be on the boat."

Zeus dropped his head. "You know I hate boats."

"I know, but we'll need your firepower. With Tessa near you, you'll be able to take out a few Elgen boats if things go south."

"I'll go," he said, "but I don't have to like it."

"Great, because you'll be in charge."

"You won't be with us?" Taylor said.

"No. They'll need me on land. I'll take Ian, McKenna, and Ostin up the coast. Ian will be able to tell us when they're ready to transport. If we encounter Elgen, McKenna and I can protect the group."

"Shouldn't I be with you?" Nichelle asked. "In case they send the Glows?"

"No," I said. "It's more likely they'll put the Glows on the transport with Jade Dragon."

"If Quentin is there he could shut down our coast guard boat before it can escape," Ostin said. "We'll be sitting ducks."

I looked at Nichelle. "You'll have to shut the Glows down first."

"I can do that," she said.

"We'll need radios," I said to Ben.

"I can get those."

I looked around the table. "What do you think?"

"What about me?" Abigail asked.

"You want in?"

She looked insulted. "What, you think I'm worthless?"

"No, your powers just aren't . . ." I searched for the right word. "*Aggressive.*"

"Neither are Ostin's," she said.

"I'm going to pretend you didn't say that," Ostin said.

"At least I *have* powers," she mumbled.

"You come with us," Jack said.

I continued, "After we stop the transport boat, Taylor, with Tessa's help, reboots everyone while Jack and Zeus go on board, grab Jade Dragon, and bring her back to our boat."

"What if they're wearing mindwave helmets?" Taylor asked.

"Then it will be easier for me to shock them," Zeus said. "Those helmets of theirs make great conductors."

I looked at Ben. "Where do we go after we have her?"

"There is a small dock here," Ben said, pointing to a spot on the map. "It is south, around the rocks from the coast guard. We can dock there."

"Okay," I said. "As soon as you have Jade Dragon, we'll leave our point here, drive down and pick you up, then drive back to the safe house."

"Who's going to drive?" Taylor asked. The question stung a little. Usually it would have been Wade.

"I'll drive," McKenna said. "I learned at the academy." Then she added, "Before purgatory."

"McKenna drives," I said. I looked around the table. "Are we good?"

Most everyone was nodding.

"That's a plan," Ostin said.

"Yeah," I said. "Let's just hope it works."

* * *

A few minutes after our meeting, Ian and I took Ben aside.

"We need to tell you something," I said. "In private."

Ben's expression fell, mirroring ours. "We can go downstairs."

After we were alone in the garage I shut the stairwell door behind us, then said, "We need to warn the voice that the Elgen might know where the ranch is."

He looked back and forth between us. "How would they know?"

"Because I told them," I said.

Ben looked stunned. "Why did you tell them?"

I felt like a fool. "After they captured us . . ." I shook my head. "I thought Hatch was my father. He asked where my mother was. And I told him."

Ben looked even more distraught. "I don't understand. Why did you think Hatch was your father?"

Ian stepped in to defend me. "It's not Michael's fault," he said. "Tara can do things to your brain. She made Hatch look like Michael's father. Michael didn't know."

Ben nodded slowly. "What did you tell him?"

"I told him that the ranch was three hours away from Los Angeles."

"That is all?"

"And I told him the weather."

He thought for a moment, then said, "I will tell the voice."

I took a deep breath, exhaling slowly. "I'm sorry. I'm really worried. I don't know what else to do."

Ben looked into my eyes then said, "There is a Chinese saying. If a problem has a solution, to worry is no use, for in the end it will be solved. If a problem has no solution, there is no reason to worry, because it cannot be solved." He put his hand on my shoulder. "We do not have time to worry. For now we have other things to use our minds for. We need to rescue Jade Dragon."

40

The Equation

That evening, as Taylor and I were finishing our shift on lookout, I told her what I'd told Ben. She tried to comfort me.

"It will be okay," she said. "America's a big place. That's not enough information to find them. Three hours away could be like Kansas. Or Nebraska." She put her arms around me and held me.

After we parted she smiled and said, "Besides, remember what your mother says. Things have a way of working out."

"You're right," I said.

After a minute she said, "There's something really important I need to tell you, too."

"What?" I asked.

"I think I can explain it better with Ostin around."

"All right," I said. "Let's go find him."

We climbed down from the roof and found Ostin sitting next

to an oscillating fan in the men's bunk room. He was translating a
Chinese magazine into English.

"Hey," I said. "We need to talk."

He looked up, his eyes wide. "What did I do?"

"You're not in trouble," I said.

"We'll need some paper and something to write with," Taylor said.

Ostin held up his pen and pad of paper. "Already got it."

Taylor walked over and locked the door, then sat down on the bed
across from Ostin. "I need to write something."

Ostin gave her his paper and pen. Taylor flipped through the pad
to a clean page and began writing. When she was finished she handed
it to Ostin.

$$s(t;t_y) = k\frac{Q}{r^2}\hat{r} \int_{R^2} m(x,y)\,e^{-2\pi i \eta \left(\frac{G_x xt + \eta G_y yt_y}{2\pi} \right)} dydx$$

Ostin looked at it for a moment, then said, "Where did you get this?"

"Jade."

"Can I have my pen back?" Ostin asked. Taylor handed it to him
and he began scratching numbers on the paper. After a moment he
said, "This is incredible." He looked at Taylor. "Do you understand
this?"

"It sounds weird since I barely made it through algebra, but I sort
of do." She looked at me. "I mean, I don't think I could explain it to
anyone, but it's, like, part of me."

Ostin went back to filling the paper with symbols, numbers, and
letters. Every now and then he'd mumble "Whoa," or "Brilliant."

"You understand what that means?" I asked Ostin.

"Most of it. Without understanding the dynamics of the MEI
machine, I can't fully understand the formula. But it's the algorithm
of the MEI waves. I would have to compare it with the Elgen's information to see the variance, but I guarantee it's different from what
the Elgen have been operating from."

"Is this what the Elgen are looking for?" I asked.

Ostin looked at me gravely. "I think so."

For a moment we were all silent as the reality of what we had sunk in. Like $E = mc^2$, this formula could change the world. Or destroy it.

"Burn that paper," I said to Ostin. "Now."

"All right," he said. He walked out to the kitchen.

"Why would she give it to me?" Taylor asked.

"Because she trusts you."

Taylor's brow fell. "But she didn't say it. She only thought it to me. That means she knew I could read her mind."

"It also means that she must know it's what the Elgen want from her," I said. I took a deep breath. "We've got to get her out of there."

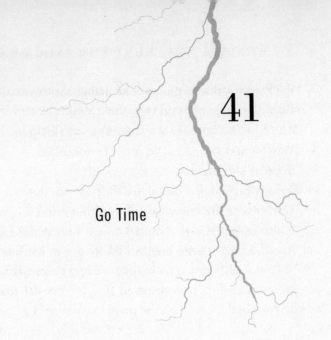

41

Go Time

The next two days passed uneventfully. We reviewed our rescue plan over and over, anticipating changes and creating alternate escape routes in case something went wrong. Ben was the only one who left the warehouse, and we all took turns watching the streets. We noticed a lot of police and military vehicles in the area.

Ben rented a boat, which he left at the small dock he had told us about. By the afternoon of our third day everything was ready. All we were waiting for was the *Volta* to arrive.

That night, a few hours after we'd gone to bed, Ben flipped on the lights in our bunk room. "It is time."

"Time to *sleep*," Ostin said groggily.

"Time to go," Ben said. "The voice called. The *Volta* is just twenty-five kilometers from the plant."

"Let's go," I said, pulling on my clothes.

Within five minutes we were all gathered downstairs in the garage. In spite of the hour everyone was wide awake. I guess fear will do that.

As we were about to get into the car Ostin said, "There's one thing we haven't talked about."

"What's that?" I asked.

"If we fail, do we sink the boat?"

"You mean with Jade on it?" Taylor asked.

"If the Elgen get that information, millions of people will die."

We all knew the answer. I looked at Taylor. "Let's not fail."

We took a different vehicle than we had before. It was a dark blue windowless van. Ben had observed that the coastal roads were being heavily patrolled, so he took the main roads through Kaohsiung before heading north to our starting point. I sat in the back of the van with Taylor. I hated that we would be separated during the rescue.

As we drove through the dark, Taylor knit her fingers with mine. "Remember our prom?" she said softly.

I smiled sadly. "Yes."

"I'd rather be there," she said.

Less than a half hour later Ben pulled off the highway and drove down smaller and smaller roads that eventually led us to a deserted, tree-lined dock. Ben parked along the road. It was a beautiful night with a full moon reflecting off the calm black sea. There was a light haze over the water, and from the moon's glow we could see the silhouette of an eighteen-foot powerboat floating alone at the dock. We all got out of the van.

"I can see the *Volta*," Ian said. "She hasn't anchored yet."

"Can you see any activity at the Starxource plant?"

"Not yet."

Ben handed me a handheld radio. "We are on channel seventeen."

"Let's test them," I said. We turned the radios on. "Can you hear me?"

Ben nodded. "Yes. Can you hear me?"

"Yes," I replied, even though I could have heard him without the radio. I put the radio in my pocket, then looked around. "We're ready." I took a deep breath. "We'd better get going."

Taylor took my hand. I must have looked as afraid as I felt because she said, "Don't worry, I'll be back. With Jade."

"Be careful," I said.

She smiled and kissed me. "Yeah, right."

Ben handed McKenna the keys to the van. "You know where to go?"

"You programmed it into the GPS, right?"

"Yes."

"Then I know."

Taylor and I hugged one last time, and then I turned to everyone else. "Good luck. *De oppresso liber.*"

"*Semper fi,*" Jack returned.

Zeus walked up to me. "Any last instructions?"

"Get the girl. Bring everyone back safe."

"I'll do it," he said. "Anything else?"

I smiled. "Yeah. Stay out of the water." We man-hugged. "See you soon."

I glanced over at Jack and he nodded at me. Then the group followed Ben to the boat. Near the dock, Taylor looked back once more. She blew me a kiss, then turned and climbed into the boat. A sick feeling came over me. Something told me I'd never see her again.

42

Not As Planned

As the boat pulled away from the dock, Ostin, McKenna, Ian, and I got back into the van. McKenna started the car while Ostin fiddled with the GPS. Ian and I sat in the seat behind them.

"Everyone ready?" McKenna asked.

"Almost," I said. I waited until the boat had vanished in the haze, then shut the door. "Let's go."

It took us only nine minutes to reach our destination. As McKenna parked along the vacant street, I checked my watch. (I had fixed the time.) It was a little after three in the morning. We waited in the car with the lights off for another twenty minutes; then my radio crackled.

"Can you hear me?" Ben asked.

"Yes. Can you hear me?"

"Yes. We are signaling the coast guard now."

I turned to Ian. "Any activity at the plant?"

"Some," he said. "There are trucks and soldiers gathering near the side exit." He shook his head. "Man, we made a mess of that place. It looks like it was hit by a hurricane."

"Hurricane Electroclan," McKenna said softly.

"Can you see a transport boat?" I asked.

"No. The only boat I can see is one of the fishing boats."

"Let's go," I said.

"Wait," Ostin said. He opened the glove compartment and brought out a pair of binoculars. "We'll need these."

Ian looked around again to make sure no one was watching, then we all climbed out of the van into the dark street. We followed the same path that we had before, creeping along the tree-lined shore. We sat down under the trees, looking out over the moonlit harbor. "There she is," Ian said. "You might be able to see her; she's out there." He pointed nearly directly west out to sea. Through the fog I could see the *Volta*'s faint silhouette. The waves had suddenly kicked up and she was pitching a little.

"That's not good," Ian said.

"What?"

"It looks like they've rearmed her. She's got serious firepower."

Ostin looked out through his binoculars. "They've installed M134 Miniguns. Those bad boys can fire four thousand rounds per minute."

"How far can they shoot?" I asked.

"As far as they want," he said. "They're usually mounted to helicopters."

I thought of Taylor and my stomach churned. "Let's just hope they think we're the coast guard."

"Speaking of which," Ian said, "there goes the coast guard boat."

A moment later a twenty-four-foot patroller sped out of the coast guard pier.

"Can you see our boat?" I asked.

"No," Ostin said.

"They're about four miles out," Ian said.

I was on edge. "Just tell me what you see."

About ten minutes later Ian said, "The coast guard is there."

We sat quietly. There was a flash of light.

"What was that?"

"Something must have gone wrong. Zeus fired on them."

My jaw was ticking. "Now what?" I asked.

"They're bringing their boat alongside the coast guard's." Another few minutes passed before Ian said, "They've got the coast guard's boat. They're driving away."

Our radio crackled. "This is Ben. We have the boat."

"Did everything go okay?"

"Mostly," he said. "What is our status?"

"The Elgen are preparing to transport. We'll tell you when they leave the plant."

"Okay," Ben said. "Good-bye."

We sat quietly in the dark for another half hour, watching the plant. "This is taking forever," Ostin said from behind his binoculars. "It's like watching grass grow."

"What's going on?" I asked.

"I'm not sure. But they now have three different trucks." He looked at me. "It's one girl. Why do they need three trucks?"

Suddenly we heard the sound of boat motors coming toward us. "What's that?" I asked.

Ian said, "Speedboats." He paused. "With really big guns."

"How many?"

"Three."

I looked at him. "Three boats? Why would they have three?"

"They're running three boats so we don't know which boat she's on," Ostin said. "That's why they also have three trucks."

We moved farther back into the darkness of the trees as the boats sped by within fifty yards of the shore. It only took them a few minutes to reach the Starxource plant. They pulled back on their throttles and idled about a hundred yards from the dock.

"Where's our boat?" I asked.

"It's about two miles out," Ian said. "Behind the *Volta*."

"How are we going to stop all three boats?" McKenna asked.

"We can't," I said. "We better let them know what's going on." I lifted my radio. "Ben, this is Michael."

"I am here."

"We've got a problem. They have three boats."

"Three?"

"Yes. And they're speedboats. You're going to have to come closer than we planned."

"Okay," he said.

"No one's moving," Ostin said. "Makes you wonder what they're waiting for."

There was suddenly a staccato series of light flashes coming from the *Volta*.

"Interesting," Ostin said. "They must be afraid that we'll intercept their radio signals so they're using light signals."

"Anyone can see those," I said.

"I know. But no one knows Morse code anymore."

"Do you?" I asked.

"Of course," he said. "I knew Morse code by the time I was five."

He watched for a moment, then said, "Someone read what I spell out . . . a-d-y-f-o-r-r-e-c-e-p-t-i-o-n-o-f-p-a-c-k-a-g-e."

"Ady, for reception of package," McKenna said.

"*Ready* for reception of package," I said, looking at Ostin. "They must mean Jade Dragon."

The three boats suddenly powered to the Elgen dock. They tied up on the near side of the fishing boat.

"This isn't going to be as easy as we thought it would be," Ostin said.

"Who thought this was going to be easy?" I said.

"How are we going to stop all three boats?" McKenna repeated.

"We don't have to," Ostin said. "There's only one girl. Ian can tell us which one she's on."

"The trucks are moving," Ian said.

I looked at Ian. "Which truck is she in?"

He looked for a moment, then said, "The first one. Wait." He turned to me. "I don't believe it."

"What?"

"There's one on every truck."

I looked at him quizzically. "One what?"

"Girl. I don't know which one she is."

"They knew you would be watching," I said. "They outsmarted us."

The radio crackled. "Hey, Michael, it's Zeus. Ben said there are three boats. Is that right?"

"Yes."

"Which one is Jade Dragon on?"

"We don't know," I said.

"They're loading the girls onto the speedboats," Ian said.

"There's a girl on each of the boats. They have three girls," I said.

"Three girls?"

"It's a decoy."

"What do we do?" Zeus asked.

"Give me a second," I said.

"That's about all we have," Ian said. "They're untying."

Taylor came on. "Should we take a chance on one of them? A one-out-of-three chance is better than nothing."

"It's too dangerous. The other speedboats are armed," I said. "Between them and the *Volta* they'll blow you out of the water."

Zeus came back on. "Michael, we keep getting radio calls from the coast guard. We can't hold out much longer. Do we go or abort?"

"Give me a second," I said again. I looked back at Ostin, who was silently looking through his binoculars at the dock. "Dude, what are you looking at?"

"That fishing boat," he said calmly.

"We're a little busy for that right now. Come on, we need your help."

Ostin was unaffected by my panic. "He's been there too long." He rubbed his chin. "And he's not unloading fish." Ostin looked over at me. "I know which speedboat she's on."

"Which one?" I asked.

"None of them," he said. "It's a shell game. The Lung Li are about deception. The three boats are the shells; the fishing boat is the magician's hand. As soon as the other boats leave, they'll load Jade Dragon onto the fishing boat and transport her to the *Volta*."

"A shell game?"

"Just like in the night market."

"But the speedboats are faster and armed."

"Exactly. They're there as decoys. If we don't fall for it, they'll return and protect the fishing boat."

The first of the three speedboats left the dock.

"I hope you're right," I said. "Because this will be over soon."

43

Shell Game

"Look," Ostin said. "The fishing boat is unmooring."

"Can you see anyone on board the fishing boat?" I asked Ian.

"I see five guards." He looked at me and smiled. "And three Glows."

"I told you," Ostin said.

"We've got them," I said. "Hatch wouldn't send his Glows out fishing at three in the morning."

I lifted the radio. "This is Michael, can you hear me?"

"This is Zeus."

"Jade Dragon isn't on any of the speedboats. She's on the fishing boat."

"Are you sure?"

"Yes. And there are Glows on board. Tell Nichelle to be ready. And be careful, the speedboats are armed. As soon as they know you're not the coast guard, they'll attack."

"Got it."

"There she goes," Ian said. "The fishing boat is pushing out."

"On our way," Zeus said.

"I have an idea," Ostin said. "I'm going to send the *Volta* a message."

"How?"

"With McKenna," he said. He turned to her. "I need you to flash your hand. If I say 'dash,' hold the light for about one second; when I say 'dot,' just flash quickly. Ready?"

McKenna nodded. "Yes."

"First letter. Dot, dot, dash."

"Just one letter?" I asked.

"*U* is an abbreviation for danger," Ostin said, his gaze fixed on the boat. There was a sudden flash back. "They got the message. Okay, here we go." Ostin began rattling off a series of dots and dashes staggered with occasional pauses.

After he finished I asked, "What did you say?"

"I said they're under attack and to defend themselves against the three boats."

Suddenly the sound of the *Volta*'s machine guns filled the air. The first speedboat burst into flames. People began jumping overboard.

"Freaking genius," I said.

"They've hit the second speedboat," Ian said.

"I'm totally going to kiss you on the lips when this is over," McKenna said to Ostin.

Ostin pumped his fist.

"And there goes the third," Ian said.

"And there we are," Ostin said, looking through his binoculars.

Our coast guard boat appeared through the haze about a hundred yards north of the *Volta*, headed straight for the fishing boat.

We heard the sound of Ben speaking over the boat's PA system, and the fishing boat slowed as the coast guard boat pulled up to its side. There were at least a half dozen flashes of electricity.

"Zeus just took out the guards," Ian said. Then a large smile crossed his face. "Jack has Jade Dragon. They're back on board."

The nose of the coast guard boat rose as it sped north up the coast

"They're going in the wrong direction," McKenna said.

Ostin lowered his binoculars. "They're putting distance between them and the *Volta*'s guns. They'll head out to sea, then turn south and head to our dock."

"Let's go get them," I said.

McKenna drove the van as close to the dock as she could, climbing the curb onto a dirt landing less than thirty yards from the water.

"Keep it running," I said. We opened all the doors. "Where are they?"

"They're coming," Ian said.

It was only a few more minutes before the rest of us saw the boat powering full speed into shore.

"He's got to slow down," McKenna said.

"I don't think he's going to use the dock," Ostin said.

Ben slowed just slightly before grounding the boat completely up on the shore. Everyone jumped off the port side of the boat and sprinted toward us. Jack was carrying a little Chinese girl. We had rescued Jade Dragon.

44

Escape

"**Y**ou drive!" McKenna shouted to Ben as he reached the van.

Everyone piled in, more panicked than celebratory. We had no idea how close the Elgen were, but knowing them, they weren't far.

I slid the side door shut, then jumped into the front passenger seat. "Go, go, go!"

Ben hit the gas and the van fishtailed a little on the dirt and bounced over the curb, sending up a spray of sparks as he scraped the front of the van on the asphalt. The streets were still vacant, and Ben sped at least eighty miles an hour toward the freeway. The freeway had traffic, and only when we had merged in with the other cars did I breathe out a sigh of relief.

"See anyone following us?" I asked Ian.

"No."

I looked at Taylor, who held Jade Dragon on her lap. It was hard to believe that such a little girl could generate so much commotion.

"Hi," I said to her. She didn't look at me.

"She thinks you're nice," Taylor said.

"How do you know that?"

Taylor cocked her head.

"Sorry," I said. I looked at Ben. "What are we going to do about those coast guard sailors still in our boat?"

"Do not worry," he said. "They will find them."

"Where are we going?"

"Back to the safe house."

No one spoke for a moment, then Zeus said, "Does anyone know why the *Volta* blew up her own boats?"

45

Life and Death

As we drove farther from the plant, the fear-borne adrenaline that had pumped through our bodies dissipated, replaced by an equally potent measure of exhaustion. Ostin even gave the phenomenon a name before falling asleep: *post-mission fatigue.*

As we entered Kaohsiung only Ben, Jack, Taylor, and I were still awake, and Ben looked as if he might doze off at the wheel. Taylor's eyes were heavy but fixed on the child she cradled in her arms.

"What's the plan now?" I asked Ben.

Ben unsuccessfully attempted to avert a yawn. "This afternoon I will drive Jade Dragon to the Taitung airport."

"That soon?" Taylor said.

"The more soon the better," he said. "The plane will be waiting. I will go after I sleep. I am too tired to drive now."

"I can help drive," Jack said.

"No," Ben said. "Only me and Jade Dragon will go. The police and army and Elgen spies will be looking for Americans. There may be road stops."

"Road*blocks*," I said, immediately scolding myself for correcting his English. "Are they flying her back to China?"

"No, they fly to America."

"What about her parents?" Taylor asked.

"The Lung Li kill her parents."

Taylor gasped. I figured that if Taylor didn't know they had been killed, Jade Dragon must not have known either. My stomach knotted as I glanced at Taylor, then back at Ben. "Where will she go? The ranch?"

"No," Ben said. "Someplace secret where they will find a family for her."

Taylor looked down at the sleeping child in her arms. "You poor sweet thing," she said softly. She looked up. "My parents would take her. I was adopted."

"Your home would not be safe," Ben said.

"I know." Taylor gently brushed her finger over Jade Dragon's cheek. I noticed that her eyes were welling up with tears. "I wish I could keep you, sweetheart."

We arrived at the warehouse as the sun peeked out over the horizon, illuminating the grounds in a pink-golden hue. I unlocked the gate and Ben pulled in past the fence, then into the warehouse. Once inside, we woke everyone.

"Do we need a lookout?" I asked, wondering if it was even possible.

"I think we are all too tired," Ben said. "I will set the alarms. We all should sleep now. We will soon have more to do."

As we climbed out of the van, Ben walked over to the garage door and manually slid a bolt through its track, then pushed some buttons on a metal control pad on the wall.

Following Taylor, I carried Jade Dragon up to the women's sleeping quarters.

"Lay her next to me," Taylor said, pushing two cots together. I laid Jade Dragon down on the bed, then Taylor lay down next to her. She gently kissed her forehead, then looked up at me and whispered, "Isn't she beautiful?"

I nodded. I was amazed at the bond the two of them had created in such a short time. I didn't know exactly what had happened between them, but whatever it was, it was probably too profound for someone who had never entered someone else's mind to understand—especially a mind as unique as Jade Dragon's. After a few minutes I said, "I'm going to get some sleep. Do you need anything?"

"No," she said. "Thank you."

"Sleep well."

As I turned to go she said, "Michael." I turned back around. Taylor was smiling. "We got her. Just like you said we would."

I smiled back. "Yeah, we did."

After leaving the room, I stopped in the kitchen for a cup of water, then went to the men's sleeping quarters. The room was dark with the lights out and the blinds drawn. The only illumination was the faint glow of Ian's and Zeus's skin. As far as I could tell everyone was already asleep except for Jack, who was sitting cross-legged on the floor next to his cot, half-concealed in shadow. His chin was up as if he was meditating. I lay down on the cot next to him.

Without looking at me he said, "What a rush."

"That's for sure."

He was quiet for a moment, then, still looking forward, said softly, "Wade would have liked Taiwan." One corner of his mouth rose in an amused half smile. "He would have wanted to learn how they make those dumplings we had." He looked up at me. "Did you know that he wanted to be a chef?"

"No."

"He was always afraid someone might find out. Sometimes I'd catch him watching those cooking shows on the Food Network. I used to make fun of him." His smile fell. "I wish I hadn't."

"He knew you were just teasing him."

"I know." Jack looked down for a moment, then back at me. "Do you believe that some part of us lives after we die?"

"You mean like a soul?"

He nodded. "Yeah, something like that."

"I think so. Why?"

"Just after the guards beat me up, I was lying there on the floor, bleeding and in pain, when I felt like someone touched me. I looked up and for just a split second, I thought I saw Wade." He rubbed his hand over his face. "I dunno. Maybe I was just delirious. They'd just hit me in the head a dozen times."

"I don't know," I said. "I've heard of things like that."

"Do you ever feel your dad near?"

My cheek began ticking. "No. Never."

"Sorry," he said. He was quiet for a moment, then said, "You should sleep."

"You too," I said.

"I will in a second. I just need to unwind a little."

I lay back on my bed. What Jack had said echoed in my mind. *Why haven't I ever felt my father like that?*

46

Saying Good-bye

I woke to the bleating of an alarm. I jumped out of bed, my heart pounding fiercely, before realizing that it was just the alarm clock that Ben had set.

"Sorry," Ben said as he shut it off.

"Is it time?" I asked.

"Yes."

"I'll go with you," I said.

"No, I must go alone."

"I just meant to get her."

He slightly bowed. "*Dwei buchi.* Sorry."

I followed him over to the women's quarters. We quietly opened the door, letting a sliver of light into the darkened room. Everyone was asleep except for Jade Dragon, who was sitting facing the door, her legs hanging over the bed, not touching the floor. She looked as if she was expecting us.

Ben mouthed something to her in Chinese. She nodded, glanced at me, then reached over and touched Taylor. Taylor rolled over but didn't wake.

I sat down on the side of Taylor's cot and gently shook her. She woke from a dead sleep. "What?"

"It's me," I said.

She looked at me through half-closed eyes. "Michael . . ."

"It's time for Jade Dragon to leave," I said.

It took only a few seconds for my words to sink in. "Oh," she said, sitting up. She looked over at Jade Dragon as tears welled up in her eyes. Jade Dragon took her hand. Without explanation, Taylor suddenly closed her eyes as if in a trance.

After a minute I said, "Taylor . . ."

"Shhh," she said.

For several minutes the two of them sat perfectly still. Then Taylor's eyes opened. "She understands. She knows she's going away without her parents." She looked at me. "She can go now."

Taylor held Jade Dragon's hand as the four of us walked downstairs to the van. Ben unbolted the garage door while I opened the van door and Taylor seat-belted Jade Dragon in behind the driver's seat.

"Keep her safe," Taylor said to Ben.

"I will," Ben said.

"When will you be back?" I asked.

"Maybe tonight. After she is gone I will talk to the voice. If I am too late I will stay in Taitung with friends and come back early tomorrow."

"When will *we* fly back?"

"I will ask the voice. It will take a few days for the plane to return. Maybe in three days. Until then no one must go out." He looked at me uneasily and I sensed that he was still shell-shocked from our last careless venture out. "It is very, very dangerous. *Fei chang, fei chang* dangerous. No one can go out for any reason."

"I promise," I said. "No one will leave the building."

He turned the ignition and the van started. "I will be back soon."

Taylor leaned forward and kissed Jade Dragon on the cheek. "*Dzai jyan,*" she said.

A tear fell down Jade Dragon's cheek. Taylor wiped her own eyes, then shut the van door as the garage door opened. I gave Ben a half wave, then he looked over his shoulder and backed the van out of the garage. The door shut behind him.

"I wish we were going with them," Taylor said.

"I know, but Ben's right. It's safer for him to go alone." I took Taylor's hand. "Are you still tired?"

"Yes. But I don't want to go back to bed or I won't sleep tonight."

"Want to go up to the roof?"

She smiled. "Sure."

I took her hand and we climbed the stairway three stories to the top of the warehouse. The stairwell's last door let out onto a flat tar-and-gravel roof with occasional vents that rose like tin mushrooms. Near the western edge of the roof, facing the harbor, was a telescope, several plastic chairs, and some faded, green-and-white-striped vinyl cushions from an outdoor sofa. It was a beautiful, clear day with only a few cotton-puff clouds, and we could see the sun's glimmering light on a sea stretching out past the Earth's gradual curve. After we settled down on the cushions Taylor said, "So now what?"

"Back to the ranch," I said.

"And after that?"

I looked up to the blue sky, then said, "We retire."

I could feel Taylor's eyes on me. "Are you serious?"

"I've been thinking a lot lately. We've shut down the academy and two power plants, and sank the *Ampere*. We rescued Jade Dragon. I think we've done our share." When she didn't say anything I looked over at her. She looked stunned.

"You want to disband the Electroclan?" she said.

"Break up the team? No. Just retire our jerseys."

Taylor smiled. "Did you really just use a sports metaphor?"

"I'm full of surprises."

"Especially this one," she said. "Retiring the Electroclan."

"I'm not saying good-bye to everyone. I just think it's time we got on with our lives."

"You know we can't go back to Idaho. The Elgen will just hunt us down."

"I know. It will have to be one of those witness protection things."

"You mean where they change our identities and move us to a different city?"

"Exactly."

"What would we do?"

"Finish school. Go to college. Be normal and boring."

Taylor sighed. "Boring sounds nice. You know, I'd like to live on a ranch. Someplace rustic. Maybe even without electricity."

"No electricity," I said. "That counts me out."

She smiled. "You're the one exception." She looked out over the horizon, her gaze following a squadron of pelicans. "I've always wondered what I would do for a living."

"Think about it," I said. "With your powers, you could be the greatest negotiator the world has ever known. You could be, like, Secretary of State."

"Not to mention the greatest mother," she said. "My kids would never lie to me."

"I'm sure they'd still try," I said. "They just wouldn't get away with it." I breathed deeply. "I'm ready for our future."

For a moment Taylor looked content; then her smile fell. "What about the Elgen?"

"It's going to be a long war," I said. "Maybe someday we'll return to it."

She looked at me quietly, then said, "Michael, why do you really want to retire?"

I didn't answer for a moment, then said, "How do you read my thoughts without even touching me?"

"That's just being a girl."

I looked down for a moment. "This morning when I left you on that boat I didn't think I would see you again." My eyes welled up. "I can't go through that again."

She took my hand. "You would leave the cause for me?"

I looked at her, then said, "You are my cause."

47

News from Home

We stayed on the roof for several hours, though at least an hour of it was spent sleeping. When we finally went downstairs everyone was in the kitchen. Jack and Zeus were playing knuckles, and Nichelle was at the stove cooking something in a wok.

"It smells good," Taylor said. "What is it?"

"Fried rice," Nichelle said. "The chef at the academy taught me how to make fried rice when I was eight. It's the only thing I can cook besides toast." She grimaced. "And tacos."

"For the record, I was sous chef," Abigail said.

"Where have you been?" Ostin asked me.

"On the roof," I said.

"I told you," McKenna said.

Taylor and I both sat down at the table.

"As long as we're all here," I said, "I want to thank everyone. Zeus, you did an amazing job leading the boat attack. You got the job done. And we didn't even celebrate you two shutting down a Starxource plant by yourselves."

Zeus smiled. "Thanks, but it was a team thing."

"And, Ostin," I said, "once again that huge brain of yours saved our bacon."

"Bacon is so good," Ostin said.

"Figuring out the Lung Li's shell-game trick was brilliant," Ian said.

"And signaling the *Volta* to blow up her own boats was genius," McKenna added. She leaned forward and kissed him on the cheek. "But then, you are a genius."

Ostin turned bright red. "*Nali*," he said.

"No idea what that means," I said. "But thanks again."

Before Ostin could explain, Taylor said, "I have something to say." She looked at me. "Michael will never say 'I told you so,' so I'm going to say it for him. On the way here everyone thought he was crazy when he told us we were picking up Nichelle. But he was right." Taylor looked at Nichelle. "I trusted Michael when he said that we had to work with you, but I never thought I would be able to forgive you for what you did to me. But you were the only one who knew I'd been kidnapped and you risked your life to save me. Thank you."

Nichelle was suddenly emotional. When she could speak she said, "You're welcome."

"It's a good thing you were with us on the boat," Tessa said. "The Glows would have had us. Quentin would have shut down our boat so we couldn't get away, and Torstyn would have melted our brains."

"I know I was hard on you," Ian said. "But I'm glad you came."

Nichelle stopped stirring the rice. "What was I going to do?" she said. "It was this or the taco stand."

"So once you get paid, where do you want to go?" I asked.

"I haven't given it much thought," she said. "I don't really have any place." She suddenly looked nervous. "I was wondering if maybe I could hang out with you guys. Join the Electroclan."

No one spoke for a moment; then Jack said, "We're down a member. I say we take a vote."

Taylor looked at me. In spite of what we'd just talked about on the roof, it was no time to discuss retirement. "You're the president," she said.

"All right," I said. "All in favor of making Nichelle—"

"*Inducting*," Ostin interjected. "All in favor of *inducting* Nichelle . . ."

"Great, now you're correcting *my* English," I said. "All in favor of *inducting* Nichelle as the newest member of the Electroclan, raise your hand."

The vote was unanimous. Nichelle smiled broadly. "Thank you for giving me the chance to be someone else."

Nichelle's fried rice was delicious. After dinner, everyone went back to bed except for me. I waited up past midnight for Ben's return, eventually falling asleep in my clothes. I woke the next morning after the sun had risen and went out to the kitchen. Ostin and McKenna were making pancakes.

"Is Ben back?" I asked.

"Not yet," McKenna said. "He probably got stopped by traffic."

Or Elgen, I thought.

The day passed excruciatingly slowly. Ben had said he'd be back early, so by three in the afternoon I thought I would lose my mind. We were sitting around the kitchen table playing cards when I suddenly lost it. "Where is he? He was supposed to be back by now."

For a moment everyone was quiet; then Taylor said what we all feared. "You don't think he was captured, do you?"

"He's smart," Abigail said. "They won't capture him."

"If he was, we have no way of knowing," Ian said.

"What if he was?" Tessa asked.

"They'll torture him to find out where we are," Zeus answered.

"They could already be on their way," I said. I looked around the room. "This isn't good. If he's not back in two hours, we prepare to leave. If he's not here by sundown, we leave."

"What do we need?" Jack asked.

"There are two cars," I said. "We'll fill them with rations and weapons. Ostin, you figure out a route."

"To an airport or harbor?"

"Whatever gets us out of Taiwan," I said. "You figure out the details."

"Zeus and I will get the weapons," Jack said.

"Hold it," Ian said, suddenly standing. "He's coming."

"Oh, thank goodness," Tessa said. "I hate packing."

Taylor, Jack, and I went downstairs to meet him. Ben pulled in and climbed out of the van, forgetting to shut the garage door.

"The door," Jack said.

Ben looked at him blankly.

Jack pointed at the open door. "You need to shut the garage door."

"*Dwei*," he said. He reached into the van and pushed the remote, then stared at us. He looked pale, like he might faint.

"Are you okay?" I asked.

"We must talk," he said. "With everyone."

We followed him upstairs and I called everyone into the kitchen. As we gathered around the room, Ben just looked silently at the floor. Taylor glanced at me with a frightened expression.

"What's wrong?" I asked.

Taylor was suddenly panicked. "Did they take her?"

Ben looked at her but didn't speak.

"Did they take Jade Dragon?" she asked.

"No," Ben said. "Jade Dragon is safe."

"Then what is it?" I asked.

Ben gripped the back of a chair. "The ranch has been attacked."

"What?" I said.

"The Elgen have attacked the ranch." He looked around at all of us, then said, "We do not think anyone survived."

It was as if all the oxygen had been sucked out of the room.

"My mom and dad . . . ," Ostin said.

Panic and anger filled my chest. "How do you know this?"

"The voice," Ben said.

"I need to talk to the voice," I said.

"You cannot. The voice has gone into hiding. He has been"—he struggled to remember the word—"compromised."

Compromised. This was my fault. I had told Hatch where the ranch was. I had told him about the voice. I had betrayed my mother and my friends. I had compromised the entire resistance. For nearly a minute I stood there, paralyzed. I looked over at Ostin. His face was red, streaked with tears. "I need to go there," I said. "I need to see the ranch."

Ben shook his head. "It is much too dangerous."

"I don't care!" I shouted. "I have to see it. I won't believe until I see it." I looked around. "No one has to go with me."

"I do," Taylor said, wiping her eyes.

"We all need to go," Jack said, his voice uneven with emotion. "We need to see what they've done. If Hatch has done this, I swear on my life, that either he dies or I do. We will avenge them."

I turned to Ben. "I don't care how you do it, but get us there. Now!"

Join the Veyniac Nation!
For Michael Vey trivia, sneak peeks, and events in your area,
follow Michael and the rest of the Electroclan at:

MICHAELVEY.COM

Facebook.com/MichaelVeyOfficialFanPage

Twitter.com/MichaelVey

Instagram.com/MichaelVeyOfficial

Look for

Book 5
Coming in Fall 2015